being brooke

new york times bestselling author

EMMA HART

Cover Photography by Romance Novel Covers

(romancenovelcovers,com)

Cover Design and Formatting by Emma Hart

Editing by Tee Tate

ISBN-13: 978-1540806383

ISBN-10: 1540806383

being brooke

new york times bestselling author
EMMA HART

Dedication

For everybody who ever bought one of my books.

I started Being Brooke almost four years ago, and I'm so glad I finally got to finish her story.

Thank you for believing in me.

one

LIFE TIP #1 : DON'T FALL FOR YOUR BEST FRIEND.

I never knew moving out would feel so good.

Of course, if you have the... *privilege*... of knowing my mother, you'd know it couldn't feel anything but good. My dropping out of college didn't go over too well—like a ten ton cliff made of shit collapsing on your head, actually—but I don't want to be a kindergarten school teacher. That's her dream, not mine. Who actually wants to teach a bunch of snotty-nosed brats?

Anyway, the bottom line: I've just moved out from my overbearing mother's home, away from my devil-may care brother and perfect princess sister into my first apartment and dropped out of college after two years.

We don't discuss that I'm ass-over-tit in debt because it was my second stint in college since my high school graduation. Although my grandmother's nest egg helped with that wasted first attempt at a degree.

Unfortunately, this leaves my job as a travel agent at the World's Worst Travel Agency as my life's sole achievement.

Yay, me.

Still, I've done it. I've moved out, all with the help of my best friend of ten years, Cain. Who is currently walking out of my new pink and white bathroom totally shirtless after his shower. I don't blush, as much as I want to, because Cain and I have the type of relationship where it's totally natural to wander around in your underwear.

Assuming, of course, we even touch on the border of

'normal' with this friendship.

It's been a long-ass ten years. When he moved from downtown Atlanta to Edge-Of-Nowhere, aka Barley Cross, GA, he was the new guy and, okay, I'll admit it, hot as hell, so Carly—my lifetime best friend—and I decided to take him under our metaphorical wings.

We've been best friends ever since.

But I'm also totally in love with him to the point I've considered photoshopping myself into pictures with him, so the best friend thing kinda sucks.

Hey. Don't judge me. We've all done it on Facebook. Mostly with Ian Somerholder or Alexander Skarsgaard. *Mmm. Alexander Skarsgaard.*

In all seriousness, there's a torturous vibe in Cain Elliott stalking out of my shower like he owns it. Hell, it's torturous him being in my life in general some days, but there's something about water that makes his dark blue eyes seem like gems and his strong facial features resemble a Greek god.

Don't even go there with the water droplet lingering on the curve of his bottom lip.

"I dunno how you did it, Brooke, but you got one hell of a shower in this place." Cain drops his shirtless self onto the sofa next to me. He wipes the water droplet from his lip— damn—and shakes his head.

I hold up my hands between us to avoid being sprayed by water, courtesy of his dark, shaggy hair. "I did it because I tested the showers on every apartment. You know I'm picky."

"You mean you showered every time?" His lips curl to one side.

I slap his arm and roll my eyes. "No, I just turned it on, dumbass."

"Well, however you did it, I might have to take all my showers here."

"I don't want your smelly male ass taking over my pink bathroom."

He pouts a little and flutters his long, girly eyelashes at me. Honestly, he's unfairly bestowed with just about everything.

Great hair, long eyelashes, captivating green eyes, plump pink lips...

I shake my head and laugh at his pathetic attempt to convince me. "I said no, Cain!" Because, seriously, if that's a regular thing, I'm gonna have to move out already.

He sighs dramatically and rests his head against the back cushions of my sofa. "You're so mean."

"Whatever." I nudge him with my foot. Hard. "Do I get the torture of you for dinner, too?"

"Shit! Dinner? What's the time?" He snaps his head up, and instantly, I know how the rest of this conversation is gonna go.

Same old, same old... Doesn't stop my heart sinking though.

"Almost five," I answer. Reluctantly.

"Uh oh."

I know that wrinkled brow, lips parted face. Inwardly, I sigh.

"I'd love to stay, Brooke, but—"

"You have to meet Nina," I mumble and look down. "I know. I get it."

I shouldn't even be pissed off. He's been here all day after all, but still... I need to sort my life out. Sue me, okay?

"I'm sorry," he says sincerely, standing and kissing the top of my head before he straightens fully. I ignore the zing that always happens every time he does that. "I'd rather eat Chinese food here until I pass out on the sofa than get dressed up for dinner. Tomorrow though, yeah? She has some parent-teacher shit to go to, so I'm a free guy. Pizza and a movie?"

"Sure." I look up and put everything I can into faking my smile. He'll see right through it, but you know. Keeping up appearances and all that.

"Aw, man, Brooke." Cain pulls his t-shirt over his head and rubs his hand down his face. His bright, emerald-green eyes flicker with guilt. "Don't look at me like that."

"I'm not looking at you like anything!"

7

"Yeah you are. You're looking at me all sad, and, hell."

"I'm not sad. I'll just look lame ordering Chinese for one, but that's fine. Maybe I'll order servings for two so I don't look so lonely."

He wavers by the door, his eyebrows pulling together. He presses his lips together. "Now you're guilt-tripping me."

"And to think, I was going to buy it for you." I sigh. "I can cope without you, Cain. Go and see Nina." The bitch girlfriend.

He's still hesitating.

"Go!" I order, pointing to the door.

He sighs and turns. "Call you tomorrow afternoon?"

"You better."

He winks over his shoulder and pulls his phone from his pocket, shutting the door behind him.

I sink back into the chair, unable to fight the dejected jolt that runs through my body.

Perfect Nina. There's always that one girl who has everything, right? The real-life Regina George in everybody's life.

Well, she's that girl to me.

Two years older than us, she's the kindergarten teacher I'll never be. She's also tall, perfectly blonde, legs as wide as my forearm, and just generally fucking perfect.

And she has Cain.

If Nina snaps her fingers, Cain goes running. Hell, if she told him to jump off a cliff, he'd find the highest one and dive into the water below.

Of course, if that happened I'd hunt the bitch down and scratch her flawless skin with my paint-chipped nails.

But the point still remains: she is everything I'm not, and I'm all too aware of it.

Mindful of my self-pity, I decide to leave the ready-made lasagna in the fridge and call for that take-out, but I decide against Chinese. I don't know any on this side of town, and given my laziness where cooking is concerned, I don't want to go out on a limb and order for one.

First impressions and all that.

Upon hanging up with Mr. Turkish Delight at the Greek deli I do know nearby, (he really is Turkish and quite nice to look at), I shuffle off into my bedroom and change into my all-in-one pajamas.

I'm twenty-four, it's a Friday night, and I'm waiting in for a take-out gyros and fries in my onesie.

My life is just so exciting I can barely stand it.

"My boss is an asshole," I announce, sliding in across from Carly and dumping my purse on the seat next to me.

"Yes, B, we established that two years ago," she says nonchalantly, flicking her brown ponytail over her shoulder. "What is it today?"

"First, I'm not selling enough vacations, then I'm not keeping the staff room clean enough. Well, I'm pretty sure I'm not the Saturday girl who's meant to clean out the staff room. I don't even use the stupid room."

"And the vacations?"

"He thinks we live in Atlanta. Hello, this is Barley Cross, population deadville. Unless Mr. Barber across the road is willing to jet set to the Maldives with a pretty little thing only after his money later this summer, Jet is just gonna have to deal with Disneyland, California. Disney World at a push, but the suckers that come in for that pricey crap ain't freaking flying." I look up at the wide-eyed teen girl with her pen poised over a notepad, clearly taken aback by my ranting.

That's sadly a regular occurrence. The ranting. And the people being shocked. Restraint isn't a skill I've ever learned—unless you count the fact I've made it just over twenty-four years and haven't been arrested for murder. With my temperament, that's worth celebrating.

That's why I have birthday parties—to celebrate making it through another twelve months of dealing with assholes and not killing any of them.

I slap my menu down on the table and force my lips to form something that resembles a smile, but in all likelihood, is closer to a constipated grimace. "I'll have a bacon cheeseburger with fries. And for goodness sake, don't go easy on any of it. Especially not the bacon. Or the cheese. Or the fries."

Yes. I know. Take-out last night, and a burger for lunch. I have a fast metabolism, so shoot me.

I also have a hint of a muffin top and a pair of ripped jeans nudging me toward getting a gym membership, but let's ignore that for now.

"Caesar salad and a bottled water," Carly orders, handing the menu to the girl without looking at her. Working in the only bank in Barley's town center, my beautiful best friend spends all day smiling at annoying people so when it comes to lunch, she avoids eye contact with anyone that isn't me.

It's why we're friends. People? No, thank you.

"It sounds like you've had a day of it already." Carly meets my eyes, their soft, oaky-brown color warm as she sympathizes with me.

"I have." I sigh and roll my napkin between my fingers.

"How did moving go? Sorry I couldn't help much."

"It's okay. It went great until Cain had to run off to deal with Miss Prissy Pants for dinner."

"I have no idea what he sees in her. She's about as attractive as a donkey's asshole mid-shit."

"Well, you said that, not me." I sniff. "But, as your best friend, I am obliged to agree with you."

"Cain would be better off with you."

I raise my eyebrows. "But we know it's never going to happen, so can we please save my little old heart the bother and not discuss that?"

Carly knows better than to bring up my long unrequited love for our mutual best friend. Way better. I've punched her for less.

"Okay, I'm sorry, I shouldn't have mentioned it," she gives in. "But since it's never going to happen, I need a favor."

My dusky blue eyes snap up to her brown ones. "No more double dates."

"Please, Brooke!" Her voice takes on a high-pitched whine. "I know the last one was..."

"A complete and utter fuck up?" I offer helpfully.

No kidding. The last guy she tried to set me up on was of the mind one should put out on the first date.

I knew the moment my knee met his dick I'd never see him again. Except that time in the grocery store when he almost dropped a bottle of wine in his haste to turn away from me.

"That's a little strong," she says hesitantly. "You were incompatible."

I snort. "I'm incompatible with exercise, Carly. That guy was a creep."

She rolls her eyes. "Listen to me. Simon is adorable. Nothing like Lord Creep-a-Lot. He's new to the bank after relocating from Atlanta after his grandmother died a couple months ago."

"Because 'guys who've relocated from Atlanta' is working out so well for me, right?" AKA, unrequited love for my bestie.

She ignores that. "He needs to get to know people."

"Why don't you take him out then?"

"Because Ian asked me."

"Ian?" I ask through a mouthful of food. "Again? Really?"

Carly looks at me disapprovingly. "He's not that bad. He's just a little... Handsy."

The waitress sets the plate in front of me, and I pull it closer to squeeze some ketchup on the surface. After a jab around the red sauce, I shove the fries in my mouth, staring at Carly.

Handsy? *Handsy?* Ian was more than handsy. He was a human octopus.

I swallow my food. "Honey, I hate to break it to you, but

his hands crawl more than the bugs Jeremy Highfield used to put down our dresses in pre-K."

She huffs, chewing her rabbit food slowly. "I know, but he's a really nice guy, so I'll give him one more chance. Besides, it's not like this town has a million choices."

"You talk like Barley Cross is the only place we'll ever live."

"Nobody in five generations of our families have ever left Barley. We won't leave. We're too rooted in climbing trees and fishing in little ponds and off the pier and stuff."

We both sigh, propping our chins up on our hands. She's kinda right. We go for college and vacation then, boom, you're back.

It's the Barley Cross Boomerang, bitch.

"Maybe a hot, rich guy stopping in to visit his grandmother will pop by the travel agents later and be dazzled by my superior wit and sweet smile," I suggest, shoving another fry into my mouth.

Carly raises an eyebrow.

I shrug. "Hey, a girl can dream. Let me do that at least."

"Yeah, but you should work on the dream of the "superior wit and sweet smile" before the hot, rich guy comes true and you screw it up."

Bitch.

She glances at the watch on her wrist and stands. "We have to get back."

"Great. Because another four hours of Jet is exactly what my patience needs."

Carly glances at me as we pay. "You're due on your period, aren't you?"

I look up to the ceiling, counting in my head. "Ten, twelve, fourteen... No. Not for a week or so. I guess I just took one too many bitch pills this morning."

She nods and we push open the diner's glass doors. "I can tell."

I screw up my face. "Am I really that bad?"

She nods again.

Oh well.

Two

LIFE TIP #2: IF YOU DON'T READ THE CALORIE COUNT, THEY'RE STILL GOING TO SHRINK YOUR CLOTHES. SADLY.

I adjust the waistband of my fat pants and debate internally whether to cook the pizza or call for Dominos.

I shouldn't actually be doing either, given the gyros last night and burger for lunch. I should be reaching into the fridge for my, ahem, ready-made lasagna.

Because that's so much healthier. Well, kinda, I guess. There are less carbs, right? Maybe.

I open the fridge and pull it out off the top shelf, then slide off the cardboard sleeve. Huh. There's actually not a huge difference in the calories, and I could exercise tomorrow, and—

The container slips right out of my hand to the floor. The lasagna inside mushes up into a mess of meat and pasta and sauce. It looks like a bucket full of puppies all projectile vomited into the container, so... Yeah. That's not happening.

Shame.

Okay. It's definitely pizza, but which one? Frozen or take-out? Hmm...

My apartment door opens, revealing my six-foot-three, muscular, handsome, builder best friend.

I need to rein it in. Hello, cheesy romance novel like.

"Oh, it's you. Come in, pal. Thanks for knocking," I drawl, swinging my gaze toward him.

He grins, looking at me standing in the middle of the kitchen. Then his green eyes drop to the lasagna on the floor. "Did you do that deliberately?"

"No." I look from him to the box. "It slipped."

He responds with a low chuckle. "Sure it did, B. I know what you're thinking, and it's Dominos every time."

I wrinkle my face as I pick up the lasagna and throw it into the trash. Now I'm gonna have to go shopping tomorrow. Damn my butterfingers.

Cain kicks the door shut, plastic bags swinging from his hands. The sound of glass clinking together has me perking up, because that sounds like wine.

How do I know? I've trained my ears to recognize it. And yes, it is a distinct sound, before you ask. This is a finely-tuned skill, that one day, a future CEO will appreciate right before they hire me.

I point at the bags accusingly. "What are they?"

He heaves them onto the counter next to me. "Wine and beer." He pulls a six pack of Coors Light and two bottles of zinfandel blush from the first bag.

Two bottles? Does he want to hold my hair while I vomit?

"Candy." He pulls a selection of bright-colored packets out of the second bag, then empties the third by grabbing the bottom and tipping up. "And way too many chips, but they were on offer, and you know I can't resist chips when they're on offer."

"Or when they're full price," I muse. "I'm amazed you bought me wine. Although if I drink all that, I'll vomit."

"Yeah, well, it was unintentional. Besides, if I bought you one bottle, I knew I'd get the "Why did you just buy one?" speech, and I'm too tired for your crap." He flashes me a panty-melting half-grin and opens a cupboard door. Then another. And another. "Uh, B? Where are your glasses?"

"In the box over there?" I point to the big pile of still packed boxes. "Or... Maybe the ones in the bedroom. I'm not sure."

What? I was working all day. And I hate unpacking

anything. Even multipacks of panties. They just sit in my dresser until I've made it through every pair, and then the package stays there until it annoys me. I'll be an excellent wife one day.

"One of those? Somewhere?" I shoot him a sweet smile. "And how can you unintentionally buy wine?"

Easily, Brooke. Very, very easily, as you well know.

"Wow. One of any box in this entire apartment. That's real helpful, Brooke. Thanks."

I don't think I like his attitude. Shithead.

"And I didn't go to the liquor aisle to buy you fucking wine," he continues. "It was a decision I made when I got the beer. I told you—I'm tired, plus I had a shitty day at work."

"Ah, yes. Catcalling all those hot women walking past while you work your muscles and your builder's butt crack is on show must be so hard." I roll my eyes as he crosses the room and takes his pocketknife from his pocket.

"I don't catcall. And I don't have a builder's butt crack." He slices open the top box open my boxes. Being a builder has its perks, and one is apparently the constant presence of a pocketknifeupon one's person.

The downside is apparently this builder doesn't show his butt crack. Someone should start a petition to make it a law. Sign me up!

I pick up the wine bottle and stare at him. "If you didn't mean to buy it, why is it chilled?"

"They had some in a fridge."

"The store doesn't have wine in the fridges."

He sighs, stands, and puts his knife back in his pocket. "Goddammit, B, do you have to argue everything?"

"As a rule, yes. If I don't, how would you know you're wrong?"

Cain pulls a wine glass out of the box and takes the bottle from me to pour it, firing me a quick, half-hearted glare. "You're exhausting, woman."

"Really? You're just figuring this out? For shame, Cain Elliott. I pride myself on being exhausting. That's how I get people to leave me alone." I take the glass he offers me, a grin stretching across my face.

He shakes his head and tries to hide his own smile. "Can you order that pizza now? I'm starvin'. Look. I'm wastin' away." He lifts his shirt slightly, his toned abs peeking out, and he pinches one whole centimeter of "fat" on his stomach.

"Yes." I drag my eyes away from his body toward the red hot Cheetos sitting on the counter. The open, half-empty packet. "Because you didn't eat on the way over, did you?"

He turns from putting his beer in the fridge. "It's past my dinner and I have a physical job. I need feeding."

"Good god, you sound like my brother," I grumble. "Except the only physical exercise Ben gets is with his right hand over the latest porno mag or whatever it is now that *Playboy* stopped publishing nudes."

"Ah, yeah. Sad times." He nods.

Men.

I grab my cell and dial Domino's to Cain's laughter and the strangely satisfying pop-hiss of him opening his beer bottle.

I love that pop-hiss. Someone needs to make empty cans for the freaks like me who just want to sit and open them for no other reason than to sigh happily at the sound over and over and—

"Hi, Brooke! What can we get you today?" the Domino's chick asks, cutting through my internal monologue.

Yeah, I order it so much they've saved my number. That's always a point of shame when I call, yet I can't stop calling... Go figure.

"Medium pepperoni passion and the BBQ one, please," I order. "Oh, but I have a new address now."

"Sure thing," the girl chimes happily. Because your job at Domino's is so good it warrants a chirpy-as-hell voice, right?

This coming from the college drop-out working at BC Travels.

Yeah, shut the fuck up, Brooke.

I reel off my address and throw my phone onto the kitchen

counter, grabbing my wine glass. I leave the kitchen and sit on the sofa, pointing to the Blu-ray box set at the side of my TV.

"Harry Potter?" Cain asks, dutifully getting up.

I nod.

He pauses, the box in hand. "I can't remember what one we got up to."

"The seventh," I reply.

"First or second?"

"No... The seventh."

"I know that." He smirks. "First or second seventh film, Brooke?"

Of course. "Oh, um, first? I think. Maybe. It's been a while."

Cain rolls his eyes and puts the appropriate disk in the Blu-ray player. "If I didn't know better, I'd say you were blonde under all that dark hair."

"But I'm not," I say pointedly, smoothing my hand over my chestnut locks. "And I never fucking will be."

"There's nothing wrong with blondes," Cain argues, a slight hint of defensiveness creeping into his voice. He picks up the DVD remote from the coffee table and sits back.

I swing my feet onto his lap. Man, it's hard not to kick him in the balls. An inch further to the right... "There's not exactly anything right with them either," I mutter into my wine glass, thinking of stick-thin blonde Nina. Perfect, flawless, blonde Nina, and her watermelon tits.

"I heard that."

Crap. "You weren't supposed to."

"I gathered that by the grumpy muttering."

I huff and grab the crispy M&M's from the table, shoving one or ten into my mouth. I don't care if he heard it. I'm tired of pretending to tolerate Queen Barbie. I've had fake plants realer than her.

And you know what? I threw them all in the trash. Where plastic belongs.

Ugh. Even *I* know I'm being petty right now.

Cain taps the arm of the sofa with the remote and presses play. As he sighs heavily, guilt creeps into my stomach at my cattiness. Well, my audible cattiness, that is.

I might be tired of tolerating her, but I do it because I love him—as my best friend. I hate her and refuse to tolerate her because I, well, love him and want him myself.

Kinda like Verruca Salt, but an angstier, grown-up version of that demanding want.

Don't care how.

I want him now.

Huff huff. Stomp, stomp.

I have *got* to grow up.

"Don't be mad, pretty B," he says, using my age-old nickname only he gets away with now. Pretty B because my mom did the Kardashian thing, except we're all named B-names instead of K-names. And she did it before it was a thing. "Please." He grabs my foot and squeezes.

I squirm, my toes protesting his touch. "I'm not mad. Do I look mad?"

"You look pretty pissed off."

"Then I'm not mad. Pissed off and mad are two different things."

"You're not looking at me." He chuckles, but I know it's more at my denial than anything else. "Look, I know you and Carly aren't Nina's biggest fans—"

"You could say that..."

"But I don't understand why you don't like her. If you just spent an hour with her..."

My doorbell rings, cutting him off. Thank god. I don't think he realizes that if I spent an hour with his girlfriend, I'd want to slice my eyeballs out with dental floss and then ask Wolverine to deafen me.

I put my glass on the coffee table and stand, deliberately not looking at him again. I seem to lose my bravado when I do that. It's easier to be a petty bitch about his girlfriend when I can't see that it bugs him, and, well, being a bitch is what's getting me through their relationship. "She's as fake as the eyelashes and hair she wears daily. I'd wager even her boobs are fake."

Cain is silent as I take the pizza from the delivery guy. Delivery Guy gives me the once over as he hands me the boxes. Ugh. I'm not interested in being hit on before dinner. Or at all, actually.

I paid for the pizza then shut the door on his perverted person. He's supposed to deliver my dinner, not look at me like I'm dessert.

"I take your silence as an admission of fake knockers." I put Cain's pizza on his lap and sit back down, crossing my legs beneath me and resting my pizza on the sofa cushion between us.

"Not everyone is born with tits that could pass as weaponry, Brooke." Cain glances at me, his eyes briefly dropping at my unfortunately on-show cleavage.

My lips curl slightly, but I reach down and yank my tank top up over them anyway. "Hey, I'm not judging the mosquito bites! I happen to be very proud of my natural D's. If my mother gave me anything good, it was the girls." I pat my boobs appreciatively.

Never mind the boob-sweat issue I have to deal with every summer or the whole sizing up a shirt to accommodate them thing.

Cain snorts, ripping his box open and dropping the lid on the floor because he knows it bothers me. "You're crazy. Remind me why we're friends again?"

I take a slice of pizza and rip a bite off. "Because your life would be so damn boring without me," I say as I chew.

"You're more of a man than I am."

"Why, thank you." I wink and take a smaller bite of pizza. "You know it's why you love me. Deep down, I'm just one of the guys."

He grins and shoves half his pizza slice in his mouth. "No, you're not," he says through his mouthful of food. God, we're classy. "You're too pretty to be one of the guys."

I hide my blush. "Aw, you big creep." I nudge his arm.

19

"I think your manners mean you cross over though. Not to mention the last time we all went out, you drunk half the guys under the table."

"They proposed the tequila. You don't drink tequila if you're a beer guy." I look at him pointedly.

He forgets I drunk him under the table that night too.

"Oh, shush!" He looks at the TV. "Hermione is on."

I shake my head and grin again. His obsession with Emma Watson is something else—only when she has long hair, though. I actually find it kinda cute, in a freaky kinda way, but only because I also love me a bit of Tom Felton.

After a few minutes of us both eating—less animal like—and watching the movie in silence, Cain's phone begins to buzz on the table. The screen lights up, and the short name on the screen makes me have to fight a frown.

I know it's Nina. It always is. It's like she has a Brooke-dar. She can sense whenever Cain and I are alone and hanging out.

My heart sinks, slowly but heavily, and I school my expression into one of not caring. I refuse to look away from the TV now.

Cain hands me his pizza box, which I take, begrudgingly, then he leans forward and grabs his phone. He waits for the buzzing to stop, then unlocks it and turns it off vibrate.

Then? Then he shoves it under the table, screen down.

Ho. Lee. Shit.

I gape at him. I can't help it.

A piece of pepperoni drops off the slice of pizza in my hand—the same one that's frozen halfway to my mouth as I stare at him in total disbelief. Did he really just do it?

"What?" Cain shrugs and takes his box back, grabbing a piece of half-eaten, meaty pizza and shoving the end in his mouth. The crust crunches as he bites down.

I swallow and glance at the coffee table. "I don't think you've ever *not* taken a call from her." I can't help the derogatory way I say 'her'. It's not intentional—honest. It's ingrained in me to be vicious to other women. I think it's a female thing. Self-preservation and all that.

"I don't think I ever haven't either." Cain tilts his head to the side and meets my gaze, a suspicious glint in his green eyes. "But the point is, we haven't done this in weeks, and I'm having too much fun to leave. Besides, we have all this junk food. If I don't help you eat it, you'll eat it all, then it'll be my fault when your pants don't fit."

Oh my god.

"Does she know you're here?" I smirk slyly and raise my eyebrows.

He shifts uncomfortably. With a cough, he puts his pizza down and grabs his beer bottle to swig from it.

Oh. My. Shitty. Life.

"She doesn't, does she?" I sit up straight, throwing my half-slice back into my box and shoving his shoulder. "Cain!"

"No," he mumbles, scratching the back of his ear. "She doesn't know."

I laugh. I can't help it. It's totally immature of me to delight in the fact he hasn't told the Prissy Princess where is he and he's ignoring her calls, but I do. It's hilarious.

And, okay. I'm smug. Totally smug. There's only one reason he hasn't told her, and that's because she hates me too.

Bitchy Best Friend Mission: Level Up!

"And tell me." I snicker, just about holding back the volcano of laughter threatening to erupt. "Where does Nina think you are?"

"She thinks I'm at Mom's." He looks at me, his lips flattening into a thin line. "Stop laughin', B. No, don't shake your damn head. I fuckin' mean it. She's a little insecure over my friendship with you and Carly, that's all. Sometimes it's easier to just tell a... little white lie."

"A little white lie? She thinks you're at your mom's!" I laugh harder and wipe at my eyes because they feel a little too wet.

"I just want the best of both worlds right now, all right?"

"What is the best of both worlds? Pizza with me and blow jobs from her?"

21

"She chooses not to eat gluten. Until she finds a gluten-free recipe she likes, I can't eat pizza when she's around."

Which is a lot.

I raise my eyebrows again. "Your girlfriend won't eat gluten but she'll happily put your dick in her mouth?"

"Brooke. Don't be a bitch." He chucks a piece of chicken from his pizza at me, his eyes narrowing.

I'm dying. I think this is it—this is how I die, laughing at Cain's lame excuses for lying to his girlfriend about spending time with me.

"Oh my fuck. This is hilarious. Seriously. Someone call Comedy Central."

"Brooke." He says my name again, this time quieter.

I stop laughing. Just about.

"I'm sorry. I just think it's funny. You want me to be nice to her but you lie to her about spending time with me." I shrug a shoulder and peel a piece of pepperoni off my pizza. I'm not even that hungry anymore.

He sighs, putting the top down on his box, and sits back. "She thinks there's something going on between us."

I laugh even harder because I might cry if I don't.

Hi, breaking heart. Grab the tissues, yo.

There's an awkward silence hanging between us now. It's not the first time someone has thought that, but given that the more time I spend with Cain, the more I seem to fall for him, it's awkward. Especially since he's lying to her just to hang out with me.

I clear my throat and look up at him. "That's ridiculous. You're my best friend. Like anything would ever happen between us. I can't put up with your shit taste in music, for a start."

"Exactly," he replies in a quieter voice, scratching behind his ear again. "It's fucking stupid. I can't stand your taste in music either. Who the fuck likes Justin Bieber?"

"People who think Kanye West should retire."

He swings his gaze to me, his lips twitching.

More awkwardness buzzes between us, and as I'm looking

right into his bright, green eyes, the awkwardness is igniting the air with something I can't put my finger on, but something I feel incredibly uncomfortable about.

I down the rest of my wine and get up to refill it. When I have, I open him a bottle of beer bring it back to the table for him.

"Thanks, Brooke." He grabs my hand and squeezes it when I sit back down. "Hey, I'm sorry for bringin' Nina up tonight."

"You didn't." I smile brightly at him even though I know he'll see right through it. "I did, I guess. Plus, she did call. Let's not think about her for the rest of the night. Okay? You can dream over Hermione while I imagine Tom Felton and Matthew Lewis fulfilling my wildest porn fantasies."

He squeezes my hand and lets go, even with an eyebrow raise. I swing back around on the sofa and rest my feet on his lap again. He pats my legs, and I drop the Domino's box on the floor to rest the M&M's between my knees. Cain leans over and grabs a huge handful, grinning at me, all awkwardness and cattiness gone.

I smile back, grabbing my own handful of M&M's, only to throw one at the side of his head. He launches one back, and I catch it in my mouth, which only makes him laugh a deep, rumbly, belly laugh that makes the hairs on my arms stand on end.

No... No.

It's definitely not a good thing if you're in love with your best friend.

I grumble and curse Carly's ability to get up at seven a.m. It's my day off, I'm stood at the corner of my street by the park and I'm wearing damn running clothes.

Yes. You heard right. Running clothes. I'm going jogging.

I figure the pair of muffins making themselves comfortable on my hips aren't gonna leave by themselves, especially not after my diet the past couple days, so I'm taking up jogging. There is a slight issue—that issue being that I don't run. At all. I'm pretty sure I can overcome it. Maybe next year is more likely, but I'll give it a go.

I hear a high-pitched yap and wonder if I have enough time to run back to my apartment and fake illness. The dark head that bobs around the corner tells me no.

I look at the ball of white and brown fluff by her feet. "Why did you bring *It*?"

"Brooke!" Carly scolds me. "She has a name, and her name is Delilah. She's not an It!"

"Carly, It hates me," I deadpan, looking at her. I'm also hating her for looking so fresh so early.

"She doesn't hate you. She just... hasn't connected with you yet."

"Oh, like she connected with my favorite pumps?" I shoot Delilah an evil glare.

Carly's dog and I have a strictly hate-hate relationship. The first time she saw me she bit me and I kicked her. I didn't mean to kick her. She bit my ankle, and it was a knee jerk reaction. Okay, so it took Carly two weeks to fully forgive me, but it was the Jack Russell's fault. Not mine. I didn't ask for the little rat to bite me. Besides her eating my favorite shoes and me hiding her favorite chew toy in retaliation—in the trunk of Cain's car—we haven't had many interactions.

But now, we're at the park and It is bigger than I remember. The little dark eyes set in the pure white fur of its face study me, and the ball of fluff growls. I poke my tongue out at it and follow Carly through the gap in the wall into the park.

"So how did last night go?" my best friend asks as we begin a light jog.

"Nina has fake tits," I share, getting straight to the point. No point boring her with the minor details.

"I knew it!" Carly punches the air, gleefully cheering.

24

"There was no way someone of her figure could have boobs like that. Was she a stripper in college?"

"Maybe. Think we could find out?"

"Do you know where she went to college?"

"Negative."

"Then it's unlikely."

"Damn." I narrow my eyes as we pass the play area. Phew. I'm getting tired already. This is torture. "Cain ignored her calls last night. And she thought he was at his mom's."

Carly giggles. "Really? He didn't tell her he was with you?"

"No, she thinks there's something going on with us."

"But there is. On your side, anyway."

I shake my head and rub my side. "No. All there is, is a teenage infatuation which refuses to pass although said teenage years already have."

"If you say so, B, but I think you should tell him."

"What? And be like, 'oh hey, Cain! I just thought I'd let you know I'm totally in love with you and I have been since we were fifteen. You're the reason my relationships have never worked. Be my boyfriend and love me always?'"

Carly snorts. "Not quite like that."

"Not at all," I protest. "I didn't tell him at fifteen, and I won't now."

"Or sixteen, or seventeen, or eighteen, or nineteen, or twenty..."

"All right, all right."

"Or twenty-one or twenty-two...Or twenty-three or twenty-four."

"Screw you, Car." I huff and push my hair from my face, slowing to a walk. I watch as It runs after a bright yellow tennis ball Carly launches a good twenty feet away. "Besides, as much as we hate her Royal Prissyness... He seems kinda happy."

Carly makes a non-committal grunting sound. "For some strange reason."

"It's the boobs," I declare. "Guys like firm boobs."

"You have firm boobs. And they're big," she argues. "And

real."

"Maybe real ones are turn offs now. I don't know. The only dates I go on are organized by you and are usually bigger disasters than I am."

And that is saying something.

Carly opens her mouth then closes it again. We pause for breath against a large oak, leaving the Devil Dog to sniff around the bottom and do her business. Dirty.

"You have a point," Carly finally agrees. "But only a small one. And talking of dates..."

Here we go. I knew this was coming.

What do I have to lose?

More dignity, but I'm running low on that anyway.

Time, but I'll do anything to avoid unpacking everything right now. And possibly more belief that I will one day move on from my unrequited love, but hey—for all I know, one day, one of these disasters she sends me on could not be such a disaster.

"Yes." I sigh with a half-hearted shrug. "I will go on this stupid date."

"You're the best!" She grins. "Simon is really nice. I'm sure you'll love him. He's clean-cut, polite, well-mannered—"

"Aren't well-mannered and polite the same thing?"

"Maybe, but he really is."

"In other words, move over Mr. Darcy?" I raise my eyebrows.

"He's pretty much perfect, B."

"Perfect guys don't exist, Carly. If his personality is that amazing, he either has one ball, a small dick, or no idea how to use it."

"Does everything come down to male anatomy with you?"

"No." I shrug. "But when guys look at me, they focus on the girls." I jiggle my boobs. "So I figure it's only polite to give their boy the same amount of attention."

Carly shakes her head and pushes off the tree. "I sometimes wonder how I stay sane around you."

"That's easy." I start jogging again next to her. "It's because

I have enough crazy for the both of us."

"By the way," Carly says casually. "That double date is tonight."

I stop. "You're kidding."

Three

LIFE TIP #3: PUT NAME TAGS IN YOUR CLOTHES SO THEY DON'T GET MIXED UP WITH YOUR MUCH HOTTER, MUCH SKINNIER SISTER'S.

*C*arly wasn't kidding.

So maybe that's why I'm currently trying—and failing—to zip my dress up the whole way. Sheesh, have I put that much weight on?

No…No. Hold your horses, Veronica. There's an answer for this.

I pull the zipper down and step out of the black dress, bringing the label up to my eyes. The little "6" on the label glares at me mockingly. The dress doesn't fit because it's not mine. Figures.

My sister has three kids and is still thinner than I am. I tell you, some people get all the luck. In my family, it's always Billie who gets it.

Unless big boobs count as luck. I'm not sure her dress would even cover my tits unzipped, let alone done up.

"Gah!" I yell and throw the dress at my bedroom wall. There isn't enough time to get Billie to bring me my black dress, so it's back to the wardrobe. Or, err, trash bag.

I really need to unpack a little.

I tip my dress bag onto my king bed and start rifling through the material. I grab my favorite white dress and groan when I see it's got more wrinkles than the residents of a senior center. With a curse to my own packing skills, I pad into the kitchen in my underwear to iron it. Living in a second-floor apartment has its perks, even when you're being forced onto yet another hell-born date.

No-one can see through my windows. I could dance around stark naked with it all hanging out if I really wanted to.

I set up the ironing board and wait for the iron to get up to temperature. As it does, I reach for the remote and turn the TV radio station up from its low hum to a much louder wall-thrumming buzz. Will.I.Am is now blasting through the speakers.

Okay, not blasting. I do have neighbors, but the music is loud enough.

I flatten the dress onto the board and, singing my heart out, and maybe shaking my butt a little, I start the daunting process of ironing my dress. I might be all grown up now, but I fucking hate ironing. In fact, I hate chores altogether. It's just a shame I have a ton of them to do these days.

Living alone – 0. With OCD Mom – 1.

"Your dancing needs some work!" Cain's voice travels above the bassy beat of Will.I.Am.

Cain's voice?

Wait.

Cain.

What?

I spin on the balls of my feet, brandishing the iron as my weapon, and shriek upon my eyes landing on him. Well, shriek is a bit of an understatement. I scream. Loud.

Cain's eyes slowly crawl down my body, from my make-up free face to my bright purple toenails and back up. I think they linger on my chest and my hips, but I could be imagining that.

My cheeks flame.

Shit.

I'm in my underwear.

At least it's nice, matching underwear. That's a comfort. I guess.

"What are you doing here?" I shout, putting the iron down and holding my dress in front of me like it'll make a difference. Like he didn't just foreplay me with his eyes.

All right. When I claimed we have the walking-around-in-underwear type of relationship, it was him in his underwear. Not me.

Cain walks past me and grabs the remote controller and presses a button. The volume of the television rapidly goes down.

"I'm here because Mom wants to know when you need your hair cut. If you'd had the music at a normal level, you would have heard me say that the first time. And heard my two calls."

"Why didn't you knock?"

"I did. Six times." He cocks an eyebrow, his lips barely resisting the same upturn.

I shrug sheepishly. "Oops."

"Then I let myself in to find you in your underwear, dancing like you're a reject from Dirty Dancing."

Ah, underwear... Bless you, Vic Secret. "Yeah, about that, turn around. I want to put my dress on."

He sighs and turns, his head slightly shaking as he does.

I slip the dress over my head and smooth it down over my ass, checking for wrinkles. None.

Damn, I'm getting good at the whole looking after myself thing.

"Okay, I'm decent." I walk into my room.

"Brooke, you'll never be decent." Cain follows me.

"I will be, just not any time soon." I grab my make-up bag. "One day, I'll be married with two point five children, a farmhouse on the outskirts of Barley Cross and a collie named Stanley."

"Stanley? Ooookay." He laughs, then pauses as I apply my foundation and stroke powder across my cheeks. "And I'm sure you will. Is that what this dress is about? Meeting Mr. Right?"

"In one of Carly's disaster dates? Not fucking likely."

"Uh oh."

"Uh oh indeed, my little builder friend, uh oh indeed." I

apply the finishing touches to my make-up and shake my hair out. "My hair is okay, right?"

"It needs a cut. I can see your split ends from here."

"Oh, gosh. Remind me to come to you next time I need an ego-boost, will ya?"

"Your sarcasm knows no bounds, Brooke Barker."

"You sound surprised, Cain Elliott."

"Not at all." He grins at me. "So? Your hair?"

"Next week. I'm off on Wednesday if she has any time. Why didn't she call me?" I sit on the bed and pull out a box of shoes.

"Because she was worried she'd go all Mommy on you and start fussin' since you're out in the world on your own now."

"I love it when she fusses over me. Someone has to." Lord knows my own mom's fussing is more of the 'go to church,' 'meet a good man!' 'get your degree,' 'settle down and start a family!' kind.

I slip a pair of nude heels onto my feet and wriggle my toes.

"I know." Cade looks at my feet. "Someone isn't in date mode."

Yeah, he knows how I pick my shoes. True friendship that is.

"No, I'm not," I agree. "I've already been running today—"

"You've been running?" He coughs out.

I glare at him. "I can run." Sort of. "And Carly brought the Demon Dog along."

"Oh, shit."

"Yes. Luckily we didn't maim or kill each other today. No shoes, ankles or puppies were hurt." I stand up and admire myself in the mirror. I'll do.

"So, who are you going on a date with?" Cain follows me into the kitchen.

"Someone called Simon. He's a banker." I raise my eyebrows. "He's perfect, according to Carly. Mom'll be thrilled. But of course, his level of perfection still remains to be seen."

Cain grunts. "I gotta get back. Mom's expecting me for dinner."

"Have fun. Tell her I said hi!"

"Will do." He waves over his shoulder and leaves my apartment. I glance at the clock. He's not the only one that should be leaving. I grab my jacket from the back of the sofa and slip my arms in.

Let Disaster Date number seven hundred and twenty-six commence.

Italia's is a small, family-run—wait for it—Italian restaurant in the town center. In fact, it's the only Italian restaurant in the town center, so it's always busy. And I wanna know why we're at the busiest restaurant instead of a nice quiet one. But I won't ask, because I'm momentarily struck dumb by the guy stood next to Ian waiting for us.

I swallow. "That's Simon?"

"That's Simon." Carly grins.

He has wavy, dark blonde hair that falls into his dark eyes a little. I'm too far away to see what color they are, but he's tall and muscular and goddamn someone get me a fan 'cause he is hot!

"Hey, Ian." Carly smiles at her date. He kisses her hand and they turn to me and Mr. Hottie. "Brooke, this is Simon. Simon, my best friend, Brooke."

Simon smiles and I put out my hand to shake his. He takes it and kisses my fingers softly. "It's a pleasure to meet you, Brooke."

"Pleasure is all mine." I shoot him a dazzling smile that, for once, is genuine.

"Shall we go and sit down?" Ian asks, touching a hand to Carly's back.

I really want to give her a rape alarm that only I can hear. We can use it as code meaning 'Handy handy! Bathroom break!' every time Ian gets too much.

Simon follows two steps behind me and pulls my chair out for me. Hot and a gentleman. This is rare—it's like the equivalent of winning the lottery or something.

"Thank you." I smile at him and he returns it. Okay, so maybe this date won't be so bad, but judging by my previous experiences, something will go wrong.

Maybe he's a nose picker. But it is a pretty nose, so...

"Everything okay?" he asks over the table.

I blink and shake off the thoughts. "Fine. I thought I saw someone I knew. I didn't." I smile and pick up the menu, even though I've been here so many times I know it by heart.

Carly nudges me under the table with her foot, and I kick her back. She narrows her eyes at me over the table.

"Be nice," she mouths.

I have an almost irresistible urge to poke my tongue out at her.

No, Brooke. No. Tonight you are civilized.

I bite my tongue to stop it poking out and to stop a giggle escaping at myself. Oh, why am I let out into public?

Carly knows I'm a hot mess. I don't know why she tries.

"So, Brooke," Simon says. "What do you do?"

"I work at BC Travels as a travel agent," I answer simply.

"She's a drop-out," Carly adds.

Thank you, Carly. I'll remember that.

"Oh? From college? Or high school?" Simon asks.

"College. I tried two different degrees, but neither were for me." I fidget uncomfortably, and decide to flip the question back on him. "Carly says you work at the bank?"

"Yeah. My grandmother just died, and since my parents both passed a few years ago, she left her estate to me," he explains. "I decided to move here from Atlanta. Not a big move, but enough for a fresh start."

"I'm sorry. That must be horrible."

"Thank you, but it was expected. She'd been sick for a long

time."

I nod like I understand and look around for a waiter. I'm one of those horrible people who hate talking about death. I just... I feel awkward.

What am I supposed to do? Pat his head? Shoulder? Take his hand? Squeeze his fingers?

Fuck me. This is why I can't be a teacher like my mom wants me to be. My compassionate bone is the floppy cock of the kindness skeleton.

AKA: useless.

"What can I get for you all today?" A waiter appears behind me and makes me jump.

I put a hand to my chest. "Georgio!" I scold, turning around to face him. "Don't do that!"

"Don't do what, Brooke?" The forty-something Italian man's eyes are twinkling with amusement.

"Scare me like that! You do it every time I come in here."

"I am sorry," he apologizes, smiling. "I forget you are, what is the word?"

"Skittish?" Carly offers.

Georgio winks at her. "That works, Carly."

"Hmph." I put my menu back. "I come here for good food and receive abuse. Georgio, what would Mamma say about your manners?"

"Mamma would kick your behind," Carly answers for him.

"Mamma is sleeping." Georgio rolls his eyes, far more reminiscent of his teenage sons than himself. "What can I get you lovely ladies and your companions?"

We order our food, and I'm about to ask for the house white when the door opens and a blast of air hits our table.

"Alessandro!" Georgio booms. "You're late!"

Thinking of the teenage sons...

"I'm sorry, Papa," Alessandro says, running through the lower part of the restaurant. "Only five minutes."

Georgio narrows his eyes, and points to the thick wooden door behind him with his pen. "Get in that kitchen and help your mamma. Pots need to be washed."

"Yes, Papa." The fifteen-year old boy hangs his head and walks past us. I catch his eye and wink at him. He smiles and scoots into the kitchen.

Georgio is frowning at me when I meet his eyes.

"What?" I ask innocently.

"You spoil that boy with your smiles," he scolds me. "You are bella, and he loves it."

"I'm teaching him to appreciate women, Georgio. He knows that if a bella woman smiles at him, he has to smile back. See? It's all good."

He frowns then smiles. "You have me there, Brooke. Now, I'll go give Mamma your order and get that wine." He taps the table with two of his fingers and leaves the main restaurant.

I shrug one shoulder and look back to my companions. Simon is looking at me quizzically. It's a kind of amused quizzical look, and I frown.

"What?" I ask.

"Nothing." He shakes his head and smiles slightly. "I've just never seen someone behave with a waiter that way. Do you know the family well?"

I laugh a little and barely stop myself from snorting. "If there's one thing you should know about Barley Cross, it's that everybody knows everybody. Oh, two things. Everybody also knows everybody's business. Honestly, if you can have sex without it being the hot topic at Bingo on a Friday night, then you've done good."

Carly's eyes bug at me across the table. "Brooke!" she chokes out.

"What?"

"You can't just say that!"

Ian laughs. "Sure she can, Carly. It's true. I bet Mrs. Lewis will ask us all about our date when she comes into the bank, and I didn't tell her."

Carly chews the inside of her lip. "Well, I suppose you have a point."

I give her a satisfied smile, and turn back to Simon. His

dark eyes are fixated on me, and I can almost see the cogs whirring in his brain.

He's no doubt realizing how crazy I am, and wondering when the hell he can get away from the odd brunette opposite him.

Such is my life.

Georgio returns with our wine, and after pouring four glasses, leaves us. Carly, Ian, Simon, and I make small talk before and during our meal. It's a comfortable kind of small talk. Carly twirls her hair around her finger and giggles at Ian's jokes. Ian plays footsies with Carly under the table and touches her at every opportunity.

Am I the only person who can see what a creep he is? Seriously?

An hour later, when we've al eaten, Alessandro brings the bill over. I give him another smile for good measure. He blushes and scoots off. I chuckle to myself as Ian leads Carly over to the counter to pay our bill.

"Georgio was right," Simon muses, his eyes finding their way back to me.

"About what?" I raise my eyebrows and tilt my wine glass slightly.

"You spoil him with your bella smiles." He gives me a pretty damn bella smile of his own.

It's my turn to blush a little. "Like I said, I'm just teaching him." I finish the rest of my wine and put my glass down, licking my lips. Simon's eyes are focused on them when I back at him. I clear my throat slightly.

He meets my eyes again and shifts. "Sorry if I wasn't the best company tonight. I'm not really a dating kinda guy."

I smile widely. "Well, contrary to popular belief, I'm not really a dating kinda gal, either, so you're in great company."

"Really? For some reason I imagined you having a long line of guys waiting to take you out."

I laugh and this time, I do snort. "Sorry." I cover my mouth with my hand while I compose myself. "No, no. I don't have any kind of line of guys waiting to date me. Carly usually has to drag them kicking and screaming."

Because I'm the one waiting in line for someone I'll never have... And being dragged kicking and screaming to dates like these.

"In that case," Simon leans forward slightly, his eyes fixed hotly on mine, his lips curved upward, "would you object to me asking you for a second date?"

I cross my legs under the table, my lips curling up slightly. Hell, he's hot, he's nice, and he's a gentleman. And I don't have any other offers.

"Not at all," I reply. "I'd love to go on another date."

four

LIFE TIP #4: SMILE. EVEN IF YOU'RE THINKING ABOUT MURDERING THE PERSON YOU'RE SMILING AT.

I smile sweetly at the couple across from me. Their hyper four-and-seven year old children are running around my table shrieking about Disneyland, while the couple themself pours over several brochures trying to decide the best value holiday for their family. Their preference? Somewhere the kids can be amused and they can have some peace.

I'm not surprised.

I'm also tempted to remind them they are looking at Disneyland, California brochures, so there's a better than average chance that the kids will be amused. For their peace, I want to suggest earplugs, but I kinda need my job, so I'll keep schtum.

"This one," the woman says after what seems like an age. She jabs a chubby finger at the package, and I nod and smile.

"Of course. Let me just check the availability of that one for you." I type it into my computer and pray to the God of Mondays that there's space on their chosen dates. I even cross my toes—and that's no easy feat in these killer shoes, I tell you.

"There's space on those dates for you," I say politely. "Would you like to book?"

"Well of course we'd like to book," the woman snaps. "Charlie! Laura! That is enough!"

I blink at the sharp tone of her voice and plaster a fake smile on my face. *Murder isn't worth the jail time, Brooke. Remember that. You're too pretty for prison.* "Of course, ma'am. Let me start that for you."

The girl—Laura, presumably—begins to cry, and Charlie stamps his feet. The high-pitched wail goes right through me. I try not to cringe at the worst delayed reaction I've seen since I egged Cain on his twenty-first birthday. He stood still for three minutes and seventeen seconds before he finally realized what I'd done.

I go through the motions of organizing, booking, planning, and taking money from the family. It takes about twenty minutes longer than it should due to the fact Charlie "broke" his foot from stamping it too hard and Laura's nose became a snot version of Niagara Falls.

I look at the clock the second they leave, sighing happily with the realization it's break time. After logging off my computer, I accept a sympathetic smile from Sarah, another travel rep, and disappear into the crummy little box Jet calls a staff room.

At least there's no Jet. A look in the cupboards reveals there's a distinct lack of cookie. And vodka. Which, after dealing with that family... the vodka is totally necessary.

I really need to start sneaking some in in a Pepsi bottle.

"Break time already, Brooke?"

I clench my teeth and turn to face my boss. "Yep."

He sneers and pushes past me to the kettle. He's actually really ugly when he sneers. It's a shame, because if he wasn't such an asshole, I'd actually consider him quite attractive with his blonde hair and blue eyes. Alas, he is an asshole, so he's about as attractive as, well, an asshole.

"How are you doing this morning?" he asks casually.

"Sold two weeks to Disneyland," I reply.

"Disneyland?"

"Couldn't afford World. I tried."

He grunts. "And that's it?"

"That's it. It is 10 a.m. on a Monday morning, Jet." I take my tea and sit at the table. "I'm not going to sell a honeymoon to the Maldives, am I?"

His blue eyes focus on me in slits. "I'm your boss, Brooke.

You will treat me with respect."

I snap my teeth together and smile tightly as he walks past me. Smile, smile, smile... And check online for people who are hiring.

Clearly, no-one ever told Jethro Peters that respect is something you earn.

"No, Mom, I'm not sitting around doing nothing," I half-lie, propping my feet up on the coffee table.

"Well with you not in college any more, Brooke, I do worry about you," she says through the phone.

"You half-kicked me out. Remember that argument?"

"I did it for your own good, darling. You're twenty-four. It's time you learned to look after yourself."

"I can look after myself just fine. I was the first to walk, first to be potty trained, and most importantly, the first to wipe my own ass," I remind her.

"Brooke!" she exclaims, her shrill tone almost deafening.

I jump, nearly dropping the phone.

"What?" I ask, righting it against my ear. "I'm just telling it how it is."

Mom sighs, and I can almost hear her wondering how she raised such a goddamn mess for a daughter. "No wonder you're single."

"Being single is a life choice. Not everyone needs a man to feel good. That's why they created vibrators."

"I... I can no longer have this conversation. I will see you on Sunday for dinner. Goodbye, Brooke." The line goes dead.

I grin.

And that is why I'm so exhausting. It gets rid of Mommy Dearest.

My mother does not talk about sex. The closest she gets is

reminding me of my relationship status and lack of higher education. The fact I don't own a degree, when my brother and sister both do means I apparently need to be looked after by someone who does have one.

Hmph. I am an independent woman, not a dependent, baby-making, barefoot housemaid. I can wash my own underwear, cook my own food—kind of—and do my own DIY. I can even work out when something is broken. Okay, that's usually because it doesn't turn on, but I can work it out and find the number for customer service.

Anyway, the point is, I do not need a man. Any man. I don't even need their help. At all.

I move to get up, and right at that moment, my TV screen goes blank and all my lights go out. My fridge is no longer whirring, and I can't see my hand in front of my face. Shit.

I really, really, hate power outages.

I sit for five minutes in the darkness, waiting for the electric to come back on. I'm starting to panic. Not because I have no heating or hot water or light, but because I just know that the ice cream in my freezer is melting as I speak. This is some power outage.

Using my phone as I move, I slip my feet into my slippers and trudge down the dark hall and staircase to the apartment below mine. There's no point trying the light, so my little phone screen will have to do.

I make it to the bottom of the stairs without tripping and mentally pat myself on the back. I knock on the door. No answer. I knock again, louder this time. No answer.

Dammit. It looks like I need a man.

I reluctantly dial Cain's number and make my way back up the stairs to my apartment.

"Yellow?" he answers.

"I need you."

"It's not often you tell me that." He chuckles. "What have you done?"

"What makes you assume that I have done something?"

"Because you usually have."

Whatever. Asshole. "I have no electricity. I think a transformer blew."

"How long has it been off?"

"Um, ten minutes."

"Are you there alone?" I can hear him moving in the background.

"Yes."

"Want me to come over?"

"Um. Yes. Please."

"See you in five."

I hang up and fall backwards onto my sofa. So much for being an independent woman.

Maybe I'll just be an independent woman during the day... when the power's on. And when there are no spiders in my tub.

Yep—definitely need a man for the bathtub spiders.

I stare into the darkness for an indeterminate amount of time, and unfortunately, my entire life flashes before my eyes. Ironic in the darkness, I know, but still. It feels like I see everything... Friendships and heartbreaks and my mother's horrified look when my sister got married to a respected doctor seven years her senior...

Except the horror was directed at me for my closest dating prospect being a chocolate fudge cake, so what do I know?

Cain lets himself into my apartment using his spare key and shines a tiny LED flashlight around. "You there, B?"

"Yup." I hold up my empty wine bottle as high as I can for his light to flick over it.

"Where are you?"

"Upside down on the couch."

"Why are you upside down on the couch?"

"Because I got bored waiting for you. And I was on the phone with my mom earlier."

Shuffling, and then, "That explains a lot. I'll be back in a minute."

I blow out a long breath, then, a minute later, I hear a couple of knocks and a loud click before my lights come back with a few flickers.

Holy shit. Did he turn the power on? How did he do that?

"How did you do that?" I ask at the sound of him shutting my door.

Cain leans on the back of the sofa next to my feet and grins, his handsome face sadly right in alignment with mine. "It wasn't the transformer. Your breaker tripped off. I just went down to the basement to turn it back on."

Lord only knows what that is, but his face is real close to me... I swing my legs around from the back cushions and sit up, only to find my face right back close to him.

I can see every dip and curve of his face. Every dark, curly eyelash that frames his gorgeous green eyes. Every little stubbly hair that decorates his jaw. The soft dimple at the edge of his mouth...

Eesh. I slide back across the sofa an inch. "What's a breaker?"

He stares at me blankly for a second before recognition flits through his startling gaze. "When the hell did I ever think it was a good idea to let you live alone?"

That's offensive. I'm twenty-four, not twelve. And all the movies I've seen show a clear affinity for hot guys in apartment blocks, or at least dodgy, sixty-something maintenance guys. Wasn't that real?

"I wasn't aware you were responsible for making that decision," I say dryly.

A small grunt leaves him. "We should have moved in together."

My heart sputters a little. Vomits, actually. And misses the toilet bowl. Or anything remote close to being able to catch it.

"So I could hear you and Nina bumpin' uglies every night? Hell no!" I stand up and walk into my kitchen. I need a drink, and, well, my mom made me drink what was left of that wine bottle.

"You think I'd do that if we lived together?" he asks tightly.

Oh, he sounds a little pissed. Good. I'm a little pissed.

"Maybe. I don't know, do I? Where else are ya gonna do it? Out the back by the dumpsters? Against a tree?"

I spin around to find him standing right in front of me. My eyes automatically find his bright green ones and fixate on them, but I'm not sure who's holding who captive. His gaze is intense, a spark of anger in the depths of it.

"Then maybe I should move in," he says tightly.

I step back, still clutching my unopened bottle of wine. Jesus, no. What a bad idea. "Why the hell would you do that?"

"To prove you wrong."

"You don't need to prove me wrong. I haven't even lived here for a week yet. Besides, I don't want Nina in my apartment." I'm not even going to bother to disguise my dislike for her. I've tried to like her. I've failed. Is it petty? Yes. Do I care? No.

Do I need to grow up a little? Eh, probably.

"It wouldn't be your apartment if I moved in," he says.

"Precisely." I slam the wine bottle down on the island in the middle of the kitchen. "This is *my* apartment, not *ours*. Completely forgetting Nina, you would drive me completely insane if you lived here. And even if you do consider it..." I pause as... it... flashes in my mind, "you'd have to fuck her in the elevator or I'd pour bleach over her head. Mind you, it'd save her the salon trip... But still. No, Cain. You're not living with me because, lord help me, I cannot stand the Barbie to your Ken."

I put my hands on my hips with a sense of finality and determination flooding my veins, my fingers brushing his as I do so.

We're standing so close that our bodies are almost touching. His hands are ghosting over mine, and there's barely room to breathe between our chests. We're so close that if I raised myself onto my tiptoes, our lips would brush the way our fingers just did.

And judging by the way his gaze keeps flitting toward my

mouth, Cain knows it.

My heart thunders against my ribs. No, no. I don't want to feel this attraction right now. I'm mad at him, damn it. I'm mad at his stupid-ass suggestion he should move in because I can't live by myself. I'm not swallowing to stop my mouth drying out because his fitted t-shirt shows his muscles to perfect and his jeans are slung low on his hips.

No. None of it. I'm not trying not to kiss him right now.

I bite the inside of my cheek and dig my fingers into my sides as he takes a deep breath. His eyes flick to my mouth where they linger on my lips for a moment, then glance back up.

"You drive me fucking crazy every single day, Brooke," he mutters, green eyes searching mine compellingly. "And you're right. Living with you would be a goddamn disaster. If we lived together, I might actually do something about it." He turns from me and stalks across my apartment, then wrenches my front door open.

I'm stunned into silence, unable to do anything but watch him as he passes through it, tugging it to slam behind him. Drive him...

I drive him crazy?

Is he crazy?

He must be. Must be totally insane.

If he had any idea what crazy meant, he'd be all up in my business, but he'd know why I'm crazy.

I want to run out the door after him and scream at him that's he's the reason I'm so crazy. That he's the reason I exist in a half-world of fucking insanity caused by nothing more or less than his bottle-blonde bitch of a girlfriend.

Until my mother calls. Again. And puts a thankful end to what was about to be a bad choice.

"Hello, Mother," I say into the phone, leaning back against the door Cain just slammed. "Another call? You're up late."

"Your brother-in-law just got a promotion!" she shrieks. "Isn't it wonderful, Brooke? He's head of the pediatric department and runs his own clinic so he'll have more time at home with Billie and the kids!"

Ah.

My brother-in-law: Marcus.

The decorated doctor.

"Wonderful, Mom," I say. "I'll call Billie tomorrow. I'm in work early so I have to go. Bye!"

I hang up and throw my phone across my apartment to the sofa. It bounces off the cushion and onto the floor. The last thing I want to hear is how perfect my big sister's life is and how she and Doctor Saint can do no wrong.

Especially not when my heart is still stuttering in my chest at my recent closeness to Cain.

I swallow and push off the door, turning back to lock it. That can't happen again.

Because I'm a little afraid of what he meant when he said I drive him crazy.

LIFE TIP #5: A GOOD HAIRCUT CAN CHANGE YOUR LIFE. SO CAN ONLINE PORN AND MASTURBATION.

I drop into the chair at Cain's mom's salon and tug the towel around my shoulders. I haven't spoken to him since he turned my power back on two nights ago, and honestly, despite the fact Carly is sitting herself in the chair next to mine, I feel a little lost.

I can't remember the last time we went over twenty-four hours without even sending a text. I'm seriously trying not to be butthurt over it, but I'm failing miserably. Coming for a haircut was supposed to make me feel better, but I don't think it's working.

It's awkward. Me and Cain. I'm used to the status quo of our relationship—I hate his girlfriends, he's skeptical of every guy I date, we joke with each other, and then we eat pizza and watch movies.

This new... level... where I want to kiss him all the time when his face is close to mine is unnerving.

Don't get me wrong. I've wanted to kiss the guy as long as I can remember. I've loved him for, like, ever, but this needing to kiss him? This temptation? Yeah...that's new.

The only good thing in this entire situation right now is that his mom isn't heading up the Nina Groupie Club either.

Mandy Elliott is three things: protective, fierce, and loyal. She has the permanent mindset that nobody will ever be good for any of her three boys, no matter how beautiful or sweet or successful they are. She especially isn't a fan of Nina, mostly because she embodies the things she hates most. She's selfish, needy, and dependent on Cain for just about everything, despite the fact they live on opposite sides of town.

Yes, I am aware I'm dependent on Cain, but not like Barbie Boiler is. I'm a damsel in distress. She's a damsel on her freaking deathbed.

Besides, if I ever get over the guy, I'll have someone else to flick my breaker for me.

Both literally and figuratively.

I'm aware I sound like a bitch. Truly, I am, and maybe my view of Nina is wildly distorted, but if anyone can look me in the eye and tell me they've never thought anything similar about the girlfriend of someone they deeply care about, then they can judge me.

Until then, settle down, Betty, because your opinion isn't needed.

"Did you change the theme for your party?" Carly asks Mandy as her stylist, Ronnie, grabs her comb.

"Oh my gosh, yes! Didn't Cain tell you?" Mandy meets my gaze in the mirror, a slight frown marring her bra. "We decided yesterday morning to change to a fifties theme."

"Oooh, fun!" Carly squeals, clapping her hands.

Ronnie taps the top of her head with her comb. "Sit still, woman. Unless you want three inches off instead of one."

Carly immediately stills, and Ronnie flashes me a wicked grin. Don't mess with Carly and her hair.

"No, he didn't say anything," I answer Mandy as she works out a knot.

"Hmm." She tugs extra hard on a particularly stubborn knot.

"Owwww!" I wince, yanking myself away from her. "What was that for?"

"Whatchu do?" Her tone is demanding as she grabs me and sets me back straight in the chair. "Y'all talk every day."

"Hey!" I say, wrapping my hand around the back of my hair where she caught the knot. "Why are you assuming it was me? Never in the history of our friendship has it been

48

me."

"She has a point," Carly adds, taking my corner. "Ninety-nine-point-nine percent of the time, it's Cain who messed up."

"Thank you." I'll ignore that zero-point-zero-one percent of the time thing.

Mandy rolls her eyes and moves my hand so she can get back to cutting. "Now, his bad mood makes sense. Nina came around for dinner last night, started talking about the kids in her class to nobody in particular, and after ten non-stop minutes, Cain snapped at her to give it a rest and went to his apartment."

Ah, yes—just in case I didn't mention it before, Cain lives in an apartment above his parents' garage. Not because he doesn't have the money to move out, but because the apartment was already there and he wants to build his house, not buy it.

I know. I don't get it either.

"He yelled at her?" Carly asks, raising her eyebrows. "He never yells at her."

Mandy shrugs and unclips a section on my hair. "I guess he's getting fed up of her rabbitin' on every damn second she can. Lord only knows I am. I had to pray for strength to deal with her before dinner, and I raised three boys born three years apart."

She has a point. We were teens when they moved to town, and those boys put her through absolute craziness. It was as soon as one left a stage, the next one started it, so on and so forth. I imagine she prayed a hell of a lot during that time, but I've never known her to pray for strength to deal with one of their girlfriends.

And Cain's brothers have dated some floozies.

Then again, Mandy never assumed said floozies would last. Is she praying because she thinks Nina might?

Jesus, she's not the only one who needs to pray...

"Maybe he's getting fed up of her shit. I know I'm fed up of hearing about her shit from Brooke," Carly continues.

"I'm going to sit on your head next time you stay with me," I warn her. "And I'm going to bounce. Hard."

Mandy's laugh as she combs my hair is loud. "You girls," she chuckles. "Don't ever change."

"I don't plan to," Carly answers. "But Brooke could use some work."

"That's it. I'm farting on your head too."

Mandy laughs again, cutting through our dumb exchange. "Now, y'all know I don't like to gossip..."

Ronnie bursts into a conveniently-timed coughing fit, making Mandy whack her with her comb.

"Of course not," I say to her with a perfectly straight face. "Never have I ever heard you gossip."

"Don't you sass me, Brooke Barker," Mandy says, snipping some of my hair.

"Sorry."

She rolls her eyes. "I heard on the Barley-vine that Nina is hoping for a little...*more*...than Cain is ready for."

Carly and I both frown in sync. Not just because of what she's saying, but because the Barley-vine—the aptly named gossip train in Barley Cross—isn't always, shall we say, accurate?

"More?" Carly asks. "Like...a ring?"

"Not *like* a ring," Ronnie answers. "A ring. She wants to get engaged, but Cain isn't ready."

"Of course he isn't ready. Cain doesn't have a girlfriend. He has a limpet." The words explode out of me before I can say anything.

"As opposed to how wonderfully unattached to him you are," my best friend shoots back dryly.

Mandy drops my hair so I can turn my chair and kick her. The side of my foot makes contact with Carly's lower leg, and she yelps.

"You asked for that." I glare at her. "He's my best guy friend. I'm supposed to be attached to him. He's supposed to do all the stuff my eventual future boyfriend will do. It's in his job description."

"Or you could just go on a second date with Simon and have him do that stuff."

"Maybe I don't want to go on a second date with Simon."

"Who's Simon?" Mandy and Ronnie ask us in unison.

Carly launches into an explanation almost identical to the one she gave me a few days ago when she was trying to talk me into the double date.

"You sound like you're trying to sell a television set that is really reliable but has no satellite or cable capabilities," I say the second she shuts up. Lord, she could sell shit to a dung beetle if given half a chance. "Simon is a perfectly nice guy."

"And that's what you say when you think the TV looks good but will perform like crap," Mandy summarizes. "Carly, girl, you know Brooke will do what she wants, with who she wants, when she wants. And we all know that until she stops being hung up on Cain, no amount of dates—bad or otherwise—are gonna convince her otherwise."

"I am not hung up on Cain!" My denial comes out a little too shrill.

Mandy raises one eyebrow, catching my gaze in the mirror. "Honey, believe me when I say there's nothin' more I'd like than for my son to come to his dang senses about you. Everybody knows you got feelings for him."

"Everybody except him." Ronnie snickers.

I huff and slide down in my chair. A quick, sharp tap from Mandy's comb has me sitting back upright again as the door opens. "Y'all're so cruel to me. If I could get over that pain in the damn ass, I would."

"Get over who?" Cain's soft voice travels through the salon.

My eyes widen, and thanks to the mirror, I know I look like a deer in headlights.

"Her vibrator," Carly answers without missing a beat. "She dropped it in the bath this morning and it's dead."

I peer at Cain in the mirror. His eyebrows are raised so high they're an inch from disappearing into his hairline, and his lips are twitching up at on side.

51

"She's really buzzed off about it," she adds, literally adding insult to injury.

Mandy chuckles behind me.

"You need to get over your vibrator?" Cain walks around the back of my chair and stands on the opposite side to his mom. "Brooke, that's dramatic, even for you."

I open my mouth but nothing comes out. I set my lips into a thin line and drop my gaze as my cheeks flame.

God damn it. See? This is why you don't fall in love with your best friend. If I weren't hopelessly and pathetically in love with him, I'd have been able to answer that question completely honestly and we'd all have moved on by now.

"Are you done yet?" I ask Mandy, ignoring Cain. "I don't feel like taking Carly's shit anymore today."

My traitorous bestie laughs.

"Nope." Mandy grabs the hair dryer. "Have to dry it."

"I can take it wet." I make to stand.

Cain grabs my shoulder and pushes me back down into the seat. "You look like a drowned rat. Sit down."

"Rather look like a drowned rat than a human mothball," I mutter, taking in his dusty appearance.

He laughs, taking the chair next to me.

I joke, but under all the dirt, it's really quite unfair how good he looks. Sure, there's a thin layer of dust covering his clothes and a few specks in his hair, but he really doesn't look like a human mothball.

I, however, look like Golem in a Wednesdsay Addams wig sitting in front of this mirror.

I'm pretty sure I only look this bad in front of a salon mirror. Either that or I'm deluding myself normally. It's probably the latter. It's already well-established I'm a walking disaster.

I want to sit grumpily as Mandy does my hair, but it's incredibly hard to be grumpy when someone is blow-drying your hair. The warmth from the dryer combined with the strangely satisfying feeling of having your hair lightly tugged as it's brushed is too soothing to ever be mad.

By the time my hair is dry, I look like a real person again, with shiny, bouncy hair.

I sigh happily, smoothing my hands down my hair. "Honestly, a good haircut is just like sex."

"You're sleeping with the wrong guys," Cain says under his breath, standing up.

"I'm not sleeping with any guys," I shoot back at him.

He pauses. "At all?"

"At all."

"This escalated quickly." Carly stands up and grabs her purse. "Here, Ronnie. Here's forty bucks. Keep the change. I need to escape the awkward."

"No!" I say too loudly. "We have to go shopping. I have nothing to wear this weekend and you need to find me something."

She sighs, leaning on the counter and burying her face into her hand. "Of course I do. Otherwise you'll end up coming like a twenties flapper and not a fifties pin up."

"It's not my fault I'm era-challenged."

"You're everything challenged."

"I beg to differ."

She quirks an eyebrow. "On what basis?"

"I sold three weeks to Disney World this morning and didn't kill the screeching twins." Okay, so the last part is touch and go...

"Brooke, if that's the best thing you have to say about yourself, Carly's gonna have to do more than take you shopping." Mandy laughs, stepping behind the reception counter. She scratches out my name and takes the money I hand her.

"This weekend?" Cain asks, mug of coffee in hand.

"You got nothin' better to do than drink my coffee, son?" Mandy questions, unamused.

"No," he answers before turning back to me. "This weekend?"

"Yes," I say slowly. "Your mom's birthday party. Remember that? The big five-oh? It's only been planned for, oh, four months."

"Ha, ha, ha." His tone is dry. "Of course I remember. I just didn't think you were going."

I frown at him, zipping up my purse. "Why wouldn't I be going?"

"Because Nina is," Carly stage-whispers to me.

Slick. Real slick. Idiot.

"Brooke, can I talk to you?" Cain turns to me with his jaw clenched. "Alone?"

I roll my eyes. "Outside." I push off the counter and walk through the salon to the sound of Carly's tutting. Yeah, I don't get it either, but whatever.

I step out onto the pavement into the blistering midday heat, shuddering as the humidity slams into me. Cain follows, shutting the door behind him.

"What do you want?" I meet his gaze. "Considering you haven't spoken to me for two days."

He scrubs his hand through his hair, looking sheepish. "What time are you going to Mom's party?"

"Why? You want me to avoid your girlfriend?"

He doesn't answer. Ironic how *that* is the answer I'm looking for.

"Oh, for fuck's sake, Cain!" The words explode out of me. "Are you kidding me? You want me to spend less time at your mom's party just so I don't run into your girlfriend?"

"Okay," he says quietly. "It sounds bad when you say it out loud."

"You mean that sounded good in your head?"

"Maybe."

A sound that's similar to a growl escapes from between my lips. "That's unreal! If your girlfriend doesn't want to be around me, then that's fine, because I don't want to talk to her either."

He winces. "Brooke..."

"No." I step toward him and jab my finger against his chest. Both anger and hurt swirls inside of me as the distance closes between us, and I hit him with a hard stare. "Listen to me, Cain. She and I will never get along, and that's fine, but don't ever try to push me out again because of her. I was here before she was, and when y'all break up, I'll still be here. I'm going to be at the party and if that's awkward for you, tough shit."

"I wasn't trying to." He grabs my shoulders before I can turn away. "Damn it, Brooke," he says much more softly.

I wriggle out of his hold, then yank at the salon door. "Carly, let's go! I need a dress for this party that will piss off my mother."

"Hell yes!" She fist bumps and spins on her heel. "Now you're talking."

I grin and step away from the door, letting it fall closed as Carly hugs both Mandy and Ronnie.

"Brooke." Cain steps in front of me and takes my face in his hands. My skin tingles as his palms connect with my cheeks and his fingertips tease my hair. His green eyes search my face before he settles on meeting my gaze and speaks quietly, "You really think I'd push you out for her?"

My heart thumps loudly.

I ignore it and bat his hands away, instantly feeling the loss of his touch in a way that's far too intimate. "Do I? Maybe. I'm not sure I know who you are right now."

six

LIFE TIP #6: SOMETIMES BEING CRUEL TO BE KIND IS A REAL BITCH. OH NO, WAIT. THE BITCH IS YOU.

"*D*amn it, damn it, damn it!" I kick the washing machine and a sharp pain shoots through my big toe and along the top of my foot. "Double fucking damn it!" I hiss, leaning back against the kitchen counter and grabbing my foot.

I should have known better than to buy a second-hand machine.

Granted, I also should have known better than to kick the freaking thing too, but alas.

Why did I buy a second hand washing machine? I've had it barely a week and it's already broken. I have good credit— you know, for someone with, like, fifteen thousand dollars of school fees to pay—so I should have just bought one on that.

Now, I can't wash my panties.

And now my phone is ringing. Fifty bucks says that's my mother. Why would it be anyone else?

I limp through my apartment and grab my cell from the sofa. Yep. My mom. Wonderful!

"Hi, Mom."

Holy shit, that was a bit too cheery.

"Hello, Brooke," she answers suspiciously. "Why aren't you in work?"

"I finished an hour ago. Why did you call if you thought I'd be working?"

She sniffs. "I was hoping I could leave a message."

Oh boy. Not as much as I wish you could have.

"Oh, well, sorry to disappoint you." Again. "Since we're

here, what's up?" I drop onto the sofa.

"I spoke to Mandy earlier. She said you got your hair cut."

"Mhmm."

"She said you and Cain are fighting."

Damn it, Mandy.

"We're not fighting," I say slowly. "I don't get along with his girlfriend and it makes it awkward."

"Brooke." My mother says my name with all the exasperation of dealing with a stubborn two-year-old. "You've never been friendly with his girlfriends. You never will be."

"It's not my fault he picks hookers and assholes."

"Brooke Barker! Must you be so crude?"

I grin at the blatant horror in her voice. "You taught me to always be honest, Mother. This is really on you."

She gasps. "There's honestly and then there's vile! That was vile."

"Sorry, it's how I feel."

"If I didn't feel the need to have this discussion with you, I'd hang up right now."

"If I say hooker a few more times, will you dump whatever conversation you plan to have with me?"

"You need to get over Cain Elliott," she says, ignoring me entirely.

I still. "That was...unexpected."

"Brooke." Her voice actually softens. Just a little. Like when you drop an ice cube on the floor and the barest slither of it cracks off. "It's devastatingly clear that Cain doesn't return your feelings. Why do you have to continue on with these emotions when there are plenty of good men out there who'd have you?"

Scratch that. The ice didn't chip. Just melted a little.

"Okay, well, first," I start, "I'm more than aware of how Cain doesn't feel about me, but that doesn't mean I can switch off the way I feel. If I could, I would have. And second, there are 'plenty of good men' who'd have me? What am I, a puppy in the pet store window? Am I purebred or a mutt?"

"Now, you're being unreasonable."

"Did you call just to remind me of how I should and shouldn't feel about my best friend or is there another point to this?"

"I see you're unwilling to discuss Cain—"

"Really? What gave it away?"

"—So I will continue onto my next point and say that, considering your grandfather will be attending, I hope you will be dressed appropriately for Mandy's party this weekend."

I pause, smacking my lips together. Appropriately? She realizes it's fifties themed, right? The era in which women were sexier than ever?

And Grandpa is there? Yeah, sure. What I'm wearing will be of concern to him. Surely she knows he's where I get my crazy?

"Sure, Mom," I lie loosely. "I'll be dressed appropriately."

For the era. Maybe not the health of her heart, but that's her own fault for not specifying the appropriateness. Right?

"Are Ben and Billie going to be there?" *Please say no. Please say no. Please say no.*

"Ben won't be, but Billie is planning on going, yes."

Wonderful! That's what I need. My sister. My perfect, skinny sister. Who I do actually happen to love very much. From a distance. Without her kids. "Great. I haven't seen her for a couple weeks."

"That's because you never call her," Mom replies with the perfect amount of disdain. "You should really call your sister."

"Uh, she doesn't call me either," I point out. "Besides, we're not each other's keepers. This isn't Jodi Picoult, Mom."

"You'd be much nicer if Jodi Picoult wrote you into a story."

"No. I'd be someone who runs away and puts her mother through hell."

"Darling," Mom drawls dryly, "It's adorable you think you

have to run away to do that."

"You're right." I grin. This is fun. "I'll just move back in."

"Now that would be hell," she agrees. "Are you bringing Simon to Mandy's party?"

"Why would I be bringing Simon to Mandy's party?"

"You went on a date, didn't you?"

Fuck it, Carly!

I sigh. "A date, Mother. One. Just one. He hasn't called me yet."

Her answering sigh rivals mine. "I might just sign you up to one of these dating shows on TV that your sister likes."

"Callontheotherlinegottagobye!" I spit the words out without taking a breath and hang up. Looking at the call time, I nod at the length of the conversation. Four minutes and fifteen seconds. That's pretty good for me.

Instead of getting up—I'm comfy, okay?—I pull up my messages and text Carly.

Me: *Did you tell my mom about Simon?*

She replies instantly.

Carly: *She asked if you were dating and I got scared*
Me: *You should be scared of me, you backstabbing bitch*
Carly: *Ah, Simon hasn't called*
Me: *Of course Simon hasn't called me. I wouldn't call me. I'm a mess.*
Carly: *I'm trying really hard to find a reason to disagree with you right now*
Carly: *What if I find you a date for Mandy's party?*
Me: *You just want to watch me burn, don't you?*
Carly: *-laughing emojis-*
Carly: *It is fun.*
Me: *If you bring me a date to Mandy's party I'm going to pull bobby pins from my hair and stick them up your ass in a long trail, one by one, while you scream at me*
Carly: *Kinky. Spoken to Cain yet?*

Me: *No. If I speak to him I'll stop being mad at him and I'm not ready for that right now*
Carly: *Your such a loser*
Me: *The most insulting part of that text message was your appalling grammar*
Me: *It's *you're, by the way*
Carly: *Go fuck yourself*
Me: *Good idea. Am gonna get the vibrator. Brb.*
Carly: *I don't know how I put up with you*
Me: *I bring you wine*
Carly: *Good point. Now go away. I have to get ready for dinner with my mom and her new boyfriend and it's scary enough without you rabbiting on*
Me: *Aw, I love you too, you shithead*
Carly: *-middle finger emoji-*

I drop my phone and laugh to myself. Well, that killed a whole five minutes.

One thing I never anticipated about living alone is the silence. I mean, seriously, it's unnerving. Every whining water pipe is a zombie who wants to eat my brains out, and every gust of wind against the windows is a ghost determined to possess my soul.

And don't even go there with the creaks outside my front door. They're clearly the work of a cannibalistic mass-murderer who wants to gouge out my heart with a wooden spoon before eating it for breakfast.

See? Unnerving. Terrifying. Fuck-this-I-need-a-roomie. Whatever.

I put my phone back down on the sofa to where it was before my mom called and get up. I really need to eat something, but I'm not so great at cooking, so... My pants will also agree that my diet is super bad, so I'm going to have to try something.

Pasta. I can't mess up chicken and pasta in a sauce, can I?

Don't answer that question. I don't want to hear the answer because I'm pretty sure I already know it.

I open the fridge and pull out the packet of chicken. The date says yesterday, so I wrinkle my nose as I slice open the cellophane top and lift the pack to my nose.

Oh good lord no! That is not good chicken!

I dump it in the trashcan and slam the top shut. It clangs through my silent apartment, and ultimately, I decide upon the pasta and the sauce. Add some cheese... So, I'm not Gordon Ramsey, but I'll take being one of the poor little shits he yells at.

Without the yelling.

I'm sensitive. Like a clitoris.

The fizz of something burning on the ceramic ring as the pan of water I just set boiling on the stoveheats up fills the kitchen area, and as it burns away into nothing, I pull the pasta and sauce out of the cupboard.

Woo. Look at me, adulting all over the place.

Settle down, Brooke, you're only boiling water.

I lean against the side while I wait for it to heat up. Can you burn water? Is that a thing that's possible? I've never heard of it before, but of course, that doesn't mean a lot... I could Google it.

I throw half the packet of pasta into the pan and relax again.

Good lord, of course you can't burn water. I can evaporate it but not burn it. What's wrong with me?

This is what happens when my life goes to shit and I'm not talking to Cain. I joke about not falling in love with your best friend—no, wait, that's not a joke.

It's awkward. He and Carly are the men in white coats to my crazy. I always have been and always will be the forgetful, scatty friend out of the three of us. Carly is the logical one, and Cain is somewhere between us both, but more than anything, he's the comfort between us.

Guy problems? We go to him.

Well. Carly does. It would be awkward for me since he is, you know, the guy problem in my life.

I sigh just as my phone buzzes from the sofa. I eye the

pasta before going to grab it and lighting up the screen. Text message from Cain.

Did I think his name too many times or something?

Cain: *I need to talk to you.*

Ha! Does he, now? I should think he wants to apologize after our conversation outside his mom's salon. And if he doesn't want to, he freaking well should. I hit reply.

Me: *People usually try to avoid talking to me.*
Cain: *I know. I'm one of them.*
Me: *You're a dick.*
Me: *Can't talk. I'm cooking.*
Cain: *K, I'll wait.*
Me: *For what?*
Cain: *You to burn it and need food.*
Me: *If you think you can buy my time with food, you're wrong.*

I put my phone on the kitchen side and grab a wooden spoon. Shoving it into the pasta bowl, I stir, and...
Shit.
It's stuck to the bottom. And burned.
Of course it is! Fuck you, life. What did I ever do to you?
Clearly I didn't put enough water in the pan. Or, you know, pay attention to it. Ugh! I pout, turn off the heat, and scrape the hot, burned pasta into the trashcan. Sure as hell, there's no water left in the pan at all.
I shouldn't have been so cocky about adulting, should I? Is burning my pasta the universe's way of keeping me humble?
Reluctantly, I pick up my phone and text Cain again.

Me: *I burned my pasta.*
Cain: *How much will an hour cost me?*

Hmm...

Me: *Mamma Alessandra's meatball lasagna.*
Cain: *I'll pick you up in ten.*

All right, maybe he *can* buy my time with food.

I scoop my hair around to one side of my neck as I sit in Cain's car. His bright, green gaze flicks toward me right as I slam the car door behind me and grab my seatbelt.

"How did you burn pasta?" he asks, amusement a thick undertone in his voice.

"I was too busy noting down all the ways I'd like to kill you in my diary," I reply with a straight face, not looking at him.

If I look at him, I'll laugh. I don't want to laugh, because I'm still mad, and if I laugh, I won't be mad. Or maybe I will—but he won't think I'm still mad.

Hmm. If I laugh, will he be lulled into a fake sense of security?

No wonder men think we're complicated. I just confused *myself* with those thoughts.

"Brooke."

"What?" I jerk my head around to him.

His lips tug up on one side. "Obviously you found a way you liked, because you're muttering under your breath."

I glare at him. "You're walking a real fine line for someone who's on my shit list."

"I've been on your shit list since I refused to give you a pencil in math class in eighth grade. You just bump me up and down it depending on how you feel about me on any given day." He laughs low, the husky sound filling the car. "Where am I today? Top or bottom?"

"Your own fucking list, asshole."

He pulls up down the street from Italia and puts the car into park. "Wow. And not even buying you food has me bumped down?"

I purse my lips and raise my eyebrows in a, "What do you think?" expression and hope he gets the message.

"Wow." He frowns slightly. "You look kind of like your mom when you do that."

I launch myself at him with my fist balled, but he laughs, grabbing my tiny fist in his much larger hand.

"Calm down, Rambo," he says in a low, slow voice.

I blink up at him, and our faces are too close together. Way too close. I can smell the mint of his gum on his breath as he exhales and it tickles my chin. My heart beats dangerously loud, feeling closer to a palpitation than anything remotely comfortable.

I swallow and sit back, tugging my fist from his grip. "I hate you so much right now."

Cain pauses, staring at me for a moment that seems to drag on. Then, he shakes his head. "Come on. Alessandro set up the roof for us."

I get out of the car. "The roof? Wow. Someone doesn't want to be seen with me."

"At one of the most romantic restaurants in town? That's not going to work out well for me."

"Oh, yeah," I say, looking down at my torn jeans and hooded sweater as I work a knot out of my hair. "This is usual date attire. I can totally see how someone would get best friends of a decade having food together confused with an actual date. Never mind that the sexiest thing about tonight will be when I get to go home and take these freaking pants off." I roll my eyes and step up onto the sidewalk.

He shoots me a look before he walks to the fire escape at the side.

"You're fucking kidding me," I say slowly.

"Brooke. Can you just humor me?"

"The fact I haven't told you to fuck yourself and walked home yet *is* me humoring you."

Cain sighs. "Just walk up the damn stairs, okay? I happen to know that Nina's parents are inside for their anniversary."

Now I know why he parked down the street. "Then why didn't you just come to my place to talk to me?"

He pauses and looks over his shoulder. The dim light from the streetlight glances over his face, highlighting his sharp, angular features, and bounces off his eyes. "Can you do this for me without arguing with me? Please?"

I inhale slowly but deeply, letting the breath fill my lungs to bursting point before letting it go raggedly. "Fine."

I shove past him and walk up the metal fire escape stairs. Each one clangs beneath my ballerina flats, mostly because I'm channeling my inner toddler and not bothering to be careful going up here at all.

"Fairy fucking elephant," Cain says quietly behind me as I step up onto the roof garden area. The gate is unlocked, so I push it open and brush past the plants that usually conceal it.

Ignoring my asshole best friend, I look around the roof. Italia's rarely advertises its roof garden, mostly because downstairs is big enough to handle a rush, and nobody likes running up and down the stairs from the main area to the roof fifty thousand times a night.

Also: tourists. If they knew this existed, we locals would never have a place to go to get Mamma Alessandra's amazing food during the high season and holidays.

It's nothing special, not really, but it feels it. Canopies and gentle lighting occupies the area, and the area Georgio ordered his son to set up for us is my favorite corner. I suspect he did that deliberately, because the two plush sofas surrounding the table have new cushions on, and there's already a bottle of my favorite wine sitting in a bucket with two glasses.

I pick up the small card and read it.

Because men are assholes.
—Mamma / Alessandra

I smile and set it back down. "Looks like Mamma's got your number," I say to Cain with a pointed look as I sit down.

He grabs the card. "Shit. That woman is good."

"So are the gossips," I counter. No doubt our conversation yesterday outside the salon was heard by no less than five members of the weekly bridge club Mamma Alessandra presides over...which means that my grandpa will have questions at Mandy's party. Not that he can talk. He only plays bridge because he has a crush on Mamma Alessandra. He's not even good at it.

Poker? Sure. Grandpa could take down the Las Vegas mob if he wanted to. But bridge? Nah.

"Yeah. The gossips are why we're upstairs," Cain says after a moment.

"I thought it's because the future in-laws are downstairs."

"They're not my future in-laws." He looks up, his stare as sharp as his tone.

"That's not what I heard."

"What you heard is probably my mom's rendition and interpretation of Nina's conversation at dinner this week," he grumbles.

I pour wine into my glass, letting him stew in silence for a minute before I pass him the bottle and say, "Is she wrong?"

He grabs the bottle a little too roughly. "I didn't text you because I want to talk about Nina."

"Yeah, well, this might be the only time I want to talk about her, so take advantage of it."

"You don't want to talk about her. You want to bathe in my discomfort."

I raise my glass to my lips and try to hide my smile behind it. "Is it that obvious?"

Cain stares at me. "I can see you smiling, Brooke. Nice try."

Whatever. At least I tried to hide it, right? "Your mom said she's angling for a ring." I turn my left hand so the back of my hand is facing him and wiggle my fingers.

He leans over and bats at my hand, only narrowly missing it. "Mom's getting carried away."

"So she doesn't want to marry you? Aw. Shame." Was that too sarcastic? It sounded too sarcastic. Shit...

"Shwamtmovewher," he says on the quietest mumble I've ever heard, averting his eyes.

"Oh, yeah, me too, I agree, enslaving the sheep would be the worst. Little Bo Peep would riot, wouldn't she?"

Cain looks up and meets my gaze. His smiles and shakes his head, then rubs his face. "You're so fucking random. Brooke. Seriously. Enslaving the sheep?"

I shrug. "Yeah, well, I don't speak grumpy. I speak fluent sarcasm, bitch, and PMS."

"I'm aware of your abilities in all three languages," he says dryly. "Nina wants me to move in with her."

I pause. Why is that more shocking than wanting marriage? Is it because it's like a trial marriage run without the expense and commitment? Because it never occurred to me that marriage would be living together?

Because if they live together that's virtually the end of our friendship?

My throat feels scratchy-dry. This is ridiculous. It could be a good thing, right? If I don't see him, then we can't be friends, and then I might just be able to get over him.

Right?

Right.

Right, right, right.

"Brooke?"

I'm saved from having to answer him when Georgio brings out a huge, steaming tray of his mom's lasagna. The rich smell of fresh Italian food momentarily jerks me out of my fog, but I can't even bring myself to give him my usual wide, bright smile.

"Thanks, G," Cain says, pulling the pan closer to the middle and grabbing the cutlery, since we always eat it straight from the pan.

Always eat it straight from the pan.

If he moves in with Nina, we'll never eat lasagna straight from the pan again. It'll be just me and Carly, and that'll be a waste, because Cain can eat half of this alone.

Georgio looks at me questioningly, but I grab my fork and pull some of the hot, melted cheese off the top. He nods once, understanding, and disappears with a light squeeze to my shoulder.

At the sound of the door closing, Cain says quietly, "Can you talk to me?"

"Are you going to move in with her?" I barely peek at him through my hair as I ask the question.

Cain's fork clangs against the pan as he sets it down. "I don't think so," he answers.

Now, I do look at him. I raise my eyebrows in question as I fork a meatball into my mouth.

"Good thing I can speak Brooke," he teases me, lips quirking. "I don't think I want to live with her. Maybe someday, but not right now. I'm still adapting to her level of...maintenance."

"Maintenance?" I ask. Then I swallow my food and ignore his raised eyebrow as he picks his fork back up. "Maintenance? What is she? A shower prone to limescale?"

This time, he laughs. Around a mouthful of food.

"Shut your mouth, you animal," I scold him.

"Rich from the one who just spoke with a mouthful of food," he shoots right back, grabbing his drink. "No, I just thought that when I moved with someone it'd be with someone who... I don't know. She spends a lot more time on the way she looks than I thought she did."

"Well, yeah," I say flatly. "You didn't think she woke up looking like that, did you?"

He shrugs.

"Boy, I have got to introduce you to the world of make-up tutorials on YouTube." I shake my head. "But I don't get it. Why does that not make you want to live with her?"

"Because I'm not that person?" he replies, it sounding more of a question than a statement. "The last time she and I went out for dinner, they gave our table away because we were late. She took so long getting ready, I ended up having to drive to four other restaurants because she said she'd taken that long to get ready and it wasn't going to waste." He pauses. "I don't know if I could take that on a daily basis."

"Yeah, but you wouldn't have to put up with mine and Carly's shit, and that's always a bonus." I try to say it upbeat, but I think it comes out a little too chirpy.

Cain eyes me. "Your fake shit isn't fooling me."

I sigh and slump. "What do you want me to say? Sure, move in with Barbie one-oh-one? Sure, I don't care if our friendship breaks down and I'm sure Carly won't mind either?"

"It wouldn't—"

"It would and you know it!" I drop my fork harshly and it clangs off the lasagna tray onto the table. I meet Cain's eyes and do my best to hold in the true strength of my emotion. I'm a big baby, I know. "She hates us, Cain, and not even in the way we hate her. I can tolerate her if I have to, but the fact you had to ask me yesterday when I'd be at your mom's party says a helluva lot about the way she feels about your friendship with me and Car."

It also says a lot about the kind of person she is. I mean, sure, I'm a bitch, but I'm a straight up bitch.

"I shouldn't have asked you that," he finally admits, unable to look at me. "I have no idea why I did. I think I panicked and tried to make it easy for myself without thinking about how it would make you feel."

"Shit," I tell him plainly. "It made me feel like complete shit."

"I got that by the way you responded. Not gonna lie, it kinda stung."

"Good." I'm not apologizing for what I said. "It was supposed to."

"You're the most honest bitch I know." He lifts his gaze to mine again, but there's no malice in it. "I deserved it. And, honestly? That probably helped me decide that moving in with her isn't a great idea. If you think I've changed, then..." He trails off and rubs his hand down his face again.

"Then what?" I ask after a moment of mutual silence.

"I care about her a lot," he answers, holding my gaze with his. "But I care about you more, Brooke. You're my best fucking friend, for god's sake. Even Carly knows I'm closest to you. I'm fucking it all up because I don't know how to handle this situation where these two sides of my life that matter to me can't collide. I don't even know if I want them to collide."

"You have to do what makes you happy. Even if it hurts other people." My words are hollow, even to me. It sounds like I've pulled them off someone's fucking happy little Pinterest board just because they sound good.

Cain shakes his head and gently sets his fork down. We've both eaten more than I thought we had, so now I'm taking that as my excuse to drink this wine. I'm thirsty from the food, not repeatedly getting my emotions fucked.

If I tell myself that enough times and all that...

"I guess I'm torn because she's not the person I ever imagined myself with." Cain toys with his wine glass, spinning it around on the spot while watching the wine swill inside it. "Even running to the store to get milk requires a full face of make-up. I thought contouring was molding a shoe stand to make it fit into someone's walk-in closet, not using so many shades of make-up on your face you look like a cast-off of the Rocky Horror Show before its all wiped together. She has more make-up than I do clothes, and shit, I don't know. I never imagined myself with someone higher-maintenance than Mariah Carey. I always imagined myself with someone like Carly...or you."

A shiver runs down my spine, but I suppress the urge to let it overtake my body.

"I tell you I'll be at your house in ten minutes and hell, I figure I'm lucky you're not wearing leggings. You probably didn't even brush your hair before you grabbed your key and left the house, let alone worried about putting make-up on."

"That's because I'm lazy," I answer. "Carly would at least grab her mascara and lip gloss to put on in the car."

"Then she'd yell at me if I turned a corner too quickly and she smudged it." He lets go of a little laugh. "It's just so fucking easy to be with you. You literally don't give a shit about what other people think of you."

"Great. I'm the cheat day on your relationship diet."

He kicks me under the table. "You keep me sane."

"Ironic, considering I drive myself crazy."

"Oh, you drive me crazy too." His grin is lopsided. "But it's crazy I can cope with. I'm used to your crazy and kinda tune it out most of the time."

I roll my eyes. "You say that like it's constant."

"It is constant. But I like it that way."

My gaze connects with his for a second before my cheeks flush a little. "So, what are you going to do about the party?"

He sighs, his shoulders slumping as he deflates. "Hope for the best when she shows up."

"Don't worry. I'm sure it'll be fine."

"Why?"

"Because Grandpa will be there." I grin.

Cain's eyes widen and he scratches his stubbled jaw. "Oh, hell."

seven

LIFE TIP #7: RESPECT YOUR ELDERS. YOU NEVER KNOW WHEN THEY'LL INSULT THE PERSON YOU HATE.

"Dad, you cannot make male anatomy out of balloons."
Mom sighs in exasperation, reaching for the balloons.

Grandpa cackles and holds the long balloon paired with two, smaller, round ones, out of her way. "Ay karumba! You can pop cherries, why not penises?"

I choke on my Diet Coke. Carly only just grabs the glass in time to stop me spilling it.

Mom's eyes bulge out of her head. "Dad!" she hisses. "That's highly inappropriate for a man of your age!"

"Is it?" Grandpa stills, the balloon penis still firmly grasped in his hand. "Dang it," he says, looking dejected.

"Balloons," Mom demands.

Grandpa pokes them in her direction. "Ehee! Good thing I've never been appropriate!" He turns to Carly. "Here, Carly. Pull my dingaling," he says, shoving the balloons in her direction.

"I'm going to regret this," she says under her breath, reaching for the balloons. She grasps the nippley bit at the end of the long balloon, pinching it, and gives a gentle tug.

"Ohoo!" Grandpa bounces out his seat with a little wiggle, his glasses almost falling off his face, which only makes him laugh harder.

"What the hell?" Cain asks, pausing in the doorway to the gazebo set up in his parents' spacious backyard.

Grandpa turns around in his chair and waves the penis balloon. "Look, son! I've got a poppable schlong!"

Cain's gaze flits between the balloons and Grandpa. Slowly, his lips curve into a smile, but his mouth and cheeks twitch as he tries to fight his amusement.

I grab my Diet Coke from the table where Carly put it and drink from it so I don't laugh too.

"I have no idea what to say to that, James," Cain wisely answers, apparently able to control his amusement.

Fifty bucks says he'd be laughing like a teenage boy if my mom weren't here, glaring at him.

Grandpa responds to him by waggling his eyebrows. Then, he cocks his finger, drawing Cain closer to him. "I tell you what, son, Donny told me a great joke at bridge last night."

Oh no.

Cain meets my gaze for a second. I widen my eyes and plead with him not to ask, but goddamn him, he does.

"All right," Cain says. "Fire away, James."

Grandpa rests his arm on the back of his chair. "What do a Boeing and a woman have in common?"

"No idea."

"They both contain a cockpit!"

I cover my hand with my mouth and look down. Oh god, oh god. *Don't laugh, Brooke. Don't do it, girl!*

Grandpa is cackling so hard I'm afraid he might hurt himself, Carly is biting her lip and looking anywhere that isn't at me or my mom, and Cain is clamping his lips together and desperately trying not to laugh.

Laughing at my grandpa does one thing: Encourage him.

"D-Dad!" Mom sputters.

Grandpa immediately sobers and looks at her. "Don't blame me, Lou. Donny told me it, and what kind of a friend to Cain would I be if I didn't share it?"

"A polite one?" Carly offers.

Grandpa spins around and points the balloon dick at her. "I saw you laughing down there, Carly Porter. Don't you tell me you didn't find that funny."

Carly freezes.

"That's what I thought." The balloon penis bobs as he

waves it at her.

"Grandpa, can you put the penis down now?" I ask gently. "The waving it around is getting alarming."

I ignore Mom's gasp at my use of the p-word.

Note to self: Next time, say cock.

Grandpa rolls his eyes. Before he puts it down, he grabs some of the string from the 'balloon table' and ties the balloons together. We all watch in a mix of silent amusement—from me, Carly, and Cain—and horror, from Mom, as he cuts the string and brandishes his now secure, poppable penis.

"Someone call that porn star fellow with the same name as me—I've found his new thwacker!" Grandpa heaves himself up out of the chair and, grabbing the roll of clear tape, hobbles over toward the door.

Where he proceeds to attach the balloons to a pole right across the top of the door.

"No!" Mom cries, scrambling up from her chair and almost slipping in the process. "Dad, do not put that...that...*thing* right there where it's the first thing anyone will see when they come in!"

"Why not?" Grandpa asks innocently, tilting his head to the side. "I thought penises were made to sit at openings. Look, Lou. I even arranged it so the balls are outside!"

"Oh, dear god," I breathe, covering my eyes with my hand.

That's it for Carly and Cain. They both burst out laughing, each of them doubling over and unable to control themselves. I can barely look at either of them while my mom sputters out many attempts at sentences that all ultimately fail.

Now I remember why we don't bring Grandpa to parties with other people.

"Good god," Eddie, Cain's dad, says from outside the gazebo. "James, what are you doing?"

I look up in time to see Grandpa turn around.

"Making penises for your old lady," he answers with a perfectly straight face.

Carly collapses forward onto the table and buries her face

in her arms. "Can't...breathe...can't..." she wheezes, her entire body shaking with each laugh.

Cain drops onto the floor next to me as his dad tries to reason with my grandfather and, at the same time, calm down my mother. "He's going to give your mom a coronary by bedtime, isn't he?"

I grimace. "How did you guess?"

"Because I've seen it happen before." He grins, leaning into me and nudging me with his elbow. "How did he come up with the penis balloon?"

"I want to say Donny, but then I feel like I'm probably not giving Grandpa enough credit." Donny is Grandpa's best friend, and the man happens to have a mind just as dirty as my grandfather's. They tend to bounce off each other's energy like a room full of toddlers. "I know he was learning how to use the computer, so maybe he Googled it."

"I can't imagine him using Google."

Given that Grandpa is currently fighting his corner for his inappropriate balloons, I can't help but agree. "This is insane."

"Agreed," Cain says, glancing at Carly. "Has her laugh always been this obnoxious?"

She sits up and kicks him, still giggling. "I heard that, you asshole."

"Yes," I answer him, quickly shifting to the side so she can't reach me with her foot. "Remember that big cat fight outside here a month ago? That was actually Carly laughing."

"I hate you so much," she snaps, glaring at me. There's no heat in her gaze though. She's all bark and no bite. Unlike her damn dog.

That thing is bark, bite, and bitch.

"Do you think your grandpa is gonna give up the balloon penis?" Cain asks.

I look up to the doorway. His dad looks as though he's run out of ideas, and my mom is physically attempting to wrestle the balloon from my grandpa.

"No," I say firmly. "Absolutely not."

I was right.

Grandpa finally got his way when Mandy came into the garden to see what his yelling was all about. She took one look at his placement of them, laughed so hard she cried, and gave him the thumbs up.

So far tonight, every single person inside the gazebo was greeted by a balloon penis over their head. They were actually directed here by them too, a fact that made Grandpa happier than I've seen him since my grandma died three years ago.

Mom didn't stand a chance. At all. And Mandy is the one person on earth she won't argue with.

Lucky Mandy.

"Your mom is gonna flip her shit when she sees how short that dress is." Carly blots out her bright red lipstick with a piece of tissue paper and meets my gaze in the mirror.

I look at myself in the full-length one attached to the wall of Mandy's spare bedroom. The black and white, polka dot dress skims the tops of my thighs, barely covering my butt by an inch. "There's nothing wrong with the length of this dress."

Not to mention hers isn't exactly a nun's habit.

"Brooke," she says slowly, dropping the tissue into the wire trash can. "You bent over five minutes ago to pull up your stocking, and I saw your underwear."

"It's not small underwear!" I protest. "Nobody's gonna see anything!"

"Except their grandma's pantaloons!"

"Maybe I like granny panties. They keep my tushy warm."

"They keep your tushy something, and what that is, is lonely."

I stick my middle finger up at her across the room and

adjust my hold-up stockings. Never mind the length of my dress—my mom is gonna flip when she sees me in these.

"Knock, knock." The sound of my sister's voice breaks through the air, but before either of us can tell her to come in, she pushes open the door and bounds into the room in all of her angelic gloriousness.

I sound like a petty bitch—which we've already established I am, thank you very much—but I'm not actually intimidated by Billie Barker-Daughtry, nor am I jealous of my big sister. Maybe I should be. My sister is, after all, two dress sizes smaller than me, married to a stupidly successful doctor, the head of a gorgeous family of tiny terrors, and the head of the PTA committee at...

Ignore that. Definitely not jealous. I don't want to be the head of anything except the Books and Booze club.

And if that doesn't exist, it should. I'm going to make it a thing. Unlike poor Gretchen Weiner—whose father invented toaster strudel, if you please—who never quite made 'fetch' a thing.

My sister, the blonde to my brunette, stops just inside the door and stares at me. Self-consciousness tingles across my skin as she peruses me with bright, baby-blue eyes.

Yeah. She got that combo too. Bitch.

"What?" I tug at the bottom of my dress.

"Are you trying to kill Mom or make Cain come to his senses?" she asks quietly.

Quiet voice or not, she's teasing the hell out of me right now.

"Both," Carly quips.

I spin and throw the hairbrush I was just using in her direction. "Neither," I correct her, turning my gaze back to Billie. "And watch your mouth!"

"Ah," she says, shutting the door. "Barbie's going to be here."

I mutter something so unintelligible I don't even know what I said. Not that it matters if Nina will be here or not. She knows better than to bring up my unrequited love. So does everyone else, not that anyone actually pays attention to me.

"I agree," Billie says sarcastically, sweeping her hands beneath her black dress with a cherry print and sitting on the edge of the bed. She smooths down the bright red collar circling her neck and clasps her hands in her lap.

If you didn't know otherwise, you'd say she was a British lady or something. She definitely got my serving of dignity as well as her own.

"Well? Is Barbie going to be here? Is that why you look like a pin-up slut?"

"That's it," I say, dropping onto the bed next to my sister. "I'm going home."

Billie puts her hand over mine as I bend to pull off one of my black heels. "No, you're not. You look hot as shit. You know I'm messing with you."

I give her my best side-eye. "Next time I see your kids, I'm feeding them pure sugar."

"No doubt." She moves on without batting an eyelid. "Have you called Simon yet?"

Carly snorts. "Like she would."

"True," Billie replies. "I don't think she's called a guy, ever. Except Cain."

I'd like a new life, please. I want to get off this one. It sucks. I want a refund.

"That's because she hasn't," Carly says, smoothing out her figure-hugging pencil skirt before she puts her hands on her hips. "She hasn't set up her own date in weeks. That's why I've taken matters into my own hands."

What?

"Oooh, yay!" Billie claps her hands together, her scarlet-red nails flashing through the air. "Who, who, who?"

Carly shoots me a devilish grin. "Simon's coming here tonight."

"What?" The word explodes out of my mouth, and I push myself up to standing. "He is what?"

"Coming here today." Her grin doesn't drop. "So is Ian."

"Are you high?" My voice is way too high and way too shrill, but is she high? "Have you lost your mind? He hasn't called me, Carly! Why the hell would you invite him here? Oh my god! You've invited him here and...and..."

"You look like a pin-up slut?" Billie offers with a wide smile.

"Ahhhh!" I throw myself face down on the bed. My second scream is muffled by the covers, and you know what? I don't even care that my dress has flapped up and my ass is on show. Not one bit. Not even a goddamn sniff.

"Are you guys okay?" Cain's voice comes through the door.

"No!" I shout, lifting my face. "I want to get off the world!" I press my face right back down again.

The door opens, and a second later he asks, "Can you pull your dress over your ass before you do that? Your underwear might scare the aliens."

"Rahhhh!" I scream into the bed and slam my fists down.

Someone—presumably Billie—pulls my dress down.

"Um," Billie says, confirming my though. "It doesn't, um, cover your ass."

I turn my face to the side. "You pushed three children out of your vagina and had at least three different people each time insert their fingers up there and you're bothered about my ass on show?"

"You're right!" The bed bounces as she moves up. "It's not my ass. I'm not showing panties bigger than the White House."

"God! I hate you people so much." I roll over and sit up, just about covering the rest of my dignity, and look at Cain.

His eyes are focused on me, and my demand to know what he wants dries up on my tongue and disappears into freaking nothing, much like my sanity. For all that's fucking good and sinful and holy and lordyshitfuckshittyshit!

Cain Elliott should not wear a suit. Ever. Especially not one that's clearly tailor-made. And gray. And did I mention it's tailor-made? Because it's hugging his body the way a koala hugs a eucalyptus tree—also the way I'd like to hug him—and no item of clothing should fit as well as his suit fits him.

Is it because the last time I saw him in a suit was our senior prom six years ago? Or is it because he's now three times the man he was then? I don't think he knew what muscles were back then, but now I know for a fact he's nothing but muscle from the hard labor of his job.

This is a five-piece suit: white shirt, gray pants, jacket, and vest, and black tie. And he even has a fucking matching fedora in his hand.

Kill me.

Right now.

Kaput.

"Well, well, well," Billie says in a strange mix of teasing and seduction. "If I weren't married, Cain Elliott..."

Cain bursts out laughing, his smile stretching right across his face. "You'd be too old for me, Bills."

"Too old? You little shit! I'm twenty-seven!"

"See? Old. That'd make you Madonna."

"Keep hold of that hat, mister. I have two kids. I know a trick or two that'd make you and your brothers blush," Billie warns.

"Make who blush?" Zeke sticks his head in the room. "Well, hello, Brooke!" He whistles low. Cain's brother, only eighteen months older than us, lands an appreciative gaze on me.

Or my legs. Whatever.

I snap my fingers by my cheek. "My face is right here, Zeke."

"Hey, Zeke," Carly calls. "You look like Danny Zuko in a suit too?"

Ezekiel 'Zeke' Elliott steps fully into the room, his large frame filling out the doorway and almost casting a shadow across the floor. He's wearing gray pants to match Cain's, but he has no jacket. His white shirt hugs his lean upper-body to a tee, and his vest is navy blue, matching his tie. "Danny Zuko wishes he were as good lookin' as me, Carly. And don't you look like a peach?"

"This peach has enough give in her skirt to stick her heel up your backside, Ezekiel Elliott, so quit it." Carly points her finger toward him. "Your flirting is wasted here."

"Why? You seein' that jerk Ian again?"

"Coming from the guy who practically jilted his fiancée at the altar." Billie rolls her eyes.

I snort.

"Hey, hey," Zeke says, holding his hands up. "She was screwing some other guy and I found out a week before the wedding. What was I supposed to do? Marry the bitch and let her bleed me dry after?"

"Bleed you dry?" Cain questions. "Your most valuable asset is the sixty-nine Mustang you put in Dad's name before you asked her to marry you."

"Ooh, big spender," I tease him.

"Hey now," Zeke says, turning his full attention back to me. His attention lasts a little too long, if you ask me. Especially at the top of my thighs where my dress doesn't quite meet the top of my hold ups when I'm sitting down.

My sister's right. I am a pin-up slut.

Shit.

Zeke brings his eyes up to mine. "Your mama just told me that guy your best friend arranged for your date tonight ain't called you back yet."

"You told my mom you were bringing him?" I exclaim at Carly at the same time Cain asks, "You have a date? Who?"

"Yes!" Carly answers, flapping her hands in front of her. "She called me! What was I meant to do?"

Billie inhales deeply.

"Not answer the phone!" I yell. "Oh my god. Now I remember why I want to get off this planet at the next stop."

I flop back on the bed, this time staying on my back. I also clamp my legs together and grab the hem of my dress to stop it riding up. Cain seeing my granny panties is one thing—hey, he's bought me tampons before—but Zeke is a whole other ballgame.

Mostly because no. No to Zeke.

Don't get me wrong, Zeke is hot as hell. His eyes are a strange oceanic mix of blue and green, but his hair is just as dark as Cain's. Slightly longer, sure, but otherwise, their faces are similar, if you discount the fact Zeke's jaw is always clean-shaven. Strangely, it doesn't make him look younger at all.

"What's wrong with Simon?" Cain asks. "Isn't he that guy you went on a date with last week? When you were doing your freaky rendition of Dirty Dancing in your underwear."

Carly snorts, but her amusement is swiftly cut short.

"Who was dancing in their underwear?"

We all still.

Oh, shitty, shit, shit.

Barbie's here.

I sit up with a helpful tug from my sister. She quickly smooths some hair from my face and secures it with a bobby pin before nodding in happiness.

Zeke rolls his eyes. "It was me, Nina. I wanted to be Baby, but Brooke dropped me, the bitch."

The excuse is so unexpected that a big laugh barks out of me. "Like I could lift you up! You're twice my freaking weight."

"I don't know," he says, looking at me with his eyes glittering. "Those thighs..."

"Don't think I won't get you and beat you down, Ezekiel, you pig."

He winks at me, knowing Nina can't see. "You beating me down? Shit, Brooke. Shouldn't you leave that talk for private?"

My jaw drops. Meanwhile, Carly and Billie are both biting their lips.

So much for their support here.

"Cain? Who was in their underwear?" Nina asks, still out of my line of sight.

I shake my head frantically, knowing that if I can't see her, she can't see me.

Cain looks at me, resignation in his green eyes before he

sighs and says, "I had to take something to Brooke's place last week before she went on a date. She had her music up too loud and I was treated to the sight of her dancing awkwardly in her underwear when I let myself in."

"Let yourself in?"

"Boy, this is awkward," Billie whispers in my ear.

I grimace in response. No kidding.

"Can we talk in private?" Nina asks from somewhere in the hall.

"Sure. Knock yourself out," Zeke says, leaning against the wall and shoving his hands in his pocket. He actually looks like a fifties gangster. He just needs the cigarette.

Cain looks at us. "They're using this room. They're not going anywhere."

"What do you mean they're not going anywhere?" Nina's voice is edged harder, yet it's shriller.

"Because we've been there for four hours already!" I finally snap. "If you wanna go whine, go do it somewhere else before I let my bitch flag fly."

"Cain!" Nina gasps. "Are you going to let her talk to me like that?"

Cain looks between me and Nina. I raise my eyebrows in a "try me," challenge, and given the shrug of his shoulders, he obviously decides that after the last couple days, Nina is the lesser of two evils.

Or he just really meant what he said when he said he cared about me more than her.

"Let's go over to my apartment," he says, turning his back on us. He disappears to the sound of her sputtering her annoyance at him not telling me to shut up.

Zeke shudders when they're out of earshot. "Well, he's up shit creek without a paddle."

"Or a boat," Carly quips.

Billie raises her eyebrows and nods. Then she turns to me, her lips curving up slyly. "I didn't know you had that in you to call her out."

"Where she's concerned, I have murder in me," I mutter.

Zeke bursts out laughing. "I think that's the fate Cain's about to face if he doesn't have a good explanation for watching you dance in your underwear."

I roll my eyes. Lord. These people. "He did not watch me dance," I say. "I was ironing in my underwear, happily singing along to Will.I.Am, and didn't hear him knock."

"If you didn't hear him knock," Carly says, "then how do you know he wasn't watching you?"

I open my mouth to reply, but all that comes out is, "Eeeeeeh." Like a strangled cat. Ten strangled cats.

Zeke laughs again. "Today is not your day, is it, Brooke?"

"It's never her day," Billie offers. "She gets maybe three good days a year, but they generally involve pizza, wine, and being alone."

"And no pants," I add. "Definitely no pants."

Zeke raises one thick, dark eyebrow. A mischievous glint in his eyes shines back at me. "Brooke, pizza, wine, and no pants? Wanna change your plans for the night?"

"You're an incorrigible flirt," I scold. "But as it happens, I'd love to change my plans. Just not to that."

Billie and Carly laugh.

He dramatically grasps his chest. "You kill me, baby." He chuckles. "As it happens, I do have another plan for you— and it'll get you out of Carly's hellish plans."

Carly gasps. "Simon is a perfectly lovely gentleman!"

"Then you date him."

"I don't want to date him."

"Isn't the first rule of Girl Code not to make your best friend date anyone you wouldn't date?"

"Ha!" Billie barks. "What do you know about girl code, Zeke? You once slept with two best friends on the same night at senior prom just because you could."

"That was me bein' helpful," he answers. "Teaching them hoes before bros and all that."

"Only guys say the hoes thing," I tell him. "It's sisters before misters."

He holds his hands up. "All right, femi-nazi. Untwist your

grandma panties."

"Can we get back to the point where you said you have a plan to get me out of a second date with the guy who said he wanted one but never called me?"

"That's right. Ouch, Carly. You bitch," Zeke says to her. "Even I know that's too far."

Carly rolls her eyes.

He returns the gesture, over-exaggerating it, of course, and looks back to me. "Be my date. I promise not to grope you or make lewd comments. Much."

Well, that's a thrilling offer. Be still my beating heart.

Oy vey.

"Brooke! You can't blow Simon off!" Carly insists, her hands back on her hips.

"I never intended on blowing him on." I tuck my hair behind my ear and ignore Zeke's choking laugh. "I intended on coming here, horrifying my mother, planning torture for Nina, and getting drunk." I turn to Cain's brother. "You got yourself a date, Zeke."

"Broooooooke!" Carly whines.

"No, Carly. You're gonna have to call him and un-invite him."

"Why do I have to be the jerk?"

"Because you're the jerk who invited him in the first place," Billie tells her. "And you know it."

Carly grabs her phone from the dresser and stalks toward Zeke. "You," she says, jabbing her finger against his chest. "I hate you."

He grins as she stomps off down the hall to call Simon. "You'd think by now she'd realize she needs to take a ticket and get in line."

One thing that might be highly surprisingly to just about

everyone who knows my mother is that she loves Zeke. His devil-may-care attitude when it comes to relationships since The Bitch is completely reasonable in her mind.

My same attitude isn't, remember?

Anyway, she feels more sympathy for him than anything. Actually, my mom loves all three Elliott boys as if they were her own. If I walked through the door with any one of them and introduced them as my boyfriend, she'd probably actually like me for once in my life.

Not that it would ever happen. Gabriel, the eldest Elliott boy, is getting married next year, Zeke is...Zeke, and Cain is, well... Cain. My best friend.

Best friend. Remember that. Best friend, not drop-dead-clitoris-calm-your-tits gorgeous.

Well... He could be both...

"See?" Zeke says into my ear, pressing a fresh glass of wine into my hand from behind me. And his hard body. Eesh. "I told you your mom wouldn't say a word about the dress when she saw you with me."

"You were right," I admit. That, and she was still trying to control Grandpa who, last I saw, was explaining to Cain's grandfather the ins and outs of creating balloon genitalia. "But I think your mom almost had a heart attack."

He laughs, slipping around to my side. "Until she realized it was just to get you out of your date."

"Don't. I thought mine was going to lose her shit when Carly said I'd blown him off."

"As you said," he says with a grin, "you never intended to blow him on."

I tip my glass of wine toward him. "Exactly!"

It really is that simple. Carly's heart is in the right place, but sometimes her actions aren't. Don't get me wrong, Simon is a perfectly nice guy.

There's just one problem.

I don't want a perfectly nice guy.

I want someone who sets my soul on fire.

I sit down on one of the chairs outside of the gazebo

where the crazy is happening. I have to arrange my skirt perfectly so that I don't flash everyone my panties—which I changed after coming under peer pressure.

Because, you know. Potentially flashing my hoo-hoo is better than granny panties.

I sigh and rest my arm on the table. I prop my chin up on my hand and sip from my wine.

Zeke stands up and turns toward the gazebo.

"Geez, am I that bad a date?" I ask him.

He laughs and squeezes my shoulder. "The worst. That's why I'm getting you something stronger."

I raise my eyebrows as he releases me and walks back inside. I'm completely alone outside, and it's actually kinda nice. There are a lot of people inside that gazebo on account of the large size of the yard, and I don't feel like I'm accidentally going to grope old Mr. Harrison's butt or something.

That, and I'm not exactly in a partying mood. It's hard to be when your best friend is on a date with Lord Octopus and your other best friend is with his girlfriend.

I really need to find more friends.

My phone buzzes inside my purse, so I reach down between my feet and pull it out.

Carly: *Houston, we have a problem.*
Me: *Oh no, what did you do?*

When she doesn't text me back instantly, I look toward the gazebo. I should probably go in there and find her. Then again, she's still on my shit list...

She saves me the trouble by darting out of the gazebo, a little wobbly on her heels. "Shit! Stupid grass!" she hisses, walking gingerly until she reaches the patio where I'm sitting.

"What's wrong with you?" I ask her, looking at her.

She huffs out a big breath and sits on the seat next to me. She gently sets down her glass of vodka cranberry and looks at me. "Two things," she says, holding two fingers up. "You want the good news or the bad news first?"

"Give me the good first."

"Really?"

"Yes. I like to enjoy a false sense of elation before my heart is ripped out. Keeps me humble."

She giggles. "Okay, the good news is: Cain and Nina aren't talking."

My eyebrows shoot up so quickly I think they might go into orbit. "They're not?"

Carly shakes her head, her voluminous curls bouncing like they're part of Tigger's tail. "Nope. Apparently she doesn't accept his excuse that he accidentally saw you in your lingerie." She says 'lingerie' with a suggestive wriggle of her dark eyebrows.

"It was accidental," I reply. "It's not my fault he decided to utilize his spare key when I was getting my groove on."

"Of course I know that, you know that, and he knows that, but she doesn't want to believe that."

"So why is she mad at him? It's obviously my fault, being the siren I am." I roll my eyes.

"Well, that's the funny part." She snorts and grabs her wine glass. "Now, this is just what Gabriel told me, okay?"

"Wait, Gabe's here?"

"Yeah, he was hiding out at Cain's to avoid the party prep. He snuck in half an hour ago dressed *literally* as Danny Zuko in the T-Birds. Which royally pissed off Nina since she's dressed like Sandy and Cain was supposed to be Danny."

So Nina's doubly pissed off. Does she have frown lines? Because if she doesn't, then I know she's nine parts silicone and one part human.

"Right. Back to me," I say.

"Right," Carly says. "So, she apparently lost her mind and screamed at Cain that it wasn't an accident he saw you in your underwear, it was entirely deliberate on your part."

"Even though I had no idea he was coming over."

"Right. She doesn't believe that. She thinks you knew he was coming over and planned the whole thing." Carly pauses.

"Which is really fucking stupid, because you can barely plan to leave your apartment on time for work."

She's not wrong. "Continue."

"Cain got pissed because she didn't believe him, but then, according to Gabe, the real cracker popped."

"The what—never mind. What then?" Lord, this is a real-life soap. I'm not sure I'm cut out for this drama. I'm kind of exhausted. It's way more fun watching people lose their shit on my Facebook feed.

"She called you a conniving slut," Carly says flatly.

"She did what?" My jaw drops. "I haven't had sex in twelve months! How can I possibly be a slut?"

"That's my argument, Mother Teresa."

"Well, I haven't had sex with a real person. A battery-operated one, sure, but still."

"Whoa," Zeke says. "I entered this conversation at the wrong time. Or the right one."

I shoot him a dark look. "Carry on, Car."

Carly gives him the same glare. "So, she called you a conniving slut, and apparently, that's when Cain lost his temper. He told her she'd been in a bad mood since she got there, and she had absolutely no right to speak about you that way. Then she got mad because he was defending you when he didn't defend her against you earlier and accused him of caring about you more than her."

Zeke whistles low.

"Exactly," Carly says, nodding in his direction and tipping her glass slightly. "So then Cain laughs and says of course he does, he's known you for ten years and her for barely a year. It's completely normal for him to do that."

"Damn," Zeke whispers, putting two shot glasses down on the table.

"Oh, it gets better." Carly holds up one finger, looking between us. "Then, Nina yells at him and asks him why, if he cares about you so much, doesn't he date you instead of her?"

"Oh shit," I mutter, grabbing my glass and swigging. "What did he say?"

Her lips twitch as she fights laughter, and her eyes sparkle. "He said he might just do that, because then he wouldn't be dating a woman with more make-up than a club full of drag queens."

My jaw drops.

Zeke doubles over, laughing loudly and infectiously. He rests his hands on his knees as his deep laugh roars out of him again and again.

Carly looks at him and then me with her eyebrows raised.

I press my lips together behind my wine glass. "Then what happened?"

"She stormed out. Cain and Gabe both thought she'd go home, but she came down here and joined the party. Gabe is sticking to Cain like glue to make sure Cain, good guy that he is, doesn't go and apologize for something that wasn't his fault."

Which is probably what Nina wants. Flaunt herself around in those skin-tight leather pants, that tight bardot-style top, and hope Cain apologizes for reacting to her bitch fit.

"Okay," I say, lifting my glass to my mouth again. "What's the bad news?" I sip.

"Nina's talking to your mom."

I turn my head to the side and spit wine across the patio. Zeke only just manages to jump out the way in time not to get splattered.

Great. Not only does Nina have the guy and is talking to my mother who will no doubt adore her, she just made me waste wine.

The wine thing might be the worst of the three, if I'm being honest.

"She's what?" I ask weakly. "Why didn't you distract my mother?"

"So she can grill me about my dating life?" Carly fires back at me, her voice a little high. "Brooke, I love you and all, but it's every girl for herself where your mother is concerned."

It's hard to deny that. So I do what any self-respecting twenty-four-year-old woman would do when faced with such a shitty situation. I grab the two shots Zeke brought out and down them, one after the other.

My throat burns as the harshness of the tequila goes down without being soothed by salt or lime.

"Shit," I mutter. "You know what this means, Carly?"

"Time to evoke the runaway plans we created in fifth grade." She nods solemnly. "At least now we have money, credit cards, passports, and a car between us. No doubt that'll be easier than raiding our siblings' piggy banks and getting the bus to London."

"Yes. Definitely easier."

"Y'all planned to run away to London in fifth grade?" Zeke questions, stacking the two empty shot glasses on the table. "How did you expect to pull that off?"

"The bus, duh," we say simultaneously. "That was a completely reasonable plan back then," Carly continues.

I nod. "We had it all planned out. Except the ocean thing, but I think we were smuggling ourselves onto a boat. That was negotiable though."

"We would have been happy with Alaska." Carly smooths her bangs from her face. "We figured the Canadian border police would let us through if we promised we were going straight back into US territory."

"What a fucking flawless plan," Zeke says dryly. "I can't possibly imagine where that could go wrong."

"Don't be a dick, Zeke." I reach across the table and smack him on the upper arm. "I know that's hard for you to grasp..."

"Hard for me to grasp." He smirks.

"Dude! You're twenty-freaking-six. Grow up."

"This is from one half of the 'Run Away To Alaska Without Being Stopped By Canada' brigade."

"You're such a prick," Carly says, draining the last of her wine glass.

Zeke raises his eyebrows. "And you've ditched your date to be out here, so now who's the prick?"

"Shh!" She presses her finger to her lips. "He thinks I'm

peeing."

"Uh, Car?" I light up my phone. "You've been peeing for twenty-minutes. That's long, even for you. And you pee like a club full of drunk girls on a good day."

"Stop it!" She taps my knee. "He's...grabby, okay? Like a toddler in a toy store. My ass is not Lego!"

Wordlessly, Zeke stands, grabs both our wine glasses, and heads toward the gazebo.

Smart, smart man. Even he knows Carly's about to lose her mind.

"I tried, Brooke. I tried to be nice to him, but no, second date and he's all over my ass like he owns it. You know who owns my ass? I do. Until he can squat like David Beckham is behind him and have my ass look this good, I own it."

"You squat like David Beckham is behind you?"

"Who else should I pretend is behind me?"

"I squat like Ryan Reynolds is behind me. Actually, no, wait. I don't squat. Or exercise."

Carly stares at me for a moment, her lips quivering. Then, her jaw twitches. And she bursts out laughing. "You're such an idiot," she manages to eke out. She reaches forward and hugs me. "I think we should get drunk."

I wrinkle my face up. "Really? With my mom here?"

Her eyes sparkle as she lifts her finger to her mouth again and pulls her phone from her bra.

Ah, bras. The invisible purse. Holding random shit since puberty.

"What are you doing?" I stare at her.

"Being the brains of our friendship."

"Careful. You might hurt yourself."

"You would know. Thinking is special for you."

"Only on Sundays and holidays." I nod. What? I don't want to give people the wrong idea. Like I'm sensible or something equally ridiculous.

"Okay, let's go." Carly stands up.

"Go where?" I grab my phone.

"Cain's. We're going on the roof."

"Without Cain?" I stand too.

She shakes her head. "He's bringing the alcohol. Oh, look, he's coming right now."

I turn toward the gazebo, and she's right. Cain, in his stupidly sexy suit, is bolting out of the gazebo and across the grass.

"Let's go. Quick. Now!" He grabs both of us and yanks us off the patio.

"Eep! Heels!" I squeal.

"Take 'em off!"

"Sake," Carly mutters as we both stop.

We pull off our heels and, grabbing the shoes by the heels, we follow him up and toward the house.

"Why'd we have to run?" I groan, the graveled path to his house cutting into the bottom of my feet.

Cain stops outside the access door to his apartment and grimaces, meeting my gaze in the semi-darkness. "Because your grandfather just told Nina she looks exactly like a whore he paid for a blow job on Main Street in nineteen-fifty-two."

93

eight

LIFE TIP #8: IF YOU PLAN TO SIT ON A ROOF WITH YOUR BEST FRIENDS AND DRINK IRRESPONSIBLY, TAKE YOUR SHOES OFF FIRST. AND WEAR BIG PANTIES.

Cain barely has the door to the stairs open before Carly and I fall against the side of the building, doubled over with laughter.

That shouldn't be funny. I know. Actually, it's horrible. But coming from Grandpa... Well, it's the context, isn't it? Not that I want to know that my grandfather hired a whore for a blow job in nineteen-fifty-two, but still.

"Shhh!" Cain whispers, grabbing us both and yanking us inside. He slams the door behind us as we lean against the wall and laugh out the last of our amusement.

Well... probably not the last-last. The *immediate* last. There's no telling when we'll randomly giggle about this again.

"Okay," Carly wheezes. "First things first. Alcohol from your apartment. Second, roof. Third, I have got to know why Grandpa Barker said that."

"Oh boy." Cain flicks the light switch and heads upstairs. "Come on, Tweedledee and Tweedledum, or no alcohol and I'm not helping you up onto the roof."

"I feel like I'm sixteen again," I trill, following him up the stairs to his apartment. "Sneaking up to your roof with alcohol."

"Except the alcohol wasn't readily available when we were sixteen," Carly says from behind me. "And, B? I can see your ass."

"Lucky you. It's a great ass." I follow Cain right into his

apartment and reach for the light switch.

"No!" he says quickly, darting in front of me and covering it with his body. "If she sees it, she'll come up, and this shit won't end well for any of us."

"You know something, Cain?" Carly says, closing the door behind her. "You're kind of a dick."

He stops. "Yeah, I know. But she pissed me off."

"Because she called me a conniving slut?" I ask cheerily as Carly heads for Cain's liquor stash.

Cain turns the key in the front door without moving away from me. His green eyes are bright as the lights coming in from the yard reflect off his face.

Unwillingly, my tongue flicks out of my mouth and wets my lips.

His gaze drops to my mouth for the barest second before he lifts it again and catches my eyes with his. "Yeah," he says slowly. "I told you the other night. She might be my girlfriend, but you're my best friend."

I drop my gaze to the rug beneath my feet and shuffle back. "You didn't have to fight my corner, you know."

"I know that, but I did anyway," he says in a low voice. "What part of what I just said don't you understand?"

Completely honestly, I shrug my shoulder. Ignoring the fact Carly has stopped rooting around in the alcohol cupboard. If Cain has noticed too, he doesn't show it.

He reaches out and pushes my hair away from my face. "Brooke." He trails a finger around the back of my ear until his hand falls away. "Unless I'm marrying someone, I'll always care about you more. Nobody gets to talk shit about you to me unless it's Carly, and that's only because I know she's already said it to your face."

"True story!" she hollers. "I have beer and tequila. I'm going to the roof. If you hear someone scream, I frog-splashed your girlfriend!"

My lips tug to the side. Even Cain manages a chuckle as I turn in time to see her deposit the alcohol in a backpack, haul it onto her back, and head for the other door.

I peer up at him through my lashes, unable to hide my smile at him shaking his head at her. "Well...thank you."

His lips twitch up.

Then he does something crazy.

He wraps his hand around the back of my neck, pulls me toward him, and presses his lips to my forehead.

The warmth of the gentle touch spreads through me like wildfire, and although I try to fight it, a shiver ricochets down my spine, making my entire body move. I shudder just as he releases me, and I don't dare look up at him. I can still feel his freaking lips on my skin.

Sure, he's done it before. He's kissed my cheek. I've kissed his hair. He's kissed my forehead.

But he's never kissed my forehead like that. He's never pressed his lips to my skin so firmly and intently that I've felt every dip and crack in his lower lip and the definitive curve of his upper one.

I've never really wanted to fall into him and push him against the wall just so he'd never take his lips from me ever, ever again.

I've never wanted him to keep his hand around the back of my neck just to keep him so close to me.

And I have no idea what to do about this.

My feelings are getting stronger, and now I'm wondering if what I felt before was really me being in love with him or the idea of being in love with him.

Because this is nothing like I've ever felt for him.

"Come on," he finally says, stepping away. "Carly's going to pitch a fit if we don't go up there now."

"You think?" I say sarcastically.

He stops despite his words and grins. "The tequila bottle isn't open, and we all know Carly can't get into children's medicine, let alone hard liquor."

"Ahh." I turn toward the door that'll lead us into the house and, ultimately, into the attic to get to the roof. "Shit. This is a lot of stairs."

"Don't worry, Drunky Smurf. I won't let you fall."

"I'm not drunk!"

"I saw you take two tequila shots one after the other. Whatever you are, it ain't sober."

"Were you spying on me?" I turn in the hallway of the main house.

Cain locks the door to his apartment, pockets the key, and then he looks at me with one eyebrow raised. "You've been here with Zeke all night. What did you expect me to do?"

"Pay attention to your girlfriend?"

"Brooke, shut up and go up to the attic before I lock you downstairs and tell your mom you got drunk and left with Jimmy Keller."

I shudder. A horrified one this time. "Please don't. Running the junkyard outside town is a perfectly respectable job, but my mom would prefer me to marry, oh, the President of the United States or something."

Cain laughs and shoves me into the attic stairs. "Go up, you fucking idiot. Or I'm going to throw you over my shoulder and carry you up while you scream."

I purse my lips. "That's a lot of steps. Will you carry me if I promise to be quiet?"

"I'm going to regret this, aren't I?"

I grin sweetly. "No. I'm not that heavy." I grab the chair from the corner of the hall and position it behind him.

He sighs resignedly. He knows exactly what's about to happen, because it's the thing he's done a thousand times before. "Come on, then. If I can hold your ass now."

"I will kick you, Cain Elliott. Don't think I won't just because you look damn good in that suit."

Oh. Shit.

He pauses. "You think I look damn good in this suit?"

"Shut up and let me climb on you."

"That isn't the right answer, B."

"Cain." My voice wavers. I swallow hard and then, "Catch!" I jump forward, launching myself off the chair toward him.

He catches me with the skill of a man who knows what I'm

doing. "I can't believe I'm carrying you up to the roof."

"I can't believe we're getting drunk on the roof. We haven't done this in years."

"That's true."

"Then again," I muse, "We haven't had to escape assholes in years."

"Not true," he says, grasping the handrail with his right hand as I hook my ankles together in front of his tight stomach. "I try to escape you on a regular basis."

I drop my foot to his groin. "Say it again, fuckhead."

"You're wonderful and I love you," he chuckles.

I know it's just a throwaway line, but my stomach flutters all the same. "You're safe. For now."

"You want me to drop you?"

"Fuck you!" I grip him tightly as he pushes open the roof door. "If you drop me and I die, I'm haunting you forever."

"Oh Jesus Christ," Carly says under her breath. "She made you carry her? What is she, sixteen?"

"Yes! I am at heart," I tell her, unhooking my legs and sliding down Cain's back until my feet hit the floor.

"At heart?" Cain peers down at me over his shoulder. "At heart and every other way possible."

"Are you calling me a child?"

"Are my balls still in danger?"

"The fact you have to ask that means they are."

"I have no idea how I put up with you two." Carly grabs the unopened tequila bottle and grabs the cap. Her knuckles go white as she twists and turns her hand around it desperately. "Cain. Open this."

I have no idea how she can't open a bottle of liquor. Honestly, it's a complete mystery. You know how some people can't open jars to save their life? That's Carly and alcohol. She can drink it like a fish, but she can't actually open it in the first place.

I've seen her call Cain and ask him to put up a shelf, only to have him open all the alcohol in her apartment and then send him home.

And you think I'm the needy one, huh?

"I have no idea how I put up with you two, she says," Cain mutters, taking the bottle. "As she hands me a bottle of tequila she can't open."

"Cain Elliott, are you sassing me?" Carly stares at him, her dark eyes glinting.

"I don't sass," he answers, handing her the bottle with the seal broken on the cap. "I screw with you. I'm not a teenage girl."

"You've been whining like it today."

"I've had a shitty day." He drops down onto the roof and stretches his legs out in front of him. He leans back on his hands, his biceps flexing before tightening.

I kinda wanna trail my nail down the curving indent of his muscle. No, not kinda. I do. I totally wanna stroke it.

What is wrong with me?

I sit down next to him as he reaches over and grabs a bottle of beer. "Did you bring a bottle opener up?"

Carly pauses. Then without answering, swigs from the tequila and shudders.

"Of course she didn't. She can't open tequila, B. Why would she think about opening beer?" Cain shoves the bottle into my hand and delves his into his pocket. His keys clink as he pulls them out, and he selects a bottle opener key chain.

Of course he has that on his keys. That's totally normal. *Cue eye roll.*

Cain pops the cap off the bottle while it's still in my hand with a half-grin. Butterflies the size of elephants thud around in my stomach, but I still manage to shoot him back a smaller smile.

"Do you think they'll notice we're gone?" Carly asks, passing the tequila bottle to me over Cain.

He shrugs. "Probably. Nina will probably decide I've run off with the two of you for a threesome."

Carly and I both shudder.

"Really? She's that crazy?" Carly asks. Unnecessarily. Nina clearly proved that point tonight already.

"Probably." Cain shrugs. "Then again, she'd have to be talking to me to accuse me of doing that."

"That's a reason to talk to you again."

"I know that. You two ignore me all the time until you get mad at me again."

"Female prerogative," I say, my gaze fixed on the label on the tequila bottle. "But at least we buy you beer to say sorry when we yell at you."

"Useless argument." Carly leans forward and meets my gaze. "She probably gives him a blowie. We can't compete with that."

Damn. She has a point there.

Cain snorts. Then he swigs from his beer. "You're kidding, right? She only apologizes for being a bitch when she wants something from me."

"That's unfair." I hand Carly back the bottle. "I already have that job. She can't be that person too."

Cain looks over at me, another grin on his face. "Exactly. The needy bitch position in my life is occupied by you. I don't have the time or patience for another one of those."

I gasp and punch him. "I'm going to push you off this roof."

"No, you're not. If you did that, you'd have nobody to help you unpack on his day off next week."

"Maybe I've already unpacked."

That causes both of them to start laughing. Into their hands. Because, you know. We're in hiding and all that.

"Yeah, all right, B," Cain says through a couple of low chuckles. "And I'm next in line to be the King of the Underworld. We both know you've barely unpacked a thing. You're probably still getting dressed out of trash bags."

I run my tongue over my top lip. Damn him. Damn them both for knowing me so well. "I've been busy," I lie.

"Vegging on the sofa watching Jerry Springer replays is not busy," Carly says, leaning forward again, her eyes glinting with silent laughter.

"It's totally busy when you're watching them too and we're

texting each other," I argue.

That is seriously time consuming. She knows that! Did he cheat? Is he the daddy? Who stole the cash? All very strong discussion points. Plus my thumbs get a work out which totally counts as exercise.

If only I burned ten calories for every text message I sent watching that show…

"Shut up and give me that," I mutter. I lean right over Cain and snatch the bottle out of her hand. I swig from it while they both laugh again. If I didn't love them so much, I'd hate them. Honestly. Sometimes it's a real fine line—like now. This is definitely one of those times.

"Cain, can I ask you a question?" Carly swings her legs around to the side and props herself up on one hand.

"Uh, sure?" he answers and turns to her, uncertainty all over his face.

She glances at me before staring at him. "Why do you stay with Nina? She clearly doesn't make you happy. If she did, you wouldn't be up here with us."

Whoa, Nelly. That came outta nowhere!

"To be fair, part of the reason I'm up here is to stop you throwing stuff at people." He smirks.

Okay. So we did that once. At Zeke's twenty-first. That was five years ago. Pish. Seriously. You throw water bombs at people from the roof *one* freakin' time…

"She has a point," I say quietly, putting the bottle down in front of me and gazing out at the yard. The sun is fully down now, and the moon is creeping up behind the trees at the end of the yard. The air is full of laughter and music and the distinct underbuzz of happy chats.

Cain sighs heavily and drops his head forward. He twirls his bottle of beer between his finger and his thumb. "I don't know," he says after a long moment. "She's not a bad person, and I guess I understand her uncertainty about my relationship with you two."

"That doesn't give her the right to be a raging bitch," Carly says, skipping over the bullshit. "Cain, you're having to sneak around to hang out with us just so she won't yell at you. You admit she doesn't want you to hang out with us and loses her shit when you do. That's not uncertainty, dude, that's fucking crap."

He sits up, crossing his legs, and rubs his hand through his hair. "I dunno, Car. Can't you just leave it alone?"

She raises her eyebrows. "When have I ever left anything alone?"

Good question. She's like a horny dog with a leg when she wants to know the answer to something.

"It's not that simple, all right?" Cain's voice is edged with something I'm not used to hearing from him—uncertainty. Vulnerability. "She's not like it all the time."

"Oh my god," Carly breathes. "She's controlling the shit out of you and you can't even see it. Let me guess, when it's good it's good, right? But when it's bad it's bad."

"Leave it." Now, his tone is harsher. "I don't need to justify my relationship to you, Carly."

"No, but you do need to listen when your friends are telling you they're concerned about it."

"In case it escaped your notice, I'm capable of handling my own shit."

"In case it escaped *your* notice, I'm only caring about you," she snaps.

I take a deep breath, slam down the tequila bottle, and grab my shoes. I get up and walk along the railed edge of the roof to the door. Neither of them say a word as I step through the door and onto the stairs.

I don't want to hear that. Not because of how I feel about Cain, but because I simply don't want to hear it. He rarely talks about his actual relationship with her, and now I know why. He just explained it without meaning to.

And you know what? Carly's right. Completely and utterly right.

"He can't even see it!" Carly slams the mug down in front of my coffee machine. "He's so goddamn dense when it comes to her. After you left and went home, he did the same thing. He texted Zeke to get him to tell Nina to leave and went to bed."

"Mhmm."

"Why can't he see it? She only apologizes when she wants something? She's not crazypants all the time? Oh, well, then, I guess that's all right." She shoves the mug into the coffee machine and jabs the button. Then she turns toward me, her dark hair billowing around her shoulders. "Because as long as she's nice to him the rest of the time, who gives a shit if she's a manipulative bitch the rest of it?"

"Mhmm."

"Goddamn it, Brooke!" She throws her arms out. "How can you not be angry about this?"

I shrug, resting my head on the side of the sofa as I look at her. "Because I can't do anything about it? I don't know, Car. He's right. He's a grown man and he can make his own dumbass choices."

She takes a deep breath and slumps back against the kitchen counter. She doesn't say a word until the coffee machine sputters the last of the coffee pod into her mug. "I just... It frustrates me so much," she says, much more quietly. "I've literally watched you quietly fall in love with him for years, and he's so blind he's stuck with someone who treats him like crap."

"Maybe that's just how she is. Maybe she doesn't even realize she's doing it."

She raises an eyebrow. "You're making excuses for her?"

I shake my head and run my hand through my hair. "No. I'm trying to understand it. Cain isn't a bad guy. He's stuck between a rock and a hard place already, and she's... I dunno,

Car."

"She doesn't even try, B. Neither does he anymore. He ran away from her last night? Are you kidding me? He's twenty-five, not thirteen. He doesn't need to hide under the bleachers to avoid the girl with a crush on him. I don't care what kind of hard place he's in—he needs to make a decision about his relationship. He's either with her or he's not. He can't run away with us every time she pisses him off."

Okay...She has a point there. I guess.

I sit up properly and hug my knee to my chest. I lean forward and rest my chin on my knee as I smack my lips together.

"What if he is trying to break up with her? If she's really that manipulative, it might not be that easy."

Carly points her teaspoon at me. "He ain't tryin' and you know it. If he were, he'd have done it already. She's obsessed with herself and I'm amazed Cain's handled it this long. She is literally the person the Biebs wrote *Love Yourself* about."

"Whatever. We can't make him do something he doesn't want to do just because we don't like his girlfriend. You know that." I sniff and glance at the TV. "I wish we could, but we can't."

She sighs and perches on the arm of the sofa. Spinning, she clasps her mug tightly and rests it on her knees as she props her feet up on the cushion. "This is more than dislike, B. His excuses yesterday were cat shit and you know it."

"Bird shit," I say. "Bird shit is worse than cat shit. You rarely know when a seagull has shit on your back."

She tips her mug toward me.

"But it still doesn't matter," I go on. "Let's face it: You're never going to like his girlfriends because you think they should be me, and I'm never going to like his girlfriends because I can't shake the way I feel about him. This is going to go around and around and around until I get over myself and get over him."

"You need to get under someone else. It'll solve the problem for a good ninety minutes."

"Yeah, right. Find me someone who isn't battery operated and can last ninety minutes and you've got a deal." I roll my eyes. "Clearly he won't listen to you, so there's nothing we can do."

"So, you'd be happy to let him marry the manipulative bitch?"

"I'm not happy he's fucking her, so I'd hardly dance on a bar if he said he was marrying her." I scratch my neck and consider my next words. "As much as I hate it, and as obvious as it is to us, we have to let him make his own mistake. How many times has he warned you off a guy you've dated and you haven't listened to him?"

She pauses. Her eye twitches, and I know I've got her. "That's totally different. That's guys I dated, not got in a relationship with. And not one of them ever had an issue with my friendship with him, because if they did, I'd have kicked them to the curb."

I will not roll my eyes. I will not roll my eyes.

There're four knocks at my door, and I stand up. "It doesn't matter if it's different," I say, walking toward the front door. "The fact is, we can't make him do anything. We only have to be here when he ultimately realizes what you said to him was right."

She huffs in response.

I open the door and still. "Mom. Hi."

Mom pushes some of her dyed, dark hair behind her ear. "Hello, dear. Can I come in?"

"Dear?" I ask without moving. "Who died?"

Her lips tug to one side. "Can I come in or not?"

Okay, so nobody died. Maybe she's been drinking Kool-Aid? Or she got drunk last night and is still a little hammered?

"Carly," Mom says, sweeping in past me although I still haven't moved. "How are you?"

"Oh, hey, Louise. I'm good, thank you. How're you?" Carly peers over at her.

"Better now my daughter let me in." Mom shoots me a disapproving look.

"Technically," I say, closing the front door. "I didn't let you in. You brought yourself in."

Carly disguises a snort with a sip of her coffee, only to cough on it. Mom thwacks her between her shoulder blades, and Carly wheezes, giving her a thumbs up. "Helpful, thanks," she manages.

"Brooke, would you make me a coffee, please?" Mom asks, taking the armchair and gracefully sitting down.

"I…Sure." *I will not argue.* I turn to the coffee machine and pull a mug out of the cupboard.

"I see you still haven't unpacked." The hint of disapproval in Mom's voice seems to scream despite her best efforts, and I just know she's casting a look of disgust around the room.

"So, Mom, what brings you by for the first time?" I say cheerily, slotting a latte pod into the machine. "Come to discuss with me my outfit yesterday and lament why I couldn't have dressed more like Billie?"

"Actually, despite the length of your dress," she hesitates, "I thought you looked lovely."

I still, my hand wrapped around the mug handle. Slowly, I turn my head so I'm looking over my shoulder, past Carly's wide-eyed expression, to my mom. "Oh, well, thank you."

"You're welcome." Mom smiles.

Yep. Someone slipped her Kool-Aid. I bet it was the blue one.

I pull her latte from beneath the machine, stir it quickly, and then carry it over to her in the front room. She takes it with a thank you before setting it on the coffee table and putting her feet down by her purse.

Awkward silence is saved only by the low hum of my guilty pleasure TV show, *Keeping Up With The Kardashians.*

Don't fucking judge me, okay? Sometimes, it's nice to watch someone else's train wreck of a life instead of lamenting my own. Plus…Khloe is kinda funny.

"I don't know how you watch this," Mom says, staring at the TV. "Their voices are highly irritating."

"I dunno," Carly says. "Their lives aren't all that. It's drama after drama after drama."

"Yeah, but at least they're rich through the drama," I point out. "I'd be able to deal with drama much better if I had a few million dollars in the bank and could shoe-shop my way through it."

"Good point." She tilts her mug toward me again.

"Goodness." Mom blinks and shakes her head, turning away from it. "So. I met Cain's girlfriend last night."

"Lucky you," I say dryly. "I hope you gave her my love."

Carly snorts, and even Mom—holy shit, even Mom suppresses a smile.

"I would have if I believed for a second I could have made it sound genuine and not like an insult," Mom says.

"Aw, Mom. You're underselling yourself. You insult me all the time and I don't realize it for a couple of hours."

"That," she replies with raised eyebrows, "is because you don't pay attention. And I prefer the term constructive criticism, Brooke."

I cross my legs beneath me. "Yeah, well, I'm sure Gordon Ramsay thinks telling people to get the fuck out of his kitchen because they're a fucking moron is constructive criticism too."

"Please watch your mouth." She purses her lips. "I didn't raise you to talk like a street worker."

"Prostitutes, Mom. You can say prostitute. Nobody will think you any less of a true Southern lady if you say it with *constructive criticism*."

Again, she fights a smile. Boy, she's in a good mood.

What did my siblings do wrong? I know it was one of them. Damn it. I'm the failure in this family. They have everything else. They can't have that too.

"Yes, well." Mom coughs into her hand and reaches for her coffee. She takes a demure sip before setting it back down. "What coffee machine is that? I like this."

I widen my eyes. "Wait. You like my coffee? Was that a compliment? Two in one day?"

"She was complimenting the machine." Carly nudges me

with her toes.

"Get your feet away from me." I twitch my leg toward her. Ew, feet.

"Yes," Mom says before we can bicker some more. "It's better than ours."

"I'll dig out the instructions." I smile. "Now, you were saying about The Girlfriend."

"The Girlfriend?" Mom raises her eyebrows. "Ah, of course. Your unrequited feelings for our Cain."

"Okay," Carly says slowly. "Now that was definitely closer to an insult than constructive criticism."

Thank you.

Mom stares at her for a moment, her dark eyes piercing into Carly until she drops her gaze. Ah, mommy dearest. Such a delight, as always.

"Yes. The Girlfriend. Nina." Mom sighs. "Personally, I thought she was a lovely girl. Successful. Her head is in the right place. Owns a nice apartment down on Barley Bay. Great job. Really nice."

So, when I die, I want to speak to Karma to find out why she's such a raging bitch to me.

Not that I didn't know my mom would love Nina. She's everything she wants me to be.

"Lovely," I choke out. "I'm sure you were thrilled to have a conversation with such a perfect young woman."

"Well, yes, I was. Then I realized she was upset, and she made the mistake of telling me why." Mom reaches forward, wraps her hands around her glass coffee mug, and peers at me over it. "Apparently she didn't realize you're my daughter, because she proceeded to launch into a mini-rant about how Cain's best friends are complete bitches, and how you, Brooke, are especially trying to break them up."

"Oh shit," Carly whispers. "Did you slap her? Tell me you slapped her."

"I did nothing of the kind." Mom glances at her. Then sips her latte. "I very calmly and very politely informed her that, if she said one more word about my daughter and her best friend, I would pull out her fake hair and strangle her with it."

Laughter bursts out of Carly, but I'm too shocked to laugh. My lips part as I stare at my mother, calmly sipping her coffee, as if she hadn't just said that she'd threatened to strangle Nina. And I blink. Harshly. A lot.

"Something in your eye, Brooke?" Mom raises one eyebrow as she looks at me sideways.

"I—no—um—I."

"Stop stuttering. It doesn't suit you."

"You threatened to strangle her with her extensions? You said that?" I explode.

"To the very word," she answers, really quite simply.

I blink some more. "And you weren't bothered that it could ruin your reputation as a perfect lady."

"On the contrary, dear." Mom sets down her coffee. "I might be a lady, but that doesn't mean I have to take anybody's shit."

Now, I choke. Did she just cuss? She did. Minutes after telling me not to.

"Language, Mother." I grin, unable to contain myself any longer. "Why?"

"Why? To teach her a lesson, of course. She learned it good, too. Don't give shit if you can't take it back."

"No, why did you threaten to strangle her?"

Mom sighs in her usual suffering way, but there's a tiny smile playing on her pearly pink lips. Her brown eyes are oddly warm as her gaze finds me. "Brooke, you might be an absolute hot mess of a twenty-four-year-old woman who drives me to insanity on a daily basis, but you're still my daughter. And nobody messes with my daughter."

"That might be the nicest thing you've ever said to me." I half-smirk, half-smile. "And also? I'm keeping that life advice. Be a lady and take no shit."

Carly nods. "I'm framing that and hanging it above my bed. And sofa. And bathtub. And basically everywhere."

"You're welcome, girls." Mom smiles as my phone buzzes. "Here," she says, passing it to me.

"Thanks." I glance at the screen. New message from Cain.

Cain: *Did your mom threaten to strangle Nina with her extensions yesterday?*

I lean over and show Mom the phone screen. "How am I answering that?"

She looks up over the top of the phone at me. "With a question, of course. Silly—you always answer a man's question with a question. It confuses them."

Look at Mom, dishing out the life advice like it's candy on Halloween.

Me: *Why do you want to know?*
Cain: *Because it's kinda funny.*
Me: *Is Nina mad at you?*
Cain: *Yeah, but mostly because I told her it was her own fault she got threatened.*

I snicker as Mom asks Carly about Ian.

Me: *There's more to that...*
Cain: *Yeah... I was pretty pissed off and told her she was lucky my mom didn't hear or she'd be, uh, strangled.*

I fall back on the sofa, laughing. Oh my freaking god. I don't think she'll be going to Mandy's for dinner anytime soon.

Carly reaches over and takes my phone from my hand. Then she laughs too, before Mom rolls her eyes.

"Let me in on the joke, for goodness sake," Mom demands, getting up. She takes my phone from Carly, her lips slowly twitching up into a smile as she reads. "Ha!" she says after a moment. "He wants to know how hard you're laughing."

I lean over and roll onto my side, grabbing my stomach as my muscles clench and burn. Tears are tickling the backs of my eyes, and I know I've finally lost it. This is it—this is when my mom and best friend call the men in white coats for me, because I've well and truly lost my mind.

It's not even that funny. I know it's not that funny. But somehow…that makes it hilarious.

That, and I'm tired. Everybody knows everything is funnier when you're tired.

"Brooke Barker!" Mom says firmly, snapping her fingers. "Pull yourself together or I'm going to text him back and tell him you wet yourself."

I instantly sober.

"Aww," Carly groans. "That's my line."

"You suck," I tell her, forcing myself to sit up.

God, my stomach hurts.

Mom passes me back my phone. I glance down at the screen. Thankfully, she hasn't replied to his last message, which leaves me free to.

Cain: *You're dying, aren't you?*

The message pops up right as I tap my thumb on the text box.

I grin.

Me: *It was touch and go there for a moment, but I survived.*
Cain: *Thank god. I'm not sure how anybody could possibly survive without you.*
Me: *You're an ass.*
Cain: *No more than you are.*

I roll my eyes and put my phone down. Mom is looking at me with a strange smirk on her face, and when I raise my eyebrows in response, she drops it and picks up her purse.

"Thank you for the coffee," she says, pulling her purse straps up onto her shoulder. "I'll call you tomorrow if you're not too busy."

"I, er, okay," is all I manage.

"Bye, girls." With that, Mom glides toward the front door, opens it, and walks through it.

The click as it shuts behind her echoes through my apartment.

"Whoa," Carly breathes after a minute. "Is it me, or has your mom been possessed by a ghost?"

"It's that or the aliens finally got to her," I agree.

"That was weird, right? It's not just me?"

I slowly shake my head. "No, no. That was really freaking weird."

LIFE TIP #9: NOT EVERYTHING IS AS IT SEEMS. EXAMPLE: YOUR PANTIES DON'T ALWAYS LAND IN THE LAUNDRY WHEN YOU THROW THEM AT IT.

There are many things I don't understand in life. Breakers that trip, for example. Or the timer on my cooker that I never manage to set correctly. Or online banking.

For the love of god, I hate online banking. It's pretty much a given that I'll never remember my freaking stupid username and have to fill out a dumbass questionnaire just to get something stupid freaking Google freaking Chrome should be remembering but is failing to.

Phew. Deep breaths, Brooke.

The thing I don't understand the most is periods. Not the end-a-sentence period. The fuck-me-this-is-agony-fuck-you-life bloody mess of a period. Obvious reasons aside, it's pointless because in order to be pregnant, one must have sex. And I'm not having any kind of sex without batteries. Or PornHub.

Still.

Mother Nature needs to get with the twenty-first century and start texting me. "Hey, Brooke! Here's your monthly reminder that your cobweb-covered vagina is spared from expanding around a person's head in eight months' time. You're not pregnant, baby!"

Yes. That. She needs to text. Or email. I don't even check my email, and anything she'd send would probably go to spam, but still. Since I'm virtually a freaking virgin again, it's a moot point for me.

You hear that, Mother Nature? Moot point! Not pregnant! Take away the cramps for the love of god!

It's unnecessary. And a week long? Really? Can't it be a day trip? Show up at eight a.m. and go home at six or something? 'Cause that'd be great, thanks.

As it is, I'm two days into this month's visitor. My uterus is conspiring to eat itself by way of cramping, and all I really want to do is lie in bed with no pants on and eat junk food.

Instead, I'm four hours into my five-hour shift at work and ready to ram my head inside a filing cabinet.

"Maybe Jamaica," the well-dressed woman in front of me says. She points one long, dark-blue fingernail to a picture in the glossy brochure. "This place looks nice."

"Joelle, I thought you wanted to go to the Bahamas, honey," her husband, Scott Fontaine, says gently.

Joelle wrinkles up her usually smooth, yet very pretty face. "I did, but it does seem rather… common, doesn't it?"

Oh lord.

"Common," he replies very flatly.

"Yes. You know Gerard and Carmella just went there last month. I wanted to go somewhere…fancier."

Scott turns to me, his eyes pleading with me to help him.

"Well, Mrs. Fontaine," I say. "We have many destinations to show you within the Caribbean. Have you considered Aruba, St. Lucia, or Puerto Rico?"

Her lips form a little 'o'. "No, I haven't. Tell me more."

I ease the brochure back and, after licking my fingers, flick through the pages to the Aruba section. "For your budget and the kind of vacation you're looking for, I would recommend one of the hotels on these four pages." I flick the page back and forth. "These are the absolute best on the island, no children, and more than enough extras to keep y'all busy while you're there."

"Oooh!"

"Thank you," Scott mouths to me.

I smile in response.

"Now, I like this," Joelle says, tapping the most expensive

hotel. "Look, sweetie! This is perfect!"

Scott slides the brochure to him. "That looks great. Can you check the availability for our dates?"

"Of course." I pull up the correct screen on my computer and type in the hotel name.

"Really? But I didn't look at St. Lucia yet." Joelle pouts.

Scott pauses. "I thought you liked this one."

"I do, but maybe I'll like one in St. Lucia more."

"It's the next location in the brochure. Page one-fifty-eight," I say without taking my eyes from the screen. "The hotel has your dates available in a master suite with an ocean view and private balcony."

"See? That sounds nice," Scott says. "Suite. Ocean view. Private balcony. How much is that, Ms. Barker?"

"Brooke, please. That's—"

"But, sweetie." Joelle lays her hand on her husband's arm. "Can I just look real quick?" She leans into him and I swear, she bats her eyelashes like a teenage girl trying to get a date to prom.

"I…" He hesitates for a moment, and I can physically see the moment his resolve wavers and snaps. "Fine. Let's look at St. Lucia too."

She beams widely, practically bouncing as she sits back up and leafs through the brochure again.

I love my job.

I love my job.

I love my job…

Carly: Don't forget we're at Mandy's again this weekend for the party.

I frown at my phone screen, sitting cross-legged on my floor, surrounded by bits of an entertainment unit.

Me: *Uh, her birthday was last weekend.*
Carly: *It's July 4th, you complete wombat.*
Me: *July 4th is this weekend?!?!?!*
Carly: *-open attachment-*

I frown again and open it. It's a picture of the calendar on the wall in her kitchen. She's got a big blue star on today's date and a big red circle around Saturday. July fourth. In three days.

Me: *Yeah, I'm gonna be sick this weekend. Cough, cough.*

I put my phone down on the floor next to me and pick up the instructions for the entertainment unit. Right now, my TV is sitting on an end table and has been since I moved it. It's not exactly ideal, and I've been putting this off long enough.

The only problem is I'm not exactly…adept…with a screwdriver. Or a hammer. Or any kind of tool, really. I tried as a kid. I really did.

Billie was the girly-girl, Ben was the nerd, and I was the one somewhere in between those things and a tomboy. I love high heels and pretty dresses, but honestly, sometimes I want sweat pants and football. Or baseball.

Mmm, baseball. Mmm, baseball *pants*.

I digress. I was the kid who always helped my dad build stuff, but I've never really had an affinity for it. In fact, the more I think about it, I've never really had an affinity for anything except junk food and wanting things I can't have.

I'm going off on a tangent. If I keep up this method, I'll be on Wikipedia looking for up conspiracy theories about the Illuminati before Googling why penguins can't fly or something. Then boom, it'll be three a.m. and I'll be asleep with my phone on my face.

"Right," I say out loud. "This isn't hard, Brooke. You can do this."

Woo! Pep talk! Yes!

I look at the first page of the instruction pamphlet where it tells me what should be coming with it. Uhhh. I don't know what I'm looking at or what any of this is.

Instinctively, I reach for my phone. I pause with my hand hovering over it. Do I call Cain? That's what I'd usually do. Just call him and have him come help me build it. Or have him build it while I watch and attempt to hand him things he doesn't need.

I shouldn't call him. It's not going to do him any good right now. Equally, I've unpacked this now and I can't leave it halfway across my living room.

I wince as I pick up my phone. I unlock it, tap 'phone,' and bring up his number. It rings three times in my ear before it clicks.

"What do you want?" Cain answers.

I gasp. "Who said I want something?"

"B," he says, closing what sounds like his fridge. "You only ever call me when you want something. Otherwise you text me."

"This is true. I, uh, I do need help."

He groans. "What did you do?"

"I unpacked my entertainment unit."

"Please tell me it's ready-built."

"Um…" I cast my gaze out at everything on the floor surrounding me. "Not exactly."

"It's flat-packed, isn't it?" he asks. "And you're sitting in the middle of it all, aren't you?"

It's kind of scary how well he knows me. "Well…"

He lets out a long breath. Kinda huffy, actually. "I just got in from work twenty minutes ago. If you feed me, I'll build it for you."

"I'm not sure if that's a deal or a guilt-trip," I say slowly. "Not to mention a sure-fire request for food poisoning. You know I can't cook."

"You haven't eaten either, have you?"

I don't answer. I don't think a fruit salad is acceptable for dinner.

"I'll see you in ten minutes," he says. "Find something for me to eat in your damn kitchen, okay?"

He hangs up before I can tell him that's a tall order. I have no idea what's in my kitchen. I have beer, if that's an acceptable dinner. I don't see why it isn't. Wine is an acceptable dinner, after all. It's only fancy grape juice.

That's my story and I'm sticking to it.

I put my phone on the sofa behind me and use it to help me up. Almost immediately my right leg buckles, tingling with that irritating and yet strangely painful sensation of a dead leg.

Freaking hell. How long have I been sitting on the damn floor? Too long is clearly the answer here. I don't want a dead leg.

Why does it hurt? It shouldn't hurt. Oh my gosh. I need a new leg. Quick, someone dial nine-one-one. It's never going to—

Oh. It's gone.

I wriggle my toes just to be sure, and yep, it's gone. So I was apparently a little over-dramatic then.

Aha! Finally, a perk of living alone. Nobody is around to experience my stupid, over-dramatic moments. Now that's one I can get on board with. Sure, I'm still a little freaked about the zombies in my pipes, but one step at a time.

I get up, this time more slowly. My legs are definitely awake again, so I leave the carnage of the flat-packed entertainment unit on the floor behind me and cross into my kitchen.

Not only do I need to unpack, but I also really need to go grocery shopping, because I turn up a grand food haul of bread, cheese, tomato soup, peppers, onions, and paprika. Okay, so there are a few other things too, but I'm seriously wondering where in the heck that paprika came from.

I'm not sure I ever bought that. Then again, Carly went shopping with me, and she way overestimates my culinary ability.

I do the best I can do in this situation. I go to Google and search *What can I make with soup peppers bread and cheese?* As I scroll through the search results, I lean back against the kitchen counter. I keep searching until I find something I think I can manage.

Red pepper and tomato soup with grilled cheese. That has to be easy, right? Especially since the recipe is calling for the soup to be made from scratch and I'm cheating with my store-bought tins. I have a blender. I can't see what can go wrong here.

Okay, I'm lying. There are at least five things that could go wrong, but I'm not going to think about those.

I take a deep breath and nod. I'm going to do this. I'm going to modify this soup and I'm going to do it well.

I'm getting good at this self-pep talk thing. Maybe I'll do it if I ever go back to college. I might actually graduate then.

I set about getting the red peppers, my cutting board, and my knife. I also pull my blender from the corner of the counter top and dust off the top. Eh, it's clean. It'll work.

When I've chopped it, I throw the pepper chunks into the blender, put the lid on, and turn on the machine. It whirs to life almost deafeningly, making me jump. *Sheesh.*

"What the hell are you doin'?"

I scream.

"Jesus!" Cain laughs loudly. "It's just me."

I turn off the blender. Then I grip the edge of the counter and flatten my other hand against my chest. "Holy shit. I think I just died and came back to life."

He raises his eyebrows. "Someone's taking a ride on the drama llama today."

If only he knew.

"You scared the life out of me." I press my hand harder against my chest and breathe deeply. "Jesus. You didn't knock, did you?"

"Nah. I figured you knew I was coming this time and you'd be fully dressed." He grins, his green eyes sparkling back at me. "Thankfully, you are. What are you making?"

"I'm flavoring soup."

"Flavoring soup," he replies flatly.

"Flavoring soup," I confirm, reaching for the cans.

"I'm not even going to ask." He shuts my front door behind him and stretches his arms above his head, making his muscles flex. "Right. Where's this damn unit?"

"Hm?" I shake my head and grab the soup cans. "It's the mess on my floor."

I pour the soup into the blender, over the mush of pepper and onion, and wrinkle my nose. Boy, this better work. If not, it's literally just grilled cheese. I put the lid on the blender and turn it on, mixing everything together for around two minutes.

"Oh no," Cain says the moment I turn it off. The horror vibrating through his tone is comical. "You bought this from Ikea, didn't you?"

"Um, yes?" I pull off the blender lid and turn around. "Is that a problem?"

He groans and leans back against the sofa. "I hate Ikea, B. You know that."

"Yeah, but their stuff is nice. And cheap. I like cheap." I pour the soup into the pan already sitting on the cooker before filling the blender with water.

"But it fucking sucks to put together," he moans, sitting up on the sofa and looking at me. "It's the worst damn furniture in the world."

I roll my eyes and turn around to face him. "You're a freaking builder by trade. I've seen you build houses. How the fuck can you be stumped by *Ikea*? It's basically created by a bunch of blond men with no sense of humor, eating meatballs around a large table."

His eyebrows go up, his lips twitching. "That's a little…stereotypical."

"Well," I say, pointing a metal spoon in his direction, "I ain't ever seen a black-haired Swedish man."

"That's like saying, 'I've never seen a great white shark, so they can't exist.'"

"Obviously they exist. I've watched Jaws."

"It could have been computerized," he reasons.

"Carry on and I won't feed you," I threaten him.

He laughs. "Then I won't build your unit."

I still, reaching for the bread from the bread bin. "Touché, asshole. Touché."

His laughter, still ringing out, trickles across my skin, teasing the hairs on my arms into standing on end. Tingles shoot down my spine, but I somehow manage to suppress the full shiver that wants to wrack my body.

I have to start fighting back my attraction to him—not to mention my feelings. I know people always say you can't fight what you feel, but I can sure as hell hide it. I've been doing it for so long that now, I need to start hiding it from myself.

"I bet you don't have beer." His voice is right behind me.

I jump again. "Will you stop freaking scaring me tonight?" I turn my head back to face him, and when I thought his voice was right behind me, I meant a foot away.

Not literally right there where there's barely an inch of air between my mouth and his.

Not literally right there where I could slip and kiss him.

Not literally right there where I *want* to *accidentally* slip and kiss him.

"It's not my fault if you're on edge," Cain says in a low voice. His green eyes flit to side to side as he searches my gaze, making me swallow. "Why are you so jumpy?"

My heart skips although I know it shouldn't. "Because you keep scaring me."

"Hmm." He puts his hand on the fridge without moving away. "Do you have beer? That's about the only thing that'll get me through Ikea furniture."

"I always have beer," I answer him, taking the chance to lightly shove my hand into his shoulder. "There are bottles of Coors in the drawer at the bottom. The bottle opener is in the drawer. Hey, can you get me the cheese?"

"And now breathe." He laughs again, taking a step back. Finally.

"Can I please have the cheese?"

He opens the door, pulls out the cheese, and hands it to

me.

"Thank you." I take it from his hand and pause. His knuckles are all cut open. They've scabbed a little in the middle of each cut, but I can still see the bright red of semi-dried blood. "What happened?"

Cain glances at his hand then back up at me. "Nothing. Accident at work." His jaw twitches as he grabs a bottle of beer and shuts the door.

I throw the cheese on the side and grab his hand before he can move away from me or hide it. He tugs back against my grip, but I tighten my fingers around his wrist and gently pull his hand toward me. I tilt his hand so I can see the cuts better.

"Sssshit," he hisses, wincing as I bend his fingers.

"Sorry." I grimace. "Cain, what did you do?"

"Accident at work. I told you that. It happens when you're building a garage and a brick falls on your hand."

"Riiiiiight. If a brick fell on your hand, your fingers would be broken. Not cut up and bruised." I look up at him through my eyelashes, absently stroking my thumb across his hand where the skin isn't broken. "What *really* happened?"

An exasperated yet helpless sigh escapes from between his lips. He sets the cold beer bottle on the side and wipes his hand on his jeans. "Nina stopped by at work today. I was in the workshop building custom bookshelves for Mrs. Mayfair's new library. Let's just say the conversation didn't go too well, and the particular shelf I was working on has a sizable dent in it."

"Cain!" I jerk his hand even closer to me and really look at it. "You punched a solid wood shelf?"

"I considered punching thin air, but I didn't think it would be as satisfying," he drawls, sarcasm dripping from every word.

"Goddamn it!" I slap his other arm. I'm not letting go of his damn hand until he realizes how dumb that was. "You can't just punch things when you're pissed off."

"Gee, Brooke, thanks for that. I sure needed that advice six hours ago."

"Do *not* use that shitty tone with me!" I stomp my foot on the ground. "She made you so mad you punched something? Jesus, Cain! That's not healthy! I don't care if it's not all the time or if she's the sugar plum fucking princess when she's not pissed off at you."

He deflates. He holds my gaze for a heartbreakingly long second before he looks away. "I know."

"When are you gonna break up with her, huh? You're not happy. I know you better than anybody and I know you're freaking miserable right now. When are you gonna wake up and see that she's not good for you?"

This is no longer about how I feel. This is about how he feels.

And I can see it. It's written in the darker than normal shadows beneath his eyes. It's chipped into the downturn of his lips, and it's swimming in the depths of his green gaze, darkening it more than eyes like his should be.

"Cain?" I say softly.

He brings his gaze back to me and says simply, "Your underwear is on the floor in front of your laundry basket."

Ten

LIFE TIP #10: BEING A HOT MESS IS HARD WORK. REALLY, REALLY HARD WORK.

I purse my lips and stare at him. "Stop trying to distract me."

"It's not a distraction," he replies, his lips turning up at the edges. "Your panties really are on the floor."

I jerk my head to the side, in the direction of the laundry basket. My eyes widen as I catch sight of my neon-orange panties lying haphazardly on my white tiles. "Oh, shit!" I drop Cain's hand like it's on fire and dart around the little island to where they are.

Cain falls back against the fridge, laughing hard.

I snatch up my pretty much luminescent undies from the floor and shove them deep into the 'color' section of the laundry basket. You know what else belongs in that section? *My goddamn cheeks.* I think my body temperature just rose by around, oh, one hundred degrees.

I can't believe I didn't notice that they didn't go in the basket when I threw them in there this morning. Or rather, attempted to throw them in there. That's what I get for pressing the snooze button on my alarm too many times. That literally was karma at play.

I don't think I've ever been so embarrassed. Why did they have to be dirty panties? Why couldn't they be clean? Or brand new with the label on? Dear god. How am I supposed to handle this?

"Well," I say out loud, forcing myself to turn around and face Cain. "That was awkward."

He rubs his hand across his mouth, still clearly laughing behind it if the crinkling at the corners of his eyes is anything to go by. "It was? I think it's hilarious."

"You would. You're not the one whose dirty undies were on show!"

"To be fair, it's not like I haven't seen your underwear before." He raises his eyebrows. "Although I suppose they were clean."

"Oh my god." I press my hands against my cheeks so he doesn't see the renewed blush from his words. "On second thought, I don't need you to build my entertainment unit."

I don't need a TV. I'm clearly entertainment enough here.

He laughs again and pushes off the counter. Unexpectedly, he wraps his arms around me and squeezes me. "Jesus, Brooke." His voice rumbles across my skin, making me plant my face into his solid chest. "If I left every time you embarrassed yourself in front of me, we wouldn't be friends anymore."

"That doesn't sound like a bad idea," I say into his t-shirt.

He squeezes me again, still chuckling. "I needed that laugh today. Thank you."

"You're welcome." I wriggle out of hold before he releases the thing I just did—the fact my heart is beating overtime, slamming itself against my ribs every other second. "Now that I've brightened your day, we're going back to your hand."

"You're still blushing."

"And you're bleeding." I give him a disapproving look as I grab his hand. "You should really wrap these. Knuckles are awkward."

"They're the body part equivalent of you."

"Awesome. I've been reduced to ten bumps of bone." I sigh and release him. "I hope I unpacked my first aid kit."

"Whoa now," he says, backing up. "The last time I let you do first aid on me, you jabbed me with scissors!"

I open my mouth to argue that, but I, um, can't. Not really. I did jab him with scissors. Sharp ones too. In my defense, he moved when I was trying to cut the sticky tape to keep the wound pad thingy on.

"Stay still this time then," I finally settle on. "No feeding if you're bleeding."

He blinks at me, his long, dark lashes, casting shadows over his upper cheeks. "You rhymed that on purpose, didn't you?"

"No," I answer, rifling through the drawer. "Aha!" I pull out the little, green bag that holds my first aid kit. "Sit down, asshole."

He does as I say. "Your bedside manner needs some work."

I smile. "And that's why I sell holidays and not surgery."

"People don't sell surgery."

"Tell that to the insurance companies." I snort, unzipping the kit. I pull out everything I think I need to wrap his hand and set to work.

He winces as I clean the wounds with anti-septic wipes, but he doesn't yell or scream at me, so I figure I'm doing good. He does watch me with a little trepidation crossing his features as I cut the bandage to size, but I make it through that without stabbing him with anything, so he relaxes when I wrap it around his hand.

"You know I'm only letting you do this because I'm hungry, don't you?" Cain says when I'm done. "I'm going to take it off the second I leave here."

I shrug. "I know, but it makes me feel better. Besides, I don't want you bleeding all over my furniture."

"I knew you had an ulterior motive for being so caring."

"And here I thought I'd gotten away with it." I sigh, but smile right after. "Okay, let me make food now."

"You're not going to poison me, are you?"

"No, but you're still going to answer my question from before you oh-so-conveniently noticed my underwear." I raise my eyebrows, looking at him pointedly. He's not fooling me—I know he saw them before he mentioned it and was saving it for a moment just like the one he said it in.

"Shit," he mutters. "If you're going to cross-examine me, I

get control of the TV controller."

"Um…" I throw my hands in the air as he throws himself over the back of my sofa and grabs the remote. "Why do you get to control *my* TV? *Friends* is on!"

"*Friends* schmends," he replies. "Look, see—*Homicide Hunter* is on."

All right. Young Joe Kenda is kinda yummy.

"Fine," I fake-snap. "But I'm soooo tearing you a new asshole."

He salutes me from his position on the sofa. He's lying down, a cushion beneath his head, and his feet crossed at the ankles while they rest on the back of the couch. He looks way too at home right now.

I'm not sure I like it.

Not to mention, I think as I cut the cheese for the grilled cheese, I kinda wanna jump on him. Not sexually, just to be annoying. I'm really good at being annoying, especially to Cain. It's definitely a skill I've perfected over the years.

I put the cheese between the bread and put the sandwiches into my sister's old George Foreman grill. I close the lid down and put the soup on really low. Then set the timer.

Cain's still lying on the sofa.

I still want to go jump on him.

I'm so going to go and jump on him.

I sneak around the island and toward the sofa. He doesn't so much as look at me as I slip between the edge of the sofa and the chair until—wham. I drop myself onto him.

He doubles up, sitting, and almost knocks me off him. I squeal as I fly forward, but he shoots his arm out and wraps it around me, yanking me back. As he lies down again, he drags me with him.

"Uft," I groan when we drop back together. "What are you doing?"

"Shhh. He's interviewing the husband." Cain doesn't even look at me. His eyes are fixed firmly on the TV, just like his arm is around my midsection.

I can't move. Literally. My back is against his stomach, my

head on his chest, and my legs at some uncomfortably awkward angle somewhere between on and off the sofa.

Kinda like how dogs sleep.

"I need to stir the soup." I wriggle is protest and try to roll over.

"Shut up, Brooke." He prods me in the side with his finger. I jerk away from him. Well, kind of. "Don't do that!"

"Don't do what? This?" He pokes me again, this time a little further down.

Right in my freaking ticklish spot.

"Nonono!" I squeal, scrambling like a drunken iguana to get away from him.

He's much stronger than me though, and he retains his grip on me as he tickles me over and over again. I can't move away from him, so I twist this way and that until I finally free one arm and manage to roll onto my stomach.

On top of him.

I'm on my stomach.

On. Top. Of. Him.

We both freeze.

My fingers twitch where they're resting against his hard chest, but his are completely still at my waist. My heart thumps a little too hard against my ribs, and I inhale as if it'll hide the franticness of the beat.

Cain's eyes, that were so dark not so long ago, are bright, still shining with his evil laughter. They search my gaze for something—I don't know what, but *something*—and his lips part the barest amount.

It's so cliché, but if the TV wasn't going, I'd swear time had stopped, that the world had briefly paused on its axis for this moment between us.

This heart-thumping, stomach-fluttering, spine-tingling moment.

This completely *wrong* moment.

"I—"

"I broke up with her," he says, cutting me off, never looking away from me. "If you'd shut up earlier, I would have

128

said that. I talked it through with Dad and when I'd calmed down, I knew it was the right choice."

My mouth forms a tiny 'o'. "Oh. You could have told me to shut up, you know."

"I know." His lips twitch up. "But you wouldn't have listened, would you?"

A piece of my hair falls from behind my ear and tickles across his cheek. He shivers and reaches up to it. The tips of his fingers graze across my cheek and then around the back of my ear as he tucks it back where it belongs.

"No." My voice is barely a whisper. "Probably not."

"Probably not?" His eyebrows go up, and now his tiny smirk becomes a full-on grin.

My heart aches. I don't trust myself to answer him, so I shake my head instead of speaking. Not that I can speak—my throat is scratchy and my mouth feels as though I've swallowed sand.

"Brooke…"

The distinct smell of burning bread and cheese hits the air.

"Oh, fuck it!" I scramble up off of him, almost hitting him in the groin, and smack my elbow against the coffee table. "Owww!"

Cain laughs and jumps up, narrowly avoiding kicking me in the head. By narrowly, I mean I ducked.

"I've got it, Clumbelina," he says from the kitchen, clicking switches and turning things off.

"Owww," I whine, hauling myself onto the sofa. I cradle my stinging elbow to my body while Cain grabs the tongs from my half-filled utensil tub.

"What," he says with barely concealed laughter, "the hell is this?" He turns, one charred grilled cheese sandwich in the air.

"Uh…Burned. It's burned."

"Smartass." He puts his foot on the pedal of my new trash can and drops it in, closely followed by the second one. "I guess I should call Carly and ask her to get dinner on her way over since the soup smells burned too."

129

"Why is Carly coming over?"

He raises an eyebrow. "Really, B? I just told you I broke up with Nina and you're asking why she's coming over?"

"Right. Of course."

Puh-lease.

Like I was paying attention to that when he was holding me and looking at me.

I was far too busy trying to stop my heart from going off the rails.

"Okay," Carly says, leaning forward. "You've eaten. You've put the little wooden maggots into the unit."

"You mean the dowels," Cain replies.

"No, I mean the little wooden maggots." She rolls her eyes. "Now, you can tell us what happened."

She's so bossy.

"Pass me that screwdriver, B." Cain points to the one he wants.

I pick it out of his toolbox and hand it to him.

"Thanks. Hold this still for me." He gets onto his knees and puts two pieces of wood together. "I don't know how much there is to tell you, Car. She knew I was in the workshop and came in. Thinking about it, I don't even know why she was mad. I think she was mad about being mad and decided to scream it out at me."

Carly snorts. "So like Brooke does on a regular basis."

"Hey!"

Cain flashes me an amused look. "Yeah, but less sarcastic hot mess and more…horror movie kind of possessed."

Eh. Given the alternative, I'll take sarcastic hot mess. It's actually a scarily accurate description of me. I did just burn grilled cheese, after all. Even if it was his fault for distracting me.

"She asked me if I was ready to apologize yet, and when I asked her what for, she lost her fucking mind." Cain moves the wood, grabs another bit the same size as the one I just held, and taps it for me to grab it again. "Dad had a customer in the office, and of course they could hear everything, so he kicked her out and told her to come back in her own time. She went back to work then."

"Then you had a male PMS moment and punched something," I remind him.

"Helpful, B, thanks."

"Ah, that explains the bandage." Carly nods. "Then what?"

Cain shrugs as he tightens the, er, big screw. "I washed my hand and got back to work. I had to remake the shelf, but whatever."

"No, with Nina, you possum."

He pauses, looking at her from the corner of his eye. "I talked it all over with Dad. The last few days have been non-stop fighting. That"—he nods toward the take out trash—"is the first thing I've eaten all day. I've barely slept for two days. And I realized you were right with what you said on Saturday."

Carly leans forward and cups her hand behind her ear. "I'm sorry, can you repeat that for the record?"

"I'm gonna kill her," Cain quickly says to me. "I said you were right. It wasn't necessarily a healthy relationship. She was trying to manipulate me into moving in with her although I said no, so I broke up with her."

I look down to hide my smile.

"I can see you smiling." He nudges his foot into mine. "Pass me that bit of wood behind you."

I do as he asks. "How did she take it?"

"About as well as teenage girls in a haunted house."

"So, lots of hysterical crying and screaming."

"I never cried and screamed," Carly protests.

"You ruined one of my t-shirts once with your mascara," Cain reminds her.

"Get on with it!"

He laughs. "She wasn't happy, and I couldn't actually explain to her the reasons why. So I hung up on her and then you called," he says to me. "So I came here and left my phone at home."

That explains why he used mine to call Carly.

"Ooooh, she's gonna be so damn mad at you!" Carly claps her hands and grins.

Cain stills and looks from her to me. "Why is she so happy about that?"

I shrug. How should I know? Carly's an enigma. "Why are you asking me? Do I look like I have a hotline to her brain?"

"You usually do."

"True, but I cut it when she started dating Ian again."

"I'm not dating Ian," she interrupts. "I told him we were done for real this time. Too much grabbing."

I told her. I so told her. Octopuses do not make good boyfriends. Or food, for what it's worth.

"So what are your reasons for breaking up with her?"

"Gee, Carly," Cain says dryly. "You should already know. You've been telling me them for past few months."

He has a point there.

I hand him the next bit of wood he points to.

"Don't be cocky." She throws an M&M at his head. "I was just asking. Of course I know all the reasons you should have broken up with her for, but I wanted yours."

Without looking up at her, Cain answers, "I wasn't happy anymore. It's that fucking simple. I don't want to be with someone I fight with every single day or who accuses me of screwing my best friends on a regular basis."

"That would put a dampener on any relationship," I reason.

Cain picks up the M&M Carly just threw at him and launches it at me. It bounces off my chin. "Don't pretend you aren't happy about it."

"Hey!" I glare at him. "I'm sorry, would you have preferred me to be happy when you were miserable with her? I'm not happy you broke up"—lies!—"I'm happy that you made a choice to be happy again."

He looks at me for a long moment, his eyes softening.

"You're totally happy they broke up," Carly butts in with a snort. "You hated Nina more than anyone else."

"I'm going to throw a hammer at you in a minute," I warn her. "And I'll hit you."

"No you won't. You'll hit the window on the opposite side of the apartment. Your aim is awful."

I shoot Cain a "help me" glance.

He simply laughs. "She's right. Your aim is horrible, B. You wouldn't hit her with a hammer anyway. You'd never find anyone else like her who'd put up with your shit."

"He's right. You wouldn't," Carly agrees.

"But neither would you, so shut it," he fires across the room at her, moving the unit. "And I still don't know why I put up with y'all's shit, but there we go."

I prop my elbow on the now-upright entertainment unit and rest my chin in the palm of my hand. "Because you love us."

He turns his face toward me. He slowly arches one of his eyebrows, his lips tugging up on that same side into a smirk that's all too kissably tempting. "Yeah. You're probably onto something there."

Carly grins. My cheeks flush at his answer and I look down at my feet.

"Move now." He leans over the unit and shoves my elbow off it. "I have to put the shelves in and then it's done."

"Great." I get up and join Carly on the sofa.

"You aren't helping me?"

I grab my almost-empty glass of wine. "No. You said you had to put the shelves in. You didn't say I had to help you."

He opens his mouth to reply, but hesitates. "Nope," he says. "Not going there."

Carly and I laugh as he grabs all six shelves and slots them into the right places. Then, without being asked to, he gets up and moves the first few things from under the end table currently housing my TV and other things. We both watch him as he moves it all to the side and onto the coffee table. Carefully, he carries the TV across the room and moves it right out the way.

"Where do you want the table?" he asks, looking over his shoulder.

"Uhh… Just put it by my bedroom door. I'll move it in there later."

"I can put it in there for you."

"No, no." I scoot to the edge of the sofa. "I'll do it. Just leave it outside."

He sighs. "Your clothes are all over the floor, aren't they?"

Carly bursts out laughing.

"I don't like you very much right now," I tell him as he walks out with the table. I lean back with a huff. "You're being mean to me."

Carly nudges me with a giggle. "You're a slob."

"I'm not a slob! I'm unorganized."

Cain comes back into the front room. "I don't know who let you get your adult card, but they must have been drunk when they signed off on it."

It's kind of hard to argue with that.

"I'm on a trial run." I push my hair from my face. "I expect my guardian angel to stop by any time to revoke it."

He lets go of a small laugh. "Help me move this."

"I got it. Trial Adult over here might stub her toe on thin air or something." Carly gets up, flashing me a grin.

It's like they think I'm a hot—wait, never mind. That train of thought is going nowhere except the utter truth.

It's a real sad state of affairs when your best friends don't trust you to move an empty entertainment unit. It's actually a miracle they allow me to live alone.

"There." Cain straightens and wipes his hands on his jeans. "Now you have a real home for your TV to watch your Kardashian crap on."

I have no idea what he has against that show. I've seen him secretly watching it and laughing his ass off at Scott more than once or twice.

"You're so horrible to me." I sniff and stand up. "Thank you," I say, kissing him lightly on the cheek without thinking.

He wraps his arm around my waist and squeezes me into him. "You're welcome, Hot Mess."

"That better not have turned into a nickname."

He grins, releasing me, and moves toward the sofa. Then he stops. "I'm going to have to plug everything in for you, aren't I?"

"Er…" I look at all the wires and electronics. "Yeah."

He nudges me and moves back to pick up the TV.

"She'd just electrocute herself," Carly teases me, snapping a hair tie off her wrist and scooping her hair back from her face.

"You're such an asshole." I flip her the bird.

"She's right. Both of you," Cain grunts. He puts the TV down. "Make yourselves useful and get me a beer."

"You could try please." I show him my middle finger too and walk into the kitchen. I pull the bottle of wine out of the fridge before I do the beer and show it to Carly.

She gets up without a word and skips over to me with our empty glasses. As I take Cain's beer from the drawer, Carly fills our glasses, draining the rest of the wine bottle into them.

"You need to do it now," she whispers, leaning into me.

"Do what?" I whisper back, grasping the bottle opener tightly. I know exactly what she's going to say.

"Tell him how you feel. Well, maybe not right this second. Next week or something. But now before you lose your chance again."

"I've never had a chance." I hook the bottle opener onto the cap, swallowing as the look in his eyes from earlier flashes in my mind. "You're delusional if you think I do now."

"I think you're the delusional one." She lifts her wine glass and looks around me to where Cain is hooking up my TV again. "I think you're ignoring what you want to see because you're afraid it's not there when it is."

"Sorry, Mrs. Sphinx, your riddles are ridiculous."

"Brooke!" She grabs my hand and pulls me further into the

kitchen. "What if you don't do it? Are you really going to mope for the rest of your life? What if the next girl he meets is perfect for him?"

I snatch my hand away, feeling my heart hardening. "Then it'll be just as well I didn't say anything. I don't fancy handing somebody my heart just to have it sliced by a blender a little while later." I pop the cap on the beer. It clinks as it comes on and bounces across the counter, flicking off the tiles at the back before finally coming to settle and lie flat.

There's something satisfying about that final, tiny clink.

I grab my wine before she can say another word and go back into the front room. Cain is lying back on the sofa, everything in place on the unit, with his feet up on top of the back cushions again.

I put the cold bottle on his stomach. "Your feet are in my spot."

"Your sass is in mine."

I whack his foot and sit in the armchair instead.

Carly takes the other one and turns to the TV. "Oh hell no! I'm not watching NASCAR! Damn it, Cain. You know the rules. Football or baseball only."

"You don't even watch the games!" He points his beer at her. "You all stare at their damn asses."

Carly grins.

"Hey!" I protest. "I watch football *and* understand it."

He cranes his neck back. "I notice you didn't protest watching baseball for their asses."

"Yeah, well, that's like saying *you* watch *The Big Bang Theory* for the science and not Kaley Cuoco."

"Shut up." He gets comfortable again. "Fine. We'll watch more murder shows."

"Yesssss." Carly snuggles into the armchair and sips her wine.

When he turns over the channel, *Homicide Hunter* is just starting again. I'm pretty sure we've seen every episode known to man—like *Friends* and *Gilmore Girls*—but unlike those two, I tend to forget who did what on this show.

Mostly because I forget I like it until someone else turns it on. Then I watch it and I realize how much I like Kenda's sass. Seriously. Watch it. He's the Sass King.

Half an hour into the program, when the commercials come on, I glance over at Cain on the sofa. His eyes are closed, and his chest is gently rising and falling. A smile tugs up at my lips, and it's then I notice Carly looking at me with a mix of sympathy and understanding in her eyes.

She finishes her wine and goes into my hallway.

I set my barely-touched glass onto the coffee table without making a noise, and gently prize the beer bottle from Cain's fingertips.

His hand twitches, but he doesn't wake when I take it and put it on the table too. He's barely touched it, but obviously, he was right when he said he'd barely slept. I've known him to fall asleep on the sofa only a handful of times. Ever. He's really not the stereotypical man who can fall asleep anywhere and everywhere. He's a straight up, bed only kinda guy.

Carly comes back into the front room with a light blanket. She passes it to me and squeezes my shoulder right before she lets it go.

I cover Cain with the blanket, taking extra care not to wake him, and silently wave goodbye to Carly. With her purse in hand, she slips out of my front door and quietly closes it.

Cain half-snores when the door clicks. I tiptoe across the room and lock the door. Then I switch everything off in the front room, leaving him in darkness. I pick up my wine glass and use my phone to guide me through the still haphazard boxes in the hallway, down to my bedroom.

I shut the door behind me before I flick on the switch. My bedroom TV is still turned on and on Netflix from when I got in from work and took the world's shortest nap, so I set down my glass and phone and go look for my pajamas.

When I find them, I change and climb into bed. A sound comes from the front room, but when there's nothing more after a second, I know it's probably Cain snoring and moving, so turn off my main light and settle into bed.

I set Netflix to play the next episode of *Friends* and snuggle under my covers.

Today was the strangest kind of crazy.

eleven

LIFE TIP #11: IF YOU'RE GOING TO SWING A BASEBALL BAT AT AN INTRUDER, MAKE SURE THEY'RE ACTUALLY AN INTRUDER FIRST.

Thud.

What the hell?

I push my covers down off my body and pause. My bedroom is visible from the vague, hazy light from the TV which is still playing a Friends episode. Holiday armadillo episode. Wow. I've been asleep for a couple hours…

Thud.

What in the shit is that noise?

A light sense of fear trickles down my spine, yet it somehow manages to grip my entire body and hold onto it. My hands are shaking as I reach beneath the bed and blindly grab for the baseball bat I know is there. After a few seconds, I drop to my knees and peek beneath the bed.

I grab the bat and stand up. I've never actually had to use this thing before on account of the fact I've never lived alone, so I don't actually know what to do with it.

Do I hold it by my side? In front of me like a gun? Do I wave it around like a nunchuck or something?

I rest it up on my shoulder and quietly open my bedroom door. Aside from the gentle light from my TV, the rest of my apartment is in complete darkness. My stomach flips repeatedly as I pad my bare feet across my hallway carpet. I can't hear a thing from the heavy beating of my heart in my ears. It thunders and echoes through my consciousness with every step I take.

"*Fuck!*"

I scream and swing the bat blindly in the darkness.

"Fuck, Brooke! What the hell?"

Ohmygod. Cain!

"Oh my god!" I drop the bat to the floor, whacking my foot with it, and cry out again. "Ow, ow, ow! Dirty motherfucking slut, that hurt!"

"Shit."

There's some slapping of a hand against the wall and then the small area floods with light. I blink harshly as my eyes struggle to adjust to the immediate onslaught of yellow light, but after a second, I'm okay.

Aside from my foot.

"What the fuck," he breathes, "are you doing swinging a fucking baseball bat around in the darkness?"

"I thought you were a burglar! Owwww!" I whine, collapsing against the wall and grabbing my foot. "I think my foot is broken."

"Oh, fucking hell." He comes toward me and loops his arm around my waist. "It's not broken. Probably bruised. Serves you right for coming at me with a baseball bat, you crazy bitch."

"I thought you were a burglar," I protest, hopping with his help.

He guides me into my bedroom, avoiding looking at my mess of clothes all over the floor, and sits me on my bed. "I was asleep on your sofa, apparently. How could you forget that?"

"I don't know." I lift my foot onto my thigh and lightly rub it. "I woke up when I heard a thud. I forgot. I was sleepy."

He turns on my bedside lamp before he raises his shoulders and smiles sheepishly. "Sorry. I banged my foot when I tried to get up. Then I walked into the sofa. It's hard navigating your maze in the dark."

"Why didn't you use—right. You didn't bring your phone."

Cain shakes his head. "I really was trying to get out without waking you. Sorry."

"No, it's fine." I put my foot down, the harsh sting now barely an ache. He's right. Not broken. "I should have woken you and not left you to sleep."

"You're telling me." He rubs the side of his neck. "My neck is burning like a bitch."

"Sorry." I grimace. "What time is it?"

"Almost two in the morning according to your microwave. I was trying to go home."

"You—what? No." I grab my phone from the nightstand and look at it. Yep. Just before five to two in the morning. "You can't go home at this time. Just stay here."

He hesitates, and while he does, I can't help but stare at him. Sure, I'm sleepy. I'm delusional at best. But oh my god, he looks oddly handsome. His hair is a mess, sticking up at all angles, and his eyes are full of a sleepy, cloudy haze. Not to mention his lips are slightly swollen as if he's been rubbing them in his sleep.

"I can't stay here," he says after a moment, standing up and shoving his hands into his pocket. "You haven't made your spare room up yet."

I've barely made my bedroom up yet, but whatever.

He's right. I know he's right. He can't sleep on the sofa, and if I offer, he'll tell me no. But he also can't go home now, because it's the middle of the freaking night. So I say as much.

"Cain, it's the middle of the night. You can't go home right now."

"My cars parked right outside the door to the building." He shrugs and takes a step back. "I'll be okay."

"Cain Elliott, if you go home right now, I'm going to hire a hit man to take you out."

He quirks a brow. "Stop me."

I throw myself at him as he darts to the door. I catch him in time and jump onto his back. I wrap myself around him the way a toddler clings to its mom's leg their first time at daycare. "No."

He staggers back, laughing huskily, and wraps his hands around my forearms. "All right, all right, I get it. Don't go out in case the boogeyman might get me."

"Exactly."

"But that doesn't solve the problem of where I'm sleeping. And can you get off me before you strangle me?"

I hit his chest and slide down his back. "Well, um. I can take the sofa."

"No."

I sigh and sit on my bed. "Keep your clothes on and your hands to yourself and you can sleep in here with me."

He jerks his face toward me. I can't read his expression at all.

"What?" I say.

"Okay, but you need to put on a bra."

I throw my arms up. "Have you tried sleeping in one of those? Isn't it bad enough that the underwires try to kill me during the day? Do you hate me so much I need to suffer that horror in my sleep too?"

"You are the most dramatic person I've ever met," he says slowly.

"You wanna wear a bra and feel my pain?"

"Not really." He smirks. "Fine, don't put on a bra, but I'm not sleeping in my jeans."

This is going from bad to worse.

I swallow. "Fine. But look." I roll over onto my knees and arrange the bed so the pillows are as far apart as they can possibly be. Then I get up and grab a clean towel from the top of my dresser. I roll it up into a long sausage and shove it in the middle, under the covers. "Your side. My side. Stay there."

He holds his hands up as he walks around the bed. "I'm not the starfisher here."

"Carry on and you can go home."

"In case it escaped your notice, Sherlock Holmes, that's what I'm trying to do."

"Shut up and get into bed. But keep your pants on until the light is off. I don't want to see that." Lies. I do want to see it. I totally want to see it.

Like, badly.

Cain rolls his eyes so hard I swear I can hear them rattling inside his eye sockets.

I shove myself under the covers and turn off my lamp on the nightstand. The room is one again bathed in only the hazy light from the television. I leave it on until I hear the light swish of his jeans hitting the floor. The bed dips right as I press the power button on the remote control, but when I go to put it back on the nightstand, I miss. It falls to the floor with a gentle thud.

"Crap," I mutter.

Cain chuckles.

"Shut it." I tug the covers right up under my chin and roll onto my side, putting my back to him. I squeeze my eyes shut, but I no longer feel tired.

I'm all too aware of Cain's warm body, separated from me by no more than a rolled-up bath towel. Still, that doesn't stop the heat from him coming across the covers and the bed sheet. Doesn't stop me knowing that he's right there, within touching distance.

I press my face into my pillow. I need to stop thinking about him. I need to stop thinking about the fact he's right here and so close to me, or I'm not going to go to sleep. *Arghhh.* Why did I tell him to sleep here? Why didn't I send him home?

"Brooke?" Cain whispers.

"Yeah?"

"Is it wrong that I don't feel bad about today?"

I roll onto my back and look up at the ceiling. "Breaking up with Nina? No. You obviously made the right choice if you feel okay."

The mattress moves as he does, and the towel nudges me as he lies on his back too. "I thought I'd at least feel bad."

"How do you feel?"

"Lighter," he answers. "It sounds awful, but if she calls me tomorrow, I know I don't have to answer it. I don't have to do shit I don't want to do anymore."

"Like build my entertainment unit." I turn my head toward him with a grin on my face.

"Like build your damn entertainment unit," he agrees, flashing me the smallest of smiles. "You don't have any other dumb furniture to build, do you?"

"Um. No?"

He sighs. "You don't sound so sure about that. What else do you need me to build?"

"I have a bookcase, a bathroom cabinet, and a dresser for my bedroom."

"B, you already have a dresser in here."

"I know that." I kick my foot to the side and connect with his ankle. "It's the one for the spare bedroom. Where else am I supposed to put my clothes until I get the new one in here?"

"Judging by their current home, the floor," he drawls.

"Shut your face. You don't have to build anything." I play with a loose thread on the cover. "I'm sure me and Carly can do it."

He shudders, vibrating the bed. "No, fuck no. If you and Carly try to build a dresser, you'll create a portal to another world or something. Or you'll just break it and call me anyway."

He might be onto something there. Carly and I aren't exactly known for our building skills. I proved that already, after all.

"Okay. I promise I'll do better to feed you next time." I pull the covers back up. "Are you really sure you feel okay?"

"I swear, I'm fine. It's like I've lost ten pounds."

"I have some spare if you want them back."

He laughs, shaking the entire bed. "If you lost ten pounds someone could snap you like a twig."

"I'd need to lose at least twenty-five for that."

"Brooke Barker, if you lose twenty-five pounds you don't

need to lose, I'm going to force-feed you cake and pizza until you put it all back on again."

I snort. "You're an idiot."

"Being an idiot doesn't change the fact I think you're perfect the way you are." He pauses, and my heart beats right out of my chest. "As long as you don't swing a baseball bat at me again."

"Don't bang around my apartment in the dark next time and I won't." I skip right over the whole 'perfect' thing, even if my heart isn't able to do it because it's going crazy. And my stomach is flipping, loop-the-looping over and over again.

It was a flippant comment. I know that. But it doesn't change the fact I'll probably still be sighing into my fucking breakfast over it next week.

"You got it. Night, Brooke." He rolls over again.

"Night, Cain," I reply softly, not moving, still staring up into the darkness, my heart echoing his words around my body with every beat.

My alarm blares out of my phone on the nightstand, rousing me fully from my awkward half-sleep state.

There's a person on top of me.

Well, not on top of me. Behind me. Against me. With an arm on top of me. And a foot.

Oh my god, Cain!

I freeze. His arm and foot aren't the only things invading my personal space.

Holy shit. Someone radio Houston because we have a problem. A big problem. And it's poking into my lower back right now.

What do I do? Do I get up and pretend I didn't feel it? Do I lie here and pretend—no, I can't pretend to be asleep. I just turned off my annoying alarm. What if he heard it?

145

Oh god, is he awake too? Is he wondering what I'm going to do? Is he pretending he's asleep and waiting for me to move?

Dear god, they don't show you this in the movies! Or the books. Two hundred books on my Kindle and of the ones I've read, none of them show you what to do when you wake up with your best friend's hard cock pressing against your back.

It's bigger than I thought it'd be.

Jesus, self! It's not a fucking birthday cake! Nor should I be contemplating the size of Cain's cock.

Now I am though, aren't I? Yep.

How much of it is touching me? Wait, how long is an inch? Can I figure out exactly how long it is right now? An inch is like half a thumb, right?

What the hell is wrong with me?

It's a good seven inches. For sure. Maybe more.

Shit my life!

"Brooke?" Cain says from behind me. "You can relax. I'm not going to whip my cock out and hit you with it."

"Oh my god!" I shove the sheets back and jump out of the bed. My cheeks are flaming, and I wrap my arms around my midsection as I turn to face him. "You knew I was awake and you lay there anyway?"

He grins, propping himself up on his elbow. "I was going to move, but then you froze, and I couldn't resist messing with you."

I give him my hardest glare. "You're such an asshole! And you violated the towel!"

He collapses onto his back, laughing his ass off. "You think I deliberately did that? It was a towel, not a fucking brick wall."

"But it poked me!" I point in the general area of his groin. "Did it have to poke me?"

He shrugs and sits up. "I told you to put a bra on."

"Cain!"

"What do you want me to say, B? I can't control where the

146

blood in my body goes when I'm sleep. I'm sorry my morning erection alarmed you, but it's no scarier than your cooking."

How is he not embarrassed right now?

"You're cute when you blush." He grins, his eyes sparkling.

"I am not blushing!" I shout, totally blushing. I slap my hands against my cheeks and run out of the room and to the bathroom. I slam the door behind me, lock it, and lean against it.

Oh god, oh god, oh god.

I should have just gotten out of bed. I'm twenty-four, for goodness sakes. I'm not seventeen. It's not the first erection I've felt. It's just...Cain's.

And I feel...warmer...than I should. Down *there*. In my vagina.

I clench my thighs together as an ache throbs through my clit.

Oh my god, my genitals are slutty.

This isn't okay. I can be attracted to him, but being turned on at the mere feeling of his erection at my back is a step too far. Isn't it? *Yes. No. Yes. No. Fuck it!*

"Brooke?" Cain knocks on the door. "Are you hiding from me?"

"No!" I say too loudly. "I'm peeing!"

"Uh-huh. Right behind the door?"

"Shit!" I push off of it.

He knocks again. "Open the door, B."

"No. I'm not sure I can ever look at you again." Because if I do, I might jump you.

"You still trying to tell me you aren't hiding or blushing?"

"I'm hiding! I'm hiding and I'm embarrassed!" I shout, cheeks flushing yet again. "I'm not coming out until you leave."

"Don't be stupid."

"Cain! Just go!"

If you don't, I might just lose my mind and tell you exactly why you need to go.

"All right," he says in a low voice. "But when I call you later, you better answer, or I'm gonna show up wearing nothing."

"Fine. Now go. Please." I really wish my cheeks would stop burning now.

It's not that I'm a prude. I'm the furthest thing from being a prude. I don't even think it's just that it's Cain and Cain's cock. It's because I wasn't expecting to wake up and get a good morning from Cain's cock.

A couple of minutes later, my front door opens and closes as he leaves.

I let go of a long, shuddery breath and move toward the sink. I grab the edge of it and lean forward, looking at myself in the mirror. My cheeks really are a light reddish color, and my eyes are shining brighter than I've seen them in a long time.

Stupid, stupid, stupid.

Brooke Alice Barker, you complete and utter fool.

I splash cold water on my face. Then I brush my teeth, and when I'm done, I head for the door and unlock it. I run my fingers through my hair and turn toward my bedroom.

"Brooke."

I scream and jump backwards. "For the love of fucking god!" I flatten myself against the wall and press my hands against my stomach. Then I throw myself toward him. "Don't. Do. That. Again!" I hit his chest with every word before taking a step back. "You're not supposed to be here!"

He holds his hands up. Just when I think he's going to walk away, he grabs my arms and pulls me toward him. I squeak as my body collides with his and I grab his shirt. He doesn't move his hands from my arms. In fact, he slides them up to my shoulders and even further until he's cupping my neck.

Cain dips his head and pushes my hair away from my ear. His hot breath tickles my skin when he lowers his mouth to my ear and whispers, "Look in the mirror, Brooke. You're a mess, but you're a fucking gorgeous mess. There's a reason I didn't want to stay, and that's it. Don't blame me for waking up with a raging hard-on when you've been lying next to me in bed for six hours."

I swallow, desperately trying to alleviate the dryness in my mouth. *That* I was not expecting. What was I expecting? I don't damn well know, but not that.

"I don't know how to reply to that." My fingers twitch, my grip tightening on his shirt, if only a little. "At all."

He blows out a long breath and rests his cheek against the side of my head.

I close my eyes. Keeping my breathing steady is getting harder and harder. I just want to lean into him and bury my face into his t-shirt and let my heart go crazy.

I don't want to have to hold onto these emotions anymore.

"Fucking hell." Cain kisses the side of my head. Then he releases me and walks across my apartment and right out of the door.

I stare after him, my stomach curling up into a sick, tight ball, and fall back against the wall.

I should have hit him with the baseball bat, shouldn't I?

Twelve

LIFE TIP #12: LOVE SUCKS HARDER THAN A HOOKER IN FRONT OF A GLORYHOLE.

I take the ball the Devil Dog drops in front of me and wince as slobber coats my fingers. Delilah wags her tail at one hundred miles per hour, her tongue hanging out of her mouth, waiting for me to throw it.

I do as she wishes, launching it across the park. She shoots off like a bat out of hell after it, yapping excitedly.

"That's it?" Carly stares at me. "He just left?"

Slowly, I nod. Our work schedules synced up well today, so after running home to get changed, we agreed to meet back at the park and, as women do, evaluate absolutely everything that happened this morning.

"He just left," I confirm.

She purses her lips and drags her gaze from me to where Delilah has just collected the ball.

"I told you. You need to tell him how you feel."

"No, I don't." I look away from her when she turns back to me. "I don't need to do anything."

"So you're just gonna keep having awkward little moments until what, you either kill your friendship or fuck it out?"

I roll onto my front and bury my face into my arms. "It's not that easy, Car, and you freaking well know it. It's not like I can just tell him how I feel. So he's attracted to me. I'm attracted to him. Hell, you're attracted to him."

"Well, he's hot, but he's more like my brother. So yes and no. I don't want to take a ride on the Cainmobile if that's what you're asking me."

"Cainmobile! Oh my god. There's something wrong with you."

"Are you talking to me or the grass?"

I groan into the blanket I brought with me. "You. How am I supposed to face him at his mom's on Saturday? Not to mention my mom stopped by work today. Grandpa wants to join a dating site and wants me and Cain to help him. Do you know how messed up that is?"

"He wants to what?" Her lips quiver as she fights a laugh.

"Join a dating website! The man is seventy-five, for the love of god! What's he gonna do if he finds a girlfriend?"

"Take her for dinner? Watch a movie? Watch TV? What do you think he's going to do?" She throws the ball for Delilah. "Oh god." She turns to me. "You were thinking he wants a…"

"Well, this is my grandpa we're talking about. Would you be surprised if you found a pot of Viagra in his bathroom cabinet?"

Carly opens her mouth, pauses, and then says, "No. No, I don't think I would be."

"See? You can understand my feelings. He puts his hip out walking down the freaking stairs, never mind any other kind of vigorous activity."

"Maybe he's lonely," she reasons, tapping her finger against her chin. "Right? He could be lonely."

"Lonely? Have you seen his diary?" I sit up and cross my legs beneath me. "He's got more of a life than I have!"

"That's not hard."

My heart jumps into my throat at the sound of his voice. "Shouldn't you be working?"

Cain laughs and drops to the grass between us. "I was, but I finished putting together Mrs. Mayfair's bookshelf, and the wood we need for her desk still hasn't been delivered, so Dad told me to go away and do something productive."

Carly blinks at him. "And you count this as productive."

"If I'm keeping you out of trouble, it is."

Just then, Delilah comes leaping back. She takes one look at Cain and yaps behind the ball. She steamrolls past me and Carly and launches her tiny self at him.

Cain laughs and catches her pretty smoothly. "Well, hello to you too, Delilah."

The dog drops the ball in his lap and licks his cheek to death.

"Great, yep, hey, I love you too," he mutters, trying to keep his mouth out of the way of her tongue.

I tilt my head to the side and smirk. "I don't know who the bigger bitch is. Your ex-girlfriend or your new one."

Carly buries her face in her hands. Her shoulders shake, and she's clearly laughing.

Yep. I can hear the tiny, snuffly snorts she does when she's fighting it.

"You're not a bitch are you, Delilah?" Cain coos when she finally stops licking him. "No, you're not. You're lovely. Unlike Brooke. Yes." He nods. The Jack Russell cocks her head at him. "Brooke's horrible. Yes she is. Here. Get the ball." He throws the ball farther than either of us have been able to so far.

"Seriously? You're bitching about me to a dog?" I smack his knee.

He shrugs. "You're the one who called her a bitch. I don't see what she's done to you."

"Don't." Carly quickly sobers. "Delilah might have almost bitten her purse when we got here. Brooke had to throw her ball to distract her."

"You threw her ball? Holy shit. Are you ill?" Cain turns to me, laughter in his eyes.

I stare at him flatly. "You're at the top of my shit list, buddy. Do you want me to make your life hell?"

"You say that like you don't already."

"I hate you."

"There's a fine line between love and hate." He winks.

Carly looks between us, her dark eyes flitting side to side before she blinks and gives the barest shake of her head. I frown at her, but if she notices, she doesn't acknowledge me.

"How far did you throw Delilah's ball?" Carly squints out in the direction her dog was running in a moment ago.

"Too far?" Cain guesses.

"Ugh." She drops her head back. "You're a shit." She gets up, tosses me a wink without him seeing, adjusts her shorts, and runs after Delilah.

Bitch!

I'm putting an ad in the paper for a new best friend. Requirements: no dog, no attitude, no inner asshole.

"She did that deliberately, didn't she?" Cain asks, grimacing.

I keep my eyes trained on some guys playing soccer. "Mhmm."

It's awkward now she's gone. She was the buffer between us.

"She needs to get better at winking. That was as discreet as a freight truck in a shopping mall on Christmas Eve." I hear his laugh rather than see it.

She needs to get better at a lot of things. Like being a friend.

"Did you really get off work early?" I ask, still not looking at him.

"I really did." He plucks a daisy from the grass and flicks it away. "I actually came out to get some stuff for Mom for the party when I saw yours. She said you and Carly were here, so I thought I'd come down too."

"Makes sense."

"Do you want me to go?"

"What?" I peer at him out of the corner of my eye. "No. Why would you say that?"

He raises his eyebrows, lips tugging up on one side. "Because you don't exactly seem comfortable with me being here right now."

I let go of a long breath, look up, then turn to him. "Honestly? I'm not. This morning was, well, really awkward, and I've been awkward all day and now you're here I'm even

more awkward and can you please stop me saying awkward?”
“Are you done?” His smile widens.
“Awkward!”
“Wanna cracker there, Polly?”
“Ugh!” I shove him in the arm. “You’re such a dick.”
“Still feel awkward?”
I purse my lips to combat the smile attempting to break out across my lips. Because yes, I do, but I also feel a hell of a lot more normal now. This is the Cain I know. The Cain I’m comfortable with. The other Cain…The one from this morning…He’s a wild card.
And wild card Cain is terrifying.
“Smile,” he goads me, a smug glint in his eyes. “You want to. You know you do.”
I shake my head.
“Smile, Brooke.”
I look down, shaking my head again.
“Come on, Hot Mess. Smile.” He accompanies that demand with a tickle to my side.
I squirm away and bite the inside of my lip. Again, I shake my head, this time harder, and he obviously takes that as a challenge, because he reaches for me for a second time.
I scramble away from him, releasing my lip but still desperately fighting to keep my smile in check. He’s faster than I am—as he always is—and grabs me. He digs his fingers into my sides, right on my most ticklish spots right above my hips, and goes to town.
My laughter erupts out of me. Still he doesn’t stop, not even as I trash left and right and bat at his hands. He’s not only faster, he’s stronger too. I do the only thing I can do—I fight back with my own hands. I run my fingers up one of his sides until he jerks, and then I tickle him right back.
“Truce!” he breathes through his hard laughter. “Brooke!”
“No! You started this, you douche monkey.”
He drops down onto his back, holding his stomach and fending me off at the same time. My assault lasts all of ten seconds before I give it and drop my head onto his chest.

Both of us are laughing so hard we've passed the healthy laugh. He probably doesn't need to work out for two days now, and me, well, I can put it off for another day at least.

I wheeze out one final laugh as he pushes my hair from my face. "That was dirty, Elliott," I tell him, planting my hand on his chest and pushing up.

Whoa.

His heart is beating so frantically I can feel it thundering against my palm. The vigor of each quick beat makes me pause, and it's pausing that makes me realize: Mine is beating just as quickly and just as harshly.

Cain pushes himself up onto his elbows. "Then you should smile when I tell you to." He looks me dead in the eye, all traces of laughter and amusement and playfulness gone. There's just a peculiar seriousness I've barely seen before shining back at me.

"Why?" I let my hand fall away. I sit up properly and cross my legs again.

My gaze scans the park for Carly, but I can't see her anywh—oh, never mind. She's by the football players. Being hit on by three of them. Wonderful. That'll be another delightful disaster date.

"Do you need a reason to smile?" Cain asks.

Yes. The problem is, you're it.

"Everybody needs a reason to smile, Cain. Maybe I already have one." I shrug a shoulder in a non-committal way.

"Yeah?" He sits up properly now, his face drawing almost level with mine. "Then what is it?"

"I'd tell you but then I'd have to kill you. Sorry." What? That's not a lie.

"Point taken." His laugh is light, yet at the same time, it's heavy. "Simon call you yet?"

"Low blow." I go to hit his thigh.

He catches my fist and gently sets my hand back on my lap. His fingertips trail over my bare leg as he takes his hand back. "Was it? I was just asking."

"You know full well he hasn't called me, so don't be a jerk

about it." I tuck my hair behind my ear.

"You're right. I've been an ass to you enough today."

I turn my face toward him. He's looking straight ahead, his face unmoving. His stubbled jaw is dirty with his unshaven dark hair, and I have the inexplicable urge to run my fingers down the curve of it just to feel the roughness against my skin.

"Cain Elliott," I say slowly and in a quiet voice. "Are you actually admitting being an asshole?"

He inclines his head toward me but he doesn't look at me. "I was an ass this morning. I should have gotten up when your alarm went off. And when I didn't, I sure as shit should have left when you told me to."

"Wow. I'm not sure you've ever admitted being wrong before."

"Shut it, you. You're the stubborn one, not me."

"Oh, please. You still think *Harry Potter and the Prizoner of Azkaban* is the best movie."

Now he looks at me. "That's because it is."

I shake my head side to side. "No. It literally cannot be the best. Do you have any idea how much stuff they got wrong? How much stuff was out of order? It makes me mad."

"I didn't read the books. You know that."

"I know, you sucky little half-blood."

"That's discrimination."

"Then read the books." I poke my tongue out at him. "But I suppose in this situation I'll admit I was a little bit of an asshole this morning."

The slow upturn of his lips is ridiculously sexy. "As opposed to your usual lovely behavior the rest of the time."

"I don't know how I put up with your shit."

"You give me shit," he points out. "It's mutual."

I sigh. He's impossible. "Fine. I should have gotten out of bed and not freaked out about…you know." I wave my hand in the direction of his crotch.

"If I were a girl I'd freak too."

"You're so big-headed."

He smirks.

"Not like that! Shit. Crap. I quit. I need a re-do of today." I slap my hand over my eyes.

Cain laughs. "Obviously you've forgotten we need to set up your grandpa's online dating profile tomorrow after work."

"Right…" I pause and look him dead in the eye. "What can I eat that'll give me food poisoning?"

He pats my cheek. "Just cook, Hot Mess. That'll do it."

Asshole.

Me: *I hate you.*
Carly: *Me? Why? What did I do?*

Ha! Like she doesn't know.

Me: *You deliberately left me alone with Cain when you knew I didn't want to be alone.*
Carly: *Are you or are you not okay again?*
Me: *I felt his penis against my back! I will never be okay again!*
Carly: *I bet if you felt it somewhere else you'd be more than okay.*
Me: *I really want to tell you that you're sick, but yeah, probably.*
Carly: *Stop being a giant baby and deal with it. So you felt his penis against your back. You want it in other places. If you're not going to tell him how you feel, you don't get to be a whiny bitch.*
Me: *I hope Mother Nature visits you at two am.*
Carly: *That's just cruel.*
Me: *—middle finger emojis—*

Thirteen

LIFE TIP #13: IF YOUR DIRTY-MINDED GRANDPA WANTS TO ONLINE DATE, DON'T LET HIM DO IT UNSUPERVISED.

"No, James." Cain takes the wireless mouse from Grandpa. "That's your height. Not your penis size."

I bury my face in a cushion.

"Why do they want my height? My penis size is much more useful on this gosh-darn thing!" Grandpa sputters, indignation screaming from every word. "Who looks at a man and says, 'Oh, fuck me, he's five foot five! Give me some of that!' huh? Now if they know I have an—"

"Your height, Grandpa!" I cry before he can finish that sentence. "It's for your height. If you put your penis size on the internet, I'm disowning you immediately."

Cain flashes me a restrained smile. "James," he says, turning to him. "Don't you think you should keep something for a surprise?"

He's a fine one to talk. I can feel the imprint of his dick on my damn back.

"I suppose." Grandpa releases a dramatic sigh. "Although Jimmy is far more endearing that my height."

"Yeah, I'm sure he's real charming." Cain answers so I don't have to.

Not that I could. I have my face in the cushion again. I can't cope with this. I didn't sign up for elderly debauchery. Mind you, I didn't sign up for this at all. I was volunteered, and I'm not happy about it. My brother would do a way better job than us.

Then again, my brother has a perpetual grip on *his* penis and an unhealthy addiction to PornHub, so maybe that's not such a good idea after all.

"Grandpa, can you just fill it out normally? Some of us have things to do." I brave looking up.

"Like what?" He looks over the back of the computer chair. "You have two friends, girl, and one of them is right here!" He cackles.

"I have more than two friends!" I protest. "I just don't happen to like the rest of them."

Cain laughs. "You don't like me most of the time."

"True story."

"What's this?" Grandpa leans in close to the screen. "Interests. Can I put Betty Rosenthal down in that section? She makes a mean brisket."

Cain hesitates. "Putting another woman as one of your general interests might not work in your favor, James. I'd stick to bridge and things like that."

"But I'm very interested in Betty." He looks at Cain and waggles his eyebrows.

"I'm sure she's very interesting."

"Her butt is in those stockings. Hooey!" Grandpa laughs again. "All right, all right. Behave. I hear you."

"Nobody said anything," I say.

He looks over at me again. "No, but I felt it in your look. You have your mother's stares, you know."

I glare at him.

"There!" He points one thick, wrinkled finger at me and adjusts his glasses. "Yep, there she is. Hi, Lou!" He waves his hand. "Can you see her, Cain? She's right there."

I look away, clamping my lips together. "Can you both hurry up? I don't want to walk home and I really do have things to do tonight."

"Why? You have a hot date?" Grandpa does the eyebrow thing for a second time.

"Yes," I say dryly. "I have a date with myself, Netflix, and a packet of margarita mix. Can we get a move on?"

"All right, all right," Cain says. "Come on, James. I think she has some lingering PMS."

I throw a pillow at the back of his head. He catches it, laughing, as it falls, and chucks it back to me. I catch it and hug it to my lap as I lean to the back of the sofa and watch them go through the sign up.

For the record, I think this is a terrible idea. Mostly because nobody will be around to supervise Grandpa on the damn thing. He needs a keeper at the best of times, and I have no idea why Mom agreed to this. She has to know he's likely to offend so many lovely old ladies that he'll get arrested.

Or maybe that's the point.

Not that him being arrested would teach him a lesson. He'd make them all laugh, they'd realize he's harmless and let him go.

No, someone needs to monitor Grandpa on this thing. And definitely no Facebook. The last thing he needs to learn about is the delightful world of unsolicited dick pics. Mostly because he'd be the sender of said pictures if he ever found out about that fun little practice.

That, or he'd expect unsolicited but appreciated old lady boob pictures.

"Should I write a dirty joke or two in this section, boy?" Grandpa asks, grasping the arm of his glasses and leaning toward the screen. "I don't want any of these prudes hitting on me."

"The first line of your bio is expressing your love for jokes and the dirtier the better," Cain says. "I'm really not sure you're going to attract any…prudes."

"Get out of here. Look at me. I'm dang handsome, me. I'm gonna attract 'em all. Even the whippersnappers."

Yep. No. This is not a good idea. Not at all.

"Maybe we should see how people take your profile first." Cain's choosing his words very carefully now. "Besides, jokes are like penises. They're not always appreciated."

He darts a glance my way.

Grandpa catches it. He puts his arm on the back of the

chair and spins right around to look at me. He fixes me with his light brown gaze before turning it to Cain. "What'sa matter, boy? She catch a sight of it and not like it?"

Cain opens his mouth to answer.

Grandpa cuts him off, looking at me. "What was it? A wee cocktail sausage?" He accompanies that with a wiggle of his pinky finger. "Wee willy winky!"

I bite the inside of my cheek as the laughter boils up inside me.

Grandpa leans toward Cain and wiggles his baby finger again.

Cain gently moves his hand away. "Turn around, James. Or I'm going to add another three inches to your height and then the ladies will know you're overcompensating."

That sobers Grandpa. If there's anything that stops his ridiculousness, it's people threatening what Cain just did. There's nothing the old man hates more than the thought of women thinking he's smaller than he is.

Actually, that logic probably applies to the younger man with him too.

Cain leans into Grandpa's side and whispers something.

Grandpa snorts which leads into a dirty chuckle. "You're right, boy. She wouldn't know what to do with a real penis."

"Hey!" I sit up. "I know what to do with a real penis!"

They both turn with raised eyebrows. "Really," Grandpa asks. "Because I haven't seen you with one for at least two years."

"Just because I don't date much doesn't mean I don't know how to slice someone's dick off with a blunt knife."

Cain winces. "Please don't."

I shoot him a look that says "You deserve it, you assdonkey," but I don't say anything.

He clearly gets the message because he turns back to Grandpa and says, "Let's finish this."

One hour later, they're finally done.

I stumble out of Grandpa's apartment block and lean against Cain's car. "That was the most traumatizing experience of my entire life."

He laughs, pressing the button on his keys to unlock the car. It beeps. "I have to admit," he says slowly, "seeing him trawl the website for some 'dead hot babes' was a little unnerving."

"No, that was the least unnerving part," I reply, getting into the car. I wait until he's sitting before I continue. "The worst part was when he saw Cornelia and declared her boobs the loveliest love mountains this side of the Rockies."

Cain shudders. "Yeah, you win. Please don't ever mention that again."

"Cornelia's love mountains."

"You're sick."

"I know." I grin and pull my seatbelt across my body. I click it into place and say, "Now, take me home. I have a hot date with Netflix."

He starts the car. "You know you're supposed to Netflix and chill with another person, right? Not by yourself."

"Who said I'd be by myself?"

"Battery friends don't count."

I shift in my seat. "Well, you've never had that kind of relationship. It's perfect. Vibrators don't answer back, yell at me for my lack of cooking skills, or wake me up awkwardly in the morning."

"It's nice to know you value your relationship with your vibrator over your one with me."

"I wasn't done. It does have a downfall. It can't build things or bring me food when I mess it up. You can do that."

He shakes his head. "You're a loser, B. You know that?"

I do. I really, really do. "Yeah, but vibrators can't break my heart, so I'd rather be a loser than heartbroken."

"Are you saying I can break your heart?"

You do. Every time you smile at me.

I flash him a grin, but my heart isn't in it. "That would imply I care, and we all know that isn't true."

Cain laughs, throwing his head back a little. "Ah, yes. The great heartless Brooke Barker. The same heartless woman who cries at just about every commercial with a puppy in it."

"Look, until you have PMS, you don't know my life."

"Doesn't count. I have to deal with you when you have PMS. It can't be worse to have it."

"Do you want me to punch you in the balls?"

"With your fist?"

"You should get a girlfriend. You're an asshole when you're single."

He shrugs, turning a corner. "I'm an asshole with a girlfriend. I just can't be this kind of asshole when I have a girlfriend. But get used to it, B. I don't plan on getting a girlfriend anytime soon. I think Nina's scarred me for life."

"Jesus, don't let that get out." I shudder. "Last time girls in this town knew you were ready to date, at least eight of them came into work and asked for your number."

"Were they hot?"

"Like the North Pole."

"Ooooh, bitchy."

I roll my eyes and sit straight in the car. We pass the turn off for my apartment, instead going the way down to the bay. "Where are we going?"

He glances across the car at me. "You're not sitting in your apartment all night, moping around. We're gonna do something fun."

"But I didn't eat yet," I whine. "I literally walked through the door when you arrived. I barely had time to get changed. I'm so hungry!"

He mutters something under his breath. "Then I'll feed you. Come on, B. We haven't done anything fun in ages."

Yeah, well, that's your own fault for getting a jealous

girlfriend. "How likely are we to run into Nina?"

He pulls into a parking lot a couple of blocks away from Italia and kills the engine. "Dunno. It's Friday. She always meets her friends on Friday, so I guess there's a chance."

I groan and lean against the door, banging my head against the window. "This isn't a good idea, Cain. If she sees us together—"

"It's none of her fuckin' business."

His hard, cold tone makes me turn my face toward him. His features are set, his brow furrowed, and his jaw tight.

"Seriously." He turns to me, his voice softer. "My whole damn relationship with her I had to hide my friendship with you and Carly. Especially you. That's bullshit, B. I'm not gonna do it anymore. But it's up to you. We can either go have stupid fun like we used to or I can turn the key and take you home. Your call."

My instinct says to take me home, but the look in his eye makes me pause.

The greenness of his eyes has always been the one thing that makes me stop. And right now, looking into his eyes, I'm doing that exact thing. There's a myriad of emotions all swirling like crazy, and I know I should tell him to take me home, but something doesn't want me to do that.

Something about the indiscernible mess of feelings in his gaze makes me want to stay and do dumb shit with him.

"Okay, but we're getting food first."

He grins at my words and pulls the key from the ignition. "Okay, let's get food first. Come on." He pushes open his car door.

What am I doing?

I undo my seatbelt. Then I get out of the car and join Cain as he heads for the exit to the parking lot. From where we are, I can see the start of the seafront and down onto the bay. The light sea breeze is a welcome respite—kinda—from the sticky heat of the early summer, and I can't help but glance out at what I can see of the horizon as the sun makes its way toward it.

"Come on," Cain says again, grabbing my elbow and steering me down toward the bay. "Let's get fries."

"Chili cheese fries?"

"Would I dare suggest anything else?"

I nudge him with my elbow and smile up at him. "I need to learn to cook. This diet isn't good for my ass."

Cain stops.

I walk a few paces before I do the same thing and turn around. "What are you doing?"

"It's not bad for your ass," he says, shrugging. "Just so you know."

I put my hands on my hips. "Did you seriously stop just to look at my ass?"

He stretches his arms out, walking again. "How am I supposed to offer a real response to your comment if I don't know whether it's bad for it or not?"

"You're way more of a perv when you're single." I brush my hair out of my face and catch up with him. "Are the fries from Zander's?"

"Do you want the fries to be from Zander's?"

"Well, yeah. He gives me extra."

Cain scoffs. "Only because he has a crush on you. You exploit that."

"Am I not supposed to?"

He looks down at me, a small smile teasing his mouth. "I can't tell if you're being serious or not, but just in case you are, probably not, no. You already exploit the shit out of me."

I flick my hair over my shoulder. "It's not my fault I was born cute. Or that you're easily exploitable."

He laughs and side-hugs me, never breaking stride. "You'll be the president one day with that attitude."

"Ha! Like that'll ever happen. I'd trip over walking up to the podium every time I had to campaign." I tuck my hands in the ass pockets of my shorts. "And I'd probably fall onto the button for nuclear bombs one day. That wouldn't be good."

"You're right." He flicks his finger against my ear, making

me jerk away. "That would be a fucking disaster. Could you imagine the shitshow this country would turn into if you were in charge?"

I actually think I'd make a good president. My first act in office would be to make Taco Tuesday a legit weekly holiday. We stop in Zander's Diner. It's not what you'd call 'cute,' and it's definitely retro, but not your stereotypical fifties diner. No, Zander's father—also named Alexander and shortened to Zander—is a huge fan of the nineties. God only knows why, and the man himself doesn't seem to be able to explain it either.

Regardless, the diner is decorated in just about everything nineties you can think of, and the music is a constant loop of cheesy pop and even cheesier R&B.

I cannot stand to eat inside this place. Luckily for me, Cain knows this, and goes straight to the counter to order while I hang back by the door. The music is quieter here, and thank god, because I don't want to spice up my life, thanks.

I spice it up enough myself just by waking up. I'm already unpredictable enough. I don't need help.

It's quiet at the take-out counter, and since we're here before their big rush in the evenings, Cain's handed two boxes within five minutes of paying. He thanks the girl behind the counter and walks back over to me.

"Here." He hands me my box of chili cheese fries before opening the door and holding it for me.

"Thanks." I smile over my shoulder as he joins me outside. "Where are we going now?"

He shrugs. "Anywhere we can sit and eat. Now I've got these, I'm hungry."

"What did you get? The same as me?"

Cain nods. "Yep. Let's go down to the beach."

We cross the street, only narrowly making it before a car comes speeding around the corner, and head for the little gate that leads to the small set of stairs.

Although the beach stretches almost the entire length of Barley Cross, we're at the wrong end of town for the better entrances. Which isn't a bad thing. The teens and all the people that will really annoy me will be at the other end of the beach, which means it'll be quiet for us.

We learned that as teenagers ourselves. Don't stick with the crowd, because that's where the cops are likely to catch you drinking. Go down the quiet end and you'll just look like a small group of teenagers drinking your Diet Coke.

Wink, wink.

I step onto the sand after Cain and immediately pull off my shoes. There's nothing worse than walking on soft sand with shoes on, and I don't want to walk on the wet sand since my ballerina pumps are white.

"Okay," I say, climbing up onto one of the giant rocks with a flatter top. "All we need is vodka in bottles of Diet Coke and we'd really be doing this right."

Cain laughs and climbs up next to me. His arm brushes mine as he gets comfortable, and even when he is, his thigh is still pressing against mine. "Damn it. Why didn't we think of that?"

"Because you have to drive, moron."

"True. Although we could have just called my mom. Or Zeke."

I lean to the side and look at him. "Okay, I was kidding. We don't actually need to be sixteen again. And Zeke would be a waste of time anyway. He always ended up drinking with us."

"True," he says as I open my box of fries.

Mmmm. They just smell so damn good.

We both eat in silence for a couple of minutes. Although I'm focused on watching the waves slowly creep up the beach from a good couple of miles out, I'm very aware of the heat of his leg against mine. His jean shorts cut off below his knee, whereas mine are much higher up. Every now and then our lower legs collide, mostly because I'm completely incapable of sitting still. The coarse hair on his legs keeps rubbing against mine, tickling my skin.

I shiver as his leg knocks against mine for the third time in at least thirty seconds. He chuckles from next to me, and if he didn't have a box of food, I'd get him back for it. The ass is doing it deliberately.

"I think you have more food than me," I tell him, peering into his box.

"You jealous?"

"Of more food? Yeah. Obviously."

He laughs and shoves three fries into his mouth. "Do you want to know what we're doing next?"

My phone rings in my pocket.

"Hold on." I pass him my box and dig my phone out. Grandpa. Oh no. "Hey, Grandpa. What's up?"

"I've got a date!" He sings down the phone. "I told her the Boeing joke!"

"Oh no. Not the cockpit one."

"Yes, that one!"

Cain's upper body shakes. He's laughing silently. No doubt it's at what is clearly a look of absolute horror on my face.

"What did she say?" I ask him slowly.

"She asked for my number. Now we're sexting."

I cough. "You're sexting a woman you just met online?"

"I am! And I tell you what, Brookey, if I thought Cornelia had nice love moun—"

"Crap! My phone's dying! Sorry, Grandpa. Gotta go!" I hang up.

Then I stare at my phone.

"Did he just say he was sexting?"

fourteen

LIFE TIP #14: LIPS ARE MADE FOR KISSING. AND DON'T GO ON A HAUNTED HOUSE TOUR WITH SOMEONE WHO REALLY HATES YOU.

"Yes," I answer Cain slowly. "Yes, he's currently sexting a woman he met online." I turn to face him. "I'm a little afraid."

Cain blinks at me. "I'm kinda proud of him. Good for him."

"Good for him?" I shove my phone back in my pocket and take my food. "Cain, he's seventy-five. He should not be sexting anyone!"

"Why not?"

"Because he's old."

"You're only as old as the woman you feel."

I blink at him. A lot.

"Got somethin' in your eye?" He grins wide. "Come on, B. He's lonely."

"I told you earlier. He isn't lonely. He has tons of friends." I huff and stick a handful of fries into my mouth. Literally a handful.

"That doesn't mean he isn't lonely," he says reasonably. "Maybe he wants something more. We all know none of the old chicks in the apartments are gonna give him what he wants."

"That's because he shouldn't want what he wants. He's a sex-mad maniac."

"He's a man. What are you gonna do about it?"

I roll my eyes. "I couldn't deal with as many people as he

does."

"Well." Cain does his box up and drops it onto the sand in front of him.

I hand him mine and he does the same, letting it fall down. I jump down from the rock and lean back against it. "Well what?"

Cain drops to his feet and turns his entire body toward me. "You'd be able to deal with people a bit better if you actually tried to like them."

"True… but there's just one problem with that."

"Which is?" He raises one dark eyebrow, his eyes bright and intent on mine.

I exhale heavily, holding his gaze and grinning. "Liking people takes a lot of energy. I'd rather use that energy for other things. Like eating four tacos and drinking an entire bottle of wine."

He smirks one of those dirty, teasing smirks. "Of course. Although I agree. I'd rather use that energy for other things too."

Now it's my turn to raise my eyebrows. "Like what?"

He takes one step toward me. "This."

He frames my face with his hands and leans in before I can stop him. Right as my eyes flutter shut of their own accord, Cain's lips find mine.

They're warm and taste like spice. He *smells* like spice. Like spice and sea air and sand.

His body is all but pressing me back against the rock. I can't breathe, because I'm not sure I can fully comprehend what's happening right now.

Until he pulls away.

Nope.

I lean forward, into him, and into that soft kiss. Into *his* soft kiss. I don't want him to pull away. Not yet. Even if he's regretting it right now, I want to keep his mouth on mine just a few seconds longer so I can commit this all to memory.

So I know I'll remember the way it feels to have his hands frame my face as his soft, pink lips lightly explore mine.

So I know I'll remember how everything I've ever imagined pales in comparison to this reality.

I don't know how long we stand here, lips together, waves crashing, seagulls crying, but I know that's it's all together too long yet not long enough at the very same time.

Cain takes a step back. His hands slowly fall away from my face, and I only open my eyes when the only evidence of him ever touching me is a lingering tingle across my cheeks.

He swallows, looking at me with a mixture of guilt and hesitation. His cheeks are even a little pink, the lightest hue you could ever imagine. Nobody else would know, but I do. I can see that tinge. I can see the difference.

I don't say anything. What am I supposed to say? Thank you for fulfilling one of my highly inappropriate dreams about you? No—I can't, and since I can't think of anything else to say, I simply press my shaking hands together in front of my stomach and wait for him to speak.

He opens his mouth twice before closing it again. He finally breaks our gaze and runs his hand through his hair, looking down. "Shit," he whispers, kicking the sand.

My heart drops like it's made of granite.

Yep.

Regret.

I look away from his too and press my hands onto my stomach. Like the simple act will stop me feeling so damn sick I can't breathe.

He kissed me, and now he regrets it.

This is why I never told him how I feel. Because of this. This fucking awful kick of regret I knew one of us would feel.

This is why you should never fall in love with your best friend. This moment right here. The lingering cloud of something that felt so right unraveling right before your eyes.

And not just a kiss.

Perhaps an entire friendship too.

"I'm sorry." Cain drags his gaze back up to look at me, and his words are reflected in his eyes. "I—I don't know why I did it."

"Don't worry about it," I reply in a voice so soft I barely recognize it as my own. "I'll walk home, okay? It's not that far from here."

"No." He stops me by flattening his hand against the rock by my head. His gaze is hot on me, almost pleading with me to look at him, but I can't.

If I do, I'm going to cry, and I'm not going to fucking cry. Not now, not where he can see me do it.

"Brooke."

I move only to swallow the lump in my throat. The same one that damn well won't go down.

I jerk away when he touches his thumb to my cheek.

"B, look at me," he says softly.

I take a deep breath and steel myself, straightening my spine. Then I look at him. And I could so easily drown in the magic of his eyes.

"I don't know why I did it." Cain repeats the horrible words again. "Except that I wanted to, okay? I don't know why I picked that moment. I just…I wanted to."

Wait, what?

"You wanted to?" My voice cracks halfway through.

He nods the barest amount. "You're probably mad at me, and it was fucking stupid. I just need you to know that I wanted to kiss you. So I did."

"I'm not mad." I wrap my arms around my stomach, still looking into his eyes. "It wasn't so bad. I mean, you don't kiss like a fish or anything."

He quirks his lips into the tiniest smile, a bright spark reappearing in his eyes. "That might be the nicest thing you've ever said to me."

"Probably. Don't expect anything that nice again. You did just attack my mouth without permission, don't forget."

He cups my chin with his hand, smiling down at me. "You're really not mad I just kissed you?"

No.

"No. Really," I assure him. Boy, keeping in my real feelings is kinda hard. Like controlling a hysterical toddler.

Funnily enough, I feel like a hysterical toddler right now. Cain's hand trails down and rests at the side of my neck. "*Really*, really?"

I half-smile at him, daring myself to touch him. So I do. I set my hands at his waist and say, "*Really*, really."

He pauses for a moment before he pulls me against him. His arms circle my shoulders, holding me tight to his hard body, and he presses his mouth to the top of my head. He's smiling against my hair. His chest is vibrating too, not to mention that too-quick beat of his heart as I wrap my arms around his waist and hug him back.

Now what?

He turns his head a little. "This is really awkward, isn't it?"

I nod into his chest.

And he laughs. He out and out laughs, his whole body shaking, the deep sound reverberating through me and dancing across my skin, making my hair stand on end just about everywhere.

"Do you still want to go home?" he asks me.

I pull back and shake my head. "It's okay. This whole thing is awkward. We may as well carry on being awkward. Is it supposed to be awkward?"

"You have a real issue with the word awkward, you know that?"

"I know. It kinda rolls off the tongue weirdly, and I like weird."

"No. You don't, do you?" he says it so dryly I have to shove at him.

"Stop it!" I snap playfully, smiling at him. "So…is this supposed to be awkward?"

I'm going to die if he smirks again.

That's it.

He smirks.

I'm dead.

"Yeah," he answers, rolling his shoulders. "You're my best friend and I just kissed you. And I'm really fucking sure I want to do it again. Somewhere nobody else can see just how badly I want to do it. So yeah. It's supposed to be fucking awkward."

"You—you want to kiss me again? Yep. This is awkward." He takes my chin in his hand and gives me a searing look. A literal red-hot look that sends shivers down my spine. "If you think kissing you is all I want to do to you right now, then you're in for a big damn shock."

I take a quick, deep breath, and let it go just as rapidly. "What were your plans for tonight?"

Cain drops his head, rubbing his hand across his mouth, and looks up at me through his dark eyelashes.

Why does he get the pretty eyelashes? This is unfair.

"If I tell you, I'm going to have to drag you there. And if I have to drag you there…" He shakes his head. Then he bends down to grab our empty boxes from our fries and straightens. "Come on. Just trust me."

"Famous last words," I mutter.

"The ghost tour?" I stare at Cain's smirking face. "*The ghost tour?*"

"What's wrong with the ghost tour?"

"What's right with it?" I shoot back. "This is the dumbest idea you've ever had. You can't really believe I'm going to survive a ghost tour. I'm the biggest wimp known to man."

"And woman and reptile and alien."

I flatten my hands against my cheeks. "You forgot arachnids. And birds."

He looks up toward the darkening sky and counts to five on a mutter. "Brooke." He drops his eyes back to mine. "Come on. You know as well as I do that it's all a tourist gimmick. It's not actually haunted."

Since we're standing outside the graveyard, I peer into it. The setting sun is barely glinting through the thick, dark green trees that surround the final resting place of hundreds of people. It has the eerie effect of casting numerous shadows across the graves, mostly old, cracked, and decaying ones covered with moss and ivy.

"Yeah, obviously," I say slowly. "But people have actually died in there." I point to the graveyard. "Didn't that girl get attacked there two years ago?"

"Well, yeah, but—"

"And didn't old Mr. Wellington walk his dog through it one night and drop dead?"

"That was proved to be from low blood sugar and he's diabetic, so—"

"And wasn't there a gang rape there not so long ago?"

He clamps his hand over my mouth. "Eight years ago, B. The girl was an accident, Mr. Wellington was already sick and old, and the gang thing was a rare occurrence."

I lick his palm, making him drop it like my face is on fire. "But they all died. I'm not going in that graveyard."

"You don't need to go in the graveyard. It's the last stop. If you get your granny panties in a twist, I promise we'll leave."

"I'm not wearing granny panties." I purse my lips. "Fine. But you know it'll be full of tourists, don't you?"

"I'm counting on it. We're in a group of twenty-five."

There are so many things wrong about this. "I hate tourists."

"B." He laughs. "You hate everybody."

"That's because people annoy me."

"Yeah, well, you annoy me, yet here I am." He raises his eyebrows with a half-smile. Then he grabs me and tugs me toward the meeting point outside the large oak tree where everyone is already gathering.

I trudge along behind him. How can I kill him? There have to be ways to torture him for this. I could make him cook for me. Or buy even more Ikea furniture. Yes! Ikea furniture. That's the best form of torture.

Of course, I'll need some money for that first, but still...

A familiar blond head catches my eye. I stop dead in the

middle of the sidewalk, almost causing someone behind me to walk into me. "Sorry," I say as Cain pulls me aside. "Shit."

"What?" He looks down at me, frowning.

My lips thin into a flat line as I meet his gaze. "Nina's here."

"Where?"

"The Arctic," I reply dryly. "Here, goofhead. The ghost tour. Over there." I point in the direction of her. I'm pretty sure we're still covered by the trees and she can't see us, but I still take a step back.

Cain cranes his neck a little. "Ah, shit." He moves back so he's standing right in front of me and meets my eyes. "You wanna go?"

Yes. But I know he doesn't. Even if the entire point of this was to make me so scared I piss myself like a newborn baby, he's excited to do it. "Let's do it." I let go of a sigh. "But it's going to be super-duper mega uber awkward."

That cracks a tiny smile from him. He leans in and tugs on my hair. "Awkward because she's there, or because I just kissed you and she's there?"

"Both. And probably because in around five minute's time I'm going to be wrapped around your body while I scream like a baby." I flash him a grin.

The darkening in his eyes makes my stomach flutter.

"Can't wait," he says in a low, husky tone.

I gulp. Literally gulp like they do in cartoons. "Let's go."

This time, I grab him by the elbow the way he did to me just a minute ago. I don't want to do this—hell, if I didn't want to do it five minutes ago, then right now, I'd rather run through the fires of hell while naked and covered in gasoline and dragging a ten ton rock.

Yeah, it's that bad.

Not only because he wants to kiss me, but because he wants to do it again. Or does he? What if I'm just a rebound? What if he is feeling worse about the break up than he's letting on? What if—

I need to stop. If I get myself worked up about this, I'm

only going to feel worse than I do right now. That might not be hard though. I'm not even sure how I feel at this exact moment. My insides are a mess of tangled up emotions.

Like headphone cords that have been stuffed in your pocket.

Yes, that's exactly it. My current emotional state is as fucked up as tangled up headphone cords. So I'm feeling pretty stable right about now.

"Ignore her, okay?" Cain whispers in my ear as he hands one of the guides' two little tickets. God knows where he got them. "I didn't know she'd be here. If I did, I wouldn't have bought the tickets."

"It's fine. I'll just hand her over to the graveyard. She might not even notice us," I reason.

Of course, that's the exact moment she turns around. As if she knows we're here and talking about her.

Nina turns her head, her blond hair flicking over her shoulder. Her gaze hovers on us for a really uncomfortable moment before it clicks. Instantly, her expression changes. Her lips turn downward as her eyes harden, and anger visibly flits across her features. Then, as quickly as she looked back, she turns her attention back to the front where the two guides are counting tickets against heads.

I tense as her friends lean in toward her. Just as I knew they would, seconds after they straighten, three heads turn toward us. I don't know her friends—Barley Cross might be small, but if you didn't already guess, I don't talk to many people.

"They're not very discreet, are they?" Cain asks quietly, a hint of amusement in his voice.

I shake my head. No, they're not. And I highly doubt they will be for the rest of the tour, either. I should have listened to my gut and not agreed to this damn thing the moment I saw Nina in the group. Now it's too late, because the guides are talking and giving an introduction to the history of our little coastal town.

I'm not listening. I already know it all. We had to learn it all in history in high school, so while I'm sure Barley Cross's almost non-existent role in the Civil War is positively thrilling to outsiders, for me, it's like watching a movie you hate over and over again.

Cain nudges me. I shake my head and realize we're moving, so I fall into step beside him. We're at the back of the group, away from Nina and her friends, but there's also the bad part of that.

They're talking.

And I know it, because as Cain just said, they're not very discreet. The constant jerking and turning of their heads back to us—to *me*—is not only annoying, but unsettling. They're really not focused on Cain, they're focused on me.

Don't think I'm a hypocrite. Okay, I am, but not here. There's nothing I've said behind someone's back—including Nina's—that I wouldn't say to someone's face. But these? No. Whatever they're saying is not something they'll ever say to me.

That somehow makes it worse.

"You're not paying attention, are you?"

I divert my attention to Cain. "Sure I am."

"B, you stopped walking."

I blink and look down at my feet as if they have the answers. "Oh." He's right. I'm not moving. I didn't even know. Is that self-preservation? Yes. That's it.

When bitches bitch, stop walking. Fucking fantastic self-preservation.

"Come on." Cain circles my shoulder with his arm and turns me around before I can protest. "Let's go do something else."

"But you want to do this." I try to stop walking.

"Not if it makes you uncomfortable." He looks down at me, the strength of his gaze forcing me to look up and meet it. "Okay?"

I stop, and this time, he lets me. "You're uncomfortable too, aren't you?"

He grimaces, squinting at me. "Yeah. A lot."

178

"Is that because of Nina or because I threatened to climb on you?"

"Honestly? A little of both."

I laugh and escape his grasp. "Cain Elliott, I think you've lost your mind."

"That's rich." He smirks. "Considering you've never had one."

Walking backward, I wiggle my finger at him. "Which makes me all the more qualified to tell you you've gone batshit crazy."

The smirk that curves on his lips is equal parts sexy, dirty, and tempting. Or is that his eyes? I don't know. I do know that he's a lot like a chocolate cake during PMS right now.

I need help. As soon as possible.

"I don't know how to reply to that," he admits, falling in alongside me on the sidewalk. He falters in his step for a moment. "Did we ever watch the seventh Harry Potter?"

"Which seventh Harry Potter?"

"The second seventh one."

I shrug and stick my hands in my back pockets again. Did we? I don't know. I'm not IMDB. Or even remotely close to having any kind of memory that could tell him a straight yes or no answer.

"I think it's in my Blu-ray." He shoves his own hands in his pockets and looks at me, almost shyly. "And my spare bedroom is made up."

"You planned this, didn't you?"

"No," he says firmly. "Happy coincidence."

"Your mom planned it, didn't she? You don't make beds. Ever."

He pulls his hand from his pocket and waves it in a 'maybe' movement.

That's the only answer I need.

And I already know that tomorrow is going to be a nightmare.

"Okay," I answer. "But only because I know your mom wants me to bake. Wait—do you have salt and vinegar chips?"

fifteen

LIFE TIP #15: DON'T WAKE UP IN YOUR BEST FRIEND'S APARTMENT THE MORNING AFTER HE KISSED YOU WHEN HE'S ON THE REBOUND. HIS MOM WILL GET IDEAS. AND SO WILL YOU.

I have few secrets in this world. The ones I do possess are highly guarded. Unless you know me. Then it's virtually impossible to keep anything from you, mostly because I have the biggest mouth known to man.

Unless it's about Cain Elliott kissing me and setting my world on fire for a mere few seconds. Then I'm schtum. Schtum, I tell you.

One of my biggest secrets is that I can bake. Don't laugh. I'm the world's worst cook, but for some reason, I can bake. Any kind of cake, cookie, or pie. It's a strange, natural skill. Not one that anyone in my family possesses, mind you. It's completely random and likely borne of nothing more than my own love of—wait, no. I hate cake unless it's chocolate.

Where the hell did this thing come from?

Never mind. Point is: I can bake. And, shock horror, I actually like to bake.

I know. It's like I'm not even me.

Baking is exactly why I'm up at six-thirty in the morning. Cain is still asleep, I think, so I'm tiptoeing through his apartment to where the coffee is in my pajamas.

I don't know what I expected to happen last night, but it wasn't a normal movie night. It wasn't Cain and I lying on the sofa at opposite ends with me batting his smelly feet away from my face.

181

The kiss threw me off. A lot. Big time. Off this planet crazy. Yet somehow, the two of us watching a movie we've seen at least fifty times, watching it the way we always have, didn't change a thing. Didn't even lend a thought to what had happened between us earlier that night.

I didn't even text Carly back when she messaged me halfway through the movie. I was afraid that if I did, I'd get suckered into a conversation and end up telling her Cain kissed me.

I want to tell her that he did, but I also want to keep it to myself.

I don't want to taint the memory by putting it into words.

Stupid, yes. I know that. Fucking hell. I'm no idiot.

Lies. I'm a total idiot.

Bleary-eyed still, I pull a coffee mug from the cupboard and shove it beneath Cain's coffee machine. I exchange the pod and hit the button on the top to make it go. It sputters pathetically, and a quick glance shows that the water tank is empty.

Of course it is.

I fill it and restart the process with the exception of replacing the coffee pod. Since nothing came out of it, nothing's been wasted. A glance at the clock tells me I have thirty minutes to get dressed into something more covering than my pajamas before making my way down to the main Elliott household.

Every holiday it's the same. One year the Elliotts hold it. The next the Barkers do. I'm not sure what or who started our crazy tradition, but I've loved it every year. I think it started the year the Elliotts moved to Barley Cross—my mom wanted to include them in everything, so include them she did.

The rest is history, as they say. Or present day, whatever.

The coffee machine spits the end of the cycle and I pull my mug from beneath it in just enough time to hear Cain awake and on the phone.

"What?" His deep, husky, sleepy voice asks. "Are

you…give it a rest, Nina."

Ahh. Fabulous.

"We're over, Nina. What I do in my time is nothing to do with you…no, really, it fuckin' ain't."

I lift my mug to my lips, looking up at the ceiling.

Toodooloo.

It sounds like his feet hit the floor. "Don't fuckin' sit here at god knows what time in the morning telling me you wanna talk when you and your band of bitches made Brooke so uncomfortable that we had to leave…yeah, *we*. What part of she's my fucking best friend don't you understand?"

Awwwwwkward.

His bedroom door opens. His voice becomes much clearer. "No, I really don't give a shit, if I'm honest. You weren't happy and neither was I. It's over so get over it." There's a seconds silence before, "Fuck me."

"It's a little early for that," I say, lifting my coffee mug to my mouth.

Cain stills.

I still.

He's wearing nothing but boxer shorts.

I. Quit. Life.

I'm actually frozen in place. I can't decide if it's his messy bedhead or his sleepy eyes. His swollen eyes or pouty lips. His wide shoulders and toned arms.

Or his fucking perfectly sculpted body, from his shoulders to his chest to his abs to the 'v' that disappears into a place that's really not hidden by his bold, blue boxer briefs.

Or his thighs, as thick as tree trunks yet still obviously solid muscle.

I'm staring. I'm staring so bad, but despite our relationship and the fact he's seen me in my underwear, I've never really seen him in his. Not totally naked without a t-shirt. And now I'm annoyed I haven't.

Cain Elliott is a walking wet dream. The type you orgasm from before you wake up.

That's right. He's a fucking rare species all right.

I can't look away. Oh god. He's watching me watch him. I've turned to stone, I know I have. I can't speak or breathe or move or holy fucking shit, what is wrong with me?

"Um, shit," Cain finally says. "I didn't think you'd be up."

"Count us even," I choke out. "You know. For the baseball bat thing and all that."

He clasps his fingers together and stretches. "Not even close in comparison, B."

"Go and put some damn clothes on!" I turn away from him, hugging my coffee close to me.

He probably thinks I'm being awkward. I hope he does. Lord knows I know I'm being awkward. Crappy, crap, crap.

"You haven't moved, have you?" I ask.

"Why are you awake? You don't have work. You're never up this early."

Nice try, asshole. I hold up one tub of blue and red sprinkles, conveniently left on his kitchen side by Mandy. "It's July Fourth. Why else would I be up early than to bake two hundred cupcakes?"

"Two…two hundred cupcakes? Isn't it usually a hundred?"

"For my mom's. Your mom's is two hundred."

Cain, apparently unbothered by his state of undress, folds his arms across his chest. "Shouldn't you have started this yesterday?"

"Yes," I answer simply. "Which is why I'm up before the birds."

He puts a mug beneath the coffee machine. "Do you want my help?"

"Are you putting some clothes on?"

"Maybe."

"Last time you helped me you burned twenty-four cupcakes."

"Yes…" He hesitates, waiting until his coffee is done until he speaks again. "But now Mom has the oven with a timer so I won't do that again."

I stare at him for a long moment. A really, really, long moment. "Put some clothes on and meet me in your mom's kitchen in ten minutes. With the attitude that you'll do exactly as you're told."

He raises his cup in a salute and winks. "Yes, mistress."

"Fifteen minutes, Cain! Fifteen! This is not fifteen minutes!" I shove the red-hot tray of burned cupcakes toward him. "This is twenty minutes."

He backs up, hands held up at his chest, palms facing me. "Fifteen? Twenty? What difference does it make?"

I drop the tray onto the kitchen island and shake off the oven mitt. It falls to the ground without a sound. Meanwhile, I grab a perfectly golden cupcake and Cain's excuse for a baked one.

"This is the difference!" I launch them both at him.

He covers his head with his hands and both cakes bounce off his fingers to the floor.

"Jesus." Zeke strolls into the kitchen, rubbing at his eyes. "What's going on in here?"

"He burned my cakes!" I yell.

"It's eight-fifteen in the morning, you psychopath!"

I throw a burned cupcake right at his head. I hit my mark and it bounces off his forehead, into the wall, and onto the floor. "I don't care!"

Zeke turns to Cain. "Can't you put her on a leash or something?"

I chuck a second cake at him. In his sleepy state, he can't avoid that either. He does, however, manage to catch it this time before it falls to the floor.

"Fucking hell!" Zeke throws the cake back in my direction, but he misses by a mile. "This happens every year, Brooke. Why don't you start on the third instead?"

"Because I'm useless and I forget." I sigh and pick the cupcakes out of tray one by one for the cooling rack.

"Woulda been a better idea than what we did yesterday," Cain grumbles. He puts a new tray of cakes into the oven and sets the timer for fifteen minutes.

"Make it twelve," I tell him, glancing over my shoulder. "And yes," I say, arranging the cakes on the rack. "You're right. It definitely would have been a better idea."

"Why? What happened?" Zeke grabs a cool cake and before I can yell at him, bites into the top of it. "Mm, 'is good."

"Thanks." There's no point being mad. He'll just eat another if I do that.

"Well, what happened last night? There's no awkward sex story, is there?"

This time, Cain grabs one of the burned cupcakes and throws it at his brother. Hard. "Fuck off, Zeke."

Zek holds his arms out.

"We saw Nina last night," Cain says. He gathers up the rest of the burned cakes and throws them in the trash. Then he launches into an explanation of what happened last night.

Zeke hits the button on the coffee machine when Cain's done. "Fuck. That sounds awkward."

"No kidding," I mutter. I prod the top of the first batch of cakes, and feeling that they're cool enough, reach for my piping bag full of red frosting. "I felt like I was in an international court of judgment or something. Except the judge and the jury were all bitches."

He chuckles and pulls his mug out from under the machine. "Were they assholes to you? Do I need to break into their apartments and put bright red hair dye into their conditioner?"

I pause, holding the icing bag poised above a cake. "How do you know about that trick?"

Cain snorts. "He jilted his cheating ex a week before the wedding. He spent three days straight Googling revenge methods before he broke up with her."

Zeke raises his eyebrows and, with a smirk, salutes me with his coffee cup.

186

I stare at them both for a moment before going back to my frosting. I don't know how to answer that, so in the interest of self-preservation, I'm simply not going to.

Although I have to give him points for the idea. That is a pretty fantastic one.

Wait...

"You did the conditioner thing, didn't you?" I ask, stepping back from the cakes. I point the icing bag at him. "Zeke!"

He grins.

That's all the answer I need.

"Blue," Cain offers. "Turquoise, to be exact."

"*Oooh*, ouch." I shudder as the timer on the oven beeps. I pull out the cupcakes and set them on the side, nudging the oven door shut with my shoulder. "Wasn't Becky, like, white blond?"

"She was. Was being the important word there for a while."

Zeke chuckles into his mug as he walks to the door. "God bless black conditioner bottles."

That man is insane. Seriously. I've never known anybody else like him.

"What time is Carly getting here?" Cain asks me. "Shouldn't she be here helping you?"

"Ha! No!" I vehemently shake my head. So much so that I get a little dizzy. "Carly can cook, but she can't bake. You know that. What happened two years ago when she insisted on helping me?"

He tilts his head to the side. "Didn't she use salt instead of sugar in the recipe?"

My stomach rolls at the thought. "Yes, yes she did."

"Hey," Zeke says, pausing in the doorway. He turns and gestures to me with his mug. "Didn't you deliberately feed me those?"

I grab one of the newly frosted cakes—a chocolate one. With a smirk, I peel off the paper casing and bite into it. Frosting smooshes against my nose, and I grin at Zeke.

You bet your ass I deliberately fed him one of Carly's

Special Cupcakes.

Yes, the caps are deliberate. That's the official name and has been ever since he threw one up.

"Bitch," Zeke fires at me before disappearing.

I put my hand in front of my face and laugh with half a mouthful of cupcake. I totally deserve that, but that prank will never get old. I'll never forget the look on his face when he bit into that cake.

"Okay," I say, my giggles petering out and wiping my nose. "I really need to get more cakes into the oven."

"Wait." Cain darts around the island toward me.

"What?" I turn back around to face him. "Oh!" I bump into him, my boobs brushing against his chest

He grabs my upper arms. "Whoa," he says quietly. "I was just—you've got…"

My skin tingles where he's touching me. Not to mention that the roughness of his hands against my arms feels kinda…nice.

"What? Got what?" I pause, waiting for him to answer. "Cain!"

"You've got, um, frosting." The smirk that tugs on his lips is stupidly sexy. "On your mouth."

I rub my fingers across my mouth. "Did I get it?"

"No, it's…here." He lifts his hand to my face, rests his fingers along my jaw, and brings his thumbs up to my lips. Then, slowly, he strokes his thumb across my top lip, tracing the same path with his eyes.

I inhale sharply, and I know he felt it, because he pauses briefly before he carries on, dragging his thumb to the edge of my mouth.

Cannotbreathecannotbreathecannotbreathe.

"Got it." Cain's low, husky voice sends tremors down my spine.

"I, uh, good." I swallow before biting the inside of my cheek. "Thanks."

"You're welcome." He's still smirking.

Not that it would make a difference if he wasn't, because

my heart would still be beating crazy hard. I still wouldn't be able to catch my breath properly or do anything other than look into his eyes the way I am right now.

I'm frozen in place, stuck between him and the kitchen counter, surrounded by freaking cupcakes in various states of creation. His green eyes are dead set on mine, shining bright, and he has the firmest grip on my chin. Yet, somehow, it feels soft. I don't know how he's doing it or why he won't let go, or why I won't make him let go, but…

"B, I…" Cain stops, his thumb twitching against my chin. "Don't fucking hate me for this," he whispers.

Right before he kisses me again.

Just like last night, it's slow and easy, the barest feather of a touch. Yet it feels like so much *more*. Like warmth and comfort and—

"Oh!"

Mandy's voice snaps me out of my mid-kiss reverie, and my entire body jerks in shock at the same time Cain releases me.

Except I'm still holding the frosting bag.

And my shocked jerk makes me squeeze it.

Right at Cain.

All. Over. His. White. Shirt.

"Oh, shit!" I squeeze the bag again and more frosting comes out.

"Jesus Christ, Brooke, put it down!" Cain looks somewhere between embarrassment and hysterical laughter. He snatches it out of my hand, and in the process, squeezes it exactly like I just did. A stream of red frosting spurts across my chest and slides down my cleavage.

"Oh. My. God!" I scramble for the sink, almost knocking over a plate of cooled cupcakes in the process, and barely manage to keep it in place as I grab the cloth. "You could have just let me put it down, Cain!"

He's standing frozen in the middle of the kitchen, his face still in the same expression it was a moment ago.

"Oh my gosh." Mandy stifles a laugh from the doorway as I dab at my chest and between my boobs. "I see I chose a bad time to refill my coffee cup."

"You!" I wave the now frosting-covered cloth at Cain. "I can't even with you!"

"Whoa." Cain's dad, Eddie, edges his way past Mandy into the kitchen. "What's going on?"

I'm still waving the cloth at Cain, so I do the only thing I can think of doing. I take aim and throw the cloth at his head. It hits him in the face with a *thwack*, and I freeze.

He, however, bursts into laughter. I stare at him as he pulls the cloth from his face and then—the bastard.

He throws it right back at me. "If you'd put it down in the first place, neither of us would be covered with it."

"Yeah, well, I didn't expect you to kiss me again, did I?"

Oopsie.

We both stare at each other. My eyes widen as my words hang in the air between us. With his parents both looking on.

Abort. Abort. Abort. Can the ground just swallow me up right now? Please? I'll pay. Anything the world wants.

"Well," Eddie says, moving past the mounds of cupcakes and ingredients and other things. "It's about damn time."

I don't even know what to say to that, so I drop the cloth back in the sink, turn around, and dip my head.

Cupcakes.

I need to make more cupcakes and pretend this didn't happen.

sixteen

LIFE TIP #16: DON'T GET DRUNK.

I collapse back against the fridge and survey the kitchen. Cake racks cover every visible inch of counter space—and, uh, the sink. A sea of red, blue, and white decorated cakes stare out at me, all adorned with little United States flags.

Bought, not made. I'm not that patient.

"Can I eat them yet?" Carly asks, walking into the kitchen with a glass of wine in her hand. "Because I'm pretty sure I'm starving."

I drop my head back again the fridge door and sigh. "Just take one. If you ask me one more time, I think I'm going to go crazy."

"That," she says, picking up one with bright blue frosting, "would imply you ever had any sanity, and we all know that isn't true."

It's hard to argue with the truth, isn't it?

"Whatever. I need to get changed. I'm covered in flour and sugar and god knows what else, and I've been in here for ten hours, so yeah." I push off from the fridge and head toward the sink where I grab the wet dishcloth. I wipe off my hands and wrists.

"You have flour on your forehead."

"Ugh." I wipe there too, but I know if it's on my forehead, it'll be all in my hair too. "I need to shower. How long do I have?"

Carly puts down her wine, pulls her phone from her

pocket, and checks it. "Little under an hour."

"Crap. Okay." I snatch up her glass and take a big gulp. "Thanks." I lift it toward her and head out of the back door.

"Hey!"

I ignore her shouts and turn around the garage to Cain's access door. I let myself in and sip the wine as I walk upstairs. Cain's apartment seems completely empty, and the door is unlocked—I have got to talk to him about that—so I go into it.

Empty was wrong.

The beats of goddamn Kanye West are escaping from down the hall and Cain's bedroom door. At least it's old school Kanye West. Think Gold Digger, not the crap he puts out these days. I can give him points for that at least. I guess.

If I had my laptop with me, I'd so play Justin Bieber—his new stuff, thank you please—at full volume and drown out Kanye.

I kick the door shut behind me and head for his spare room. Knowing I had to make enough cupcakes to feed an elementary school, I packed enough stuff to last me, well, a week before leaving my apartment yesterday.

I take another big gulp of wine, set it on the nightstand, then grab my little bag with all my toiletries in it. There's no way I'm using Cain's shampoo. I don't even think he *uses* real shampoo, come to think of it.

A walk into the bathroom and a glance at the little shelf in his shower unit tells me everything. Yep. No shampoo.

He's more low maintenance than I thought. I've seen toddlers—aka my nieces and nephew—require more pampering than Cain Elliott.

I slide the lock on the bathroom door. A few minutes later, I'm standing beneath a steaming hot stream of water from the shower head. I can physically feel the grime from baking all day in a hot kitchen washing off me in the heat, and nothing has ever felt this good.

Except going to sleep after a bottle of wine. Or eating a six-pack of Krispy Kreme donuts by yourself. Or sex.

Definitely up there with sex.

Maybe. I don't know. I might have forgotten what sex feels like.

I pause.

Well. Real sex. Plastic, battery-operated sex I'm familiar with.

Let's be real: The closest I've come to real sex in months is kissing Cain.

Kissing Cain.

That sounds like the chick-flick of my dreams. Probably because it is.

Wonderful.

Now I'm standing in the shower, wet and naked, thinking about kissing Cain.

I turn off the water and open the shower door before I do something stupid like slip because I'm thinking about him. That's an entirely believable thing for me to do, after all. So I save myself by stepping out onto his extraordinarily fluffy bath mat and pulling a towel from the rack.

Oh, oh, it's warm.

Heated towel rack, rather.

Hmm. Maybe he was onto something when he said we should live togeth—

No. He wasn't. No, no, he wasn't. Definitely not onto something or anything. Onto nothing. That's right, nothing. Nothing.

He was on to nothing.

Nada.

Nope.

Nay.

I flip my head forward with a groan and wrap my hair in a second towel. When I flip it back up, I have a perfectly twirled towel turban, and I smile with satisfaction as I catch a glance of myself in the mirror.

I have no make-up lines.

I had no make-up on this morning when I made the cakes. That means I had no make-up on when Zeke came in.

Or when Cain kissed me.

I grip the edge of the sink and lean back against it, using one hand to hold in place the towel that's wrapped around my body.

Again. When he kissed me *again.*

If I was confused before, now I'm completely messed up. I've seen myself without make-up. It's not nice. I wouldn't kiss me without make-up. But he did.

Maybe I'm a better kisser than I am a natural beauty. That has to be the explanation for it.

Yep. I'm taking that and I'm running with it.

I push off the sink with a shake of my head. I'm going crazy over the fact he kissed me and flipping back and forth between his obvious rebound and his obvious insanity. I need to just ask him why the hell he's kissing me and if he doesn't have an answer to stop before it goes too far and our friendship is ruined forever.

In fact, I'm going to do it right now.

Well. When I have some clothes on, I mean.

Which I didn't bring into the bathroom with me.

I sigh, clutch the towel tighter, and grab up my dirty clothes. Tucking them under my arm snugly, I reach for the lock and slide it back, then open the door.

"Don't lie to me, Cain. Your mom saw you kiss her." Carly's voice trails across the apartment to where I'm standing in the bathroom with the door cracked open.

I freeze. I shouldn't stand here and listen, but it's pretty well established I literally never do the things that I should, so...

"Can't you drop it?" Cain responds.

Something clangs.

"No, I can't freaking drop it! My best friends are kissing and I'm confused," Carly replies.

"There's nothing to be confused about. And keep your damn voice down. The shower's off." His voice is much quieter, and I close my eyes.

"Cain," Carly says, barely above a whisper. "If you're using her as a rebound from Nina, I swear, I love you, but I will personally rip off your fucking balls and choke you with them."

"You really have to work on dropping stuff people don't want to talk about, you know that?"

"Stop deflecting," she whisper-snaps. "This isn't a joke, okay?"

"You think I don't know that?" he replies harshly, his voice at the same level as hers.

I'm straining to hear them now, which is a good thing since I shouldn't be listening at all.

"I know it's not a joke," Cain continues in the same low voice. "This isn't just a random fucking girl, Car. This is Brooke. And, *shit.*"

"You're right. She's not a random girl. She's your best damn friend."

"You don't get it, and I can't explain it to you, so leave it alone."

"No. Don't you dare fuck with her feelings, because she's been screwed by them long enough where you're concerned."

My entire body freezes. Except my eyes. They widen. Oh—and my heart. That's in my goddamn throat.

Shut up, Carly. Shut. Up.

"What's that supposed to mean?" Cain asks after a second. "She's been screwed by her feelings long enough where I'm concerned."

"Nothing," she replies quickly. "I don't even know why I said that."

Buy it. Buy it. Buy it.

A light bang, and then, "She didn't hate Nina for no reason, did she?" Cain's voice is flat.

Carly. Run away. Now.

"I, er, um. Shit, look, an eagle!"

Five seconds later, the front door opens and closes as she obviously runs away.

Hey, look. It's like she heard me.

"Fuck!" Something bangs immediately after Cain's snap of

the cuss word.

It brings me crashing back into reality. I need to get out of this bathroom before he hurts himself. Again.

"Are you all right?" I ask, hovering in the doorway.

He spins around in a flash. His jaw twitches, a sure fire sign he's not being completely truthful, and he says, "Yeah. Banged my foot."

"Ah. Right. After you cussed?"

"It was a preemptive fuck." He reaches up and rubs his hand across the back of his neck. "I didn't know you were here 'til I heard the shower."

"Yeah, I was going to ask, but I couldn't think past the shit that was coming from your room. The shower was the only way to drown it out."

"I'm going to ignore the comment about my taste in music—"

"Which is positively traumatizing."

"—and remind you that you're standing in front of me in a towel and it's not very long."

I slap one hand down to cover my apparently on-show vagina, but all I connect with is fluffy towel.

"Gotcha." He grins, throwing in a wink for good measure.

"You're an ass." I turn around and head for the spare room.

"Brooke? Your ass is on show."

"Fuck off, Cain!"

"No, for real. The towel is bunched up."

I flip the bird over my shoulder and shut myself in the spare room with a slam of the door. Then catch sight of my half-bare ass in the mirror, beneath the towel that, like he said, is bunched up.

"Brooke?" Cain says from outside the bedroom door. "Don't worry. It's a great ass."

And just like that, any embarrassment disappears, and I burst out laughing.

He's not wrong.

Why did my sister have to bring her kids? And her in-laws? Don't get me wrong. I adore my nieces and my nephew, but only in small doses. They're loud and shouty and exhausting. And a constant reminder of all the reasons why I dropped out of college and dropped the misguided dream of becoming a teacher.

I'm sorry. My mom's dream of becoming a teacher.

I dream about pizza and wine and not wearing pants.

I know, I know. I'm going places. Like Weight Watchers, probably.

I sip my cocktail. I have no idea what's in it. It's one of what Cain's mom would call her specialties—making endless jugs of various cocktails without a name or recipe attached. Oh, actually, I lie. This year, we have names. According to the card propped up in front of the jug on the table, the blue delight I'm currently sipping on is called 'Cocksucking Cowgirl.'

I don't even know how to answer that. Apparently she's taken advice from my grandpa to name them. I wonder if Mom's seen these…

"Hide me." Billie grabs my arm from behind. Thankfully not the one where I'm holding my cocktail.

"Whoa," I say, shaking my arm in an attempt to extract her claw-like grip. "Why do I need to hide you? And who from?"

"A good wingwoman doesn't ask questions."

"Happily married people don't have wingwomen."

"Fine, good sisters don't ask questions."

"True." I tilt my glass at her. "But we both know I'm a shit sister."

Billie pauses, then jerks her head side to side with an "Eh, yeah," expression on her face. "My in-laws are driving me insane. My mother-in-law saw the cocktail names, and when Grandpa introduced himself as the genius behind the names, she went pale. Brooke, I thought she was going to pass out on me. I've never seen her so terrified."

"That still doesn't explain why I need to hide you." *I knew it was Grandpa.*

"Because she hasn't seen them all, and they get worse!"

"They're worse than 'Cocksucking Cowgirl?'"

Billie's eyebrows shoot up, and she holds her hands out in front of her. "There's the 'Screaming Oh,'" she says, ticking it off on her pointer fingers. "'The Blow Whoa,' the 'Cherry Popper,' and the…" She takes a deep breath and covers her eyes with her hand. "'The Salami Slammer.'"

That's it. I can't.

For the second time today, I burst out laughing. Salami Slammer? That's the most random thing I've ever heard in my entire life. Where does the old guy even come up with this shit? I just…I don't know.

At least I know where I get my crazy from.

My mom's line. I'm sure she's thrilled at that.

"Bill, that still doesn't explain why I need to hide you." I run my hand through my hair as I swallow down the last of my giggles. "Sure, Grandpa's cocktail names are, um, dirty, but these are your in-laws. They know you're not like Grandpa."

"No, but they're like *Mom*," she hisses.

"Then why in the hell did you bring them?"

"Marcus invited them and Mandy said it was okay. I couldn't refuse, could I?"

I tilt my head to the side. "Um, yes?"

"Brooooooooke!"

"Eeesh, you sound like Bella."

"Ack, and here I was convincing myself my daughter brattiness comes from you." Billie sighs and looks over her shoulder to where her kids are running riot with some of the other neighborhood kids. "Quick, talk to me. They're looking at me."

I glance past her to where her mother-in-law is looking at her with pursed lips. She catches sight of me, and being the awkward turtle that I am, I raise my hand in a strange wave-type thingy.

Billie glares at me. "All right. I'm pulling out the big guns."

I snort. "Please."

"I spoke to Carly about half an hour ago."

I freeze for a split second before deciding that my glass is too full and that alcohol should be in my stomach. So I move for self-preservation and down half the glass.

Ha. Ha. Oy. Strong!

I shudder as the alcohol burns my throat, but I still stalk the few feet toward the table and grab the jug full of... Fuck it. I want the Salami Slammer. So the Salami Slammer I have. I fill my glass to the brim and I'm already sipping by the time my sister catches up with me and shoves me to the side. It takes everything I have not to let my drink spill, so I save it by taking another mouthful and stepping backward.

Thank god I'm barefoot, that's all I'm saying. She's manhandling me.

"Hey, what the hell?" I snap at her.

"Shhh." She presses her finger against my lips, grabs my hand, and drags me back toward the house.

Ugh. I don't want to go inside. Going inside means we have to talk. I don't want to talk, and definitely not about what she wants to talk about.

Doesn't she know I already talk to myself about this crap? I can't see how she'd have better advice than I do.

"Don't you have children to watch? A husband to give attention to? In-laws to convince you're not from a family of heathens?" I ask when Billie shoves me into the kitchen and closes the sliding door.

My sister turns to me. "Cain *kissed* you?"

"Cain did what?" Zeke casually strolls into the kitchen, Gabe following right behind him.

Like his brothers, Gabriel Elliott is tall, dark, and handsome. I'm not sure I need to elaborate more on that to explain the current level of male hotness in the room.

"Cain kissed you?" Gabe opens the fridge, looking at me

199

with a smirk. "Great. It's only fucking taken him ten years."
I swallow.
"Wait," Billie says. "What do you mean, ten years?"
"Do we have to do this right now?" I interject. "Shouldn't
we be out there? Celebrating independence and shit?"
Zeke snorts and takes a beer from his brother, but he
doesn't answer.
"Speak. Now." Billie uses the Mom Voice.
Both guys step back.
"Ain't it obvious?" Gabe asks. He pops the ring of his beer
can, the satisfying pah-cha-hiss filling the room. "Cain's had a
crush on her for years."
"Her is sitting right here." I wave my arm. "And no he
hasn't."
Zeke meets my eyes. "Yeah, he has. He's never done
anythin' about it because of your friendship."
"But apparently that's irrelevant now." Gabe smirks.
"Because he's done somethin' about it."
"He hasn't done anything!" I slap my hand against the
table, making my glass jump. "He kissed me *on the rebound.*
Because I'm a fucking idiot who didn't and can't tell him no."
"That's not what he said to Carly," Billie adds softly.
"I know what he said to Carly!" I turn to her. "I heard the
fucking conversation, Bill! What he said and what Carly
thinks he said are likely two completely different things. He's
on the rebound and that's the end of it."
"What if he ain't?" Gabe pulls a chair out from the table,
spins it, and turns it around. He sits on it backward. "Trust
me, Brooke. Everything I know about my brother says he
ain't on the rebound."
"Well, then, you know wrong."
Billie raises her eyebrows. "Really, Brooke? You're gonna
tell Cain's brother he doesn't know what he's talking about?"
"Yes!" Both of my hands slam against the table, and I
shove myself back and stand. "Yes, okay? I am. This isn't new
for me. It's old damn pain being pulled up just to be shoved
back down again. This is straight up bullshit and I don't care

how I feel or how I've felt or how you all think he feels. I don't care how Carly took his words. This isn't simple and this isn't easy. He's my best friend. He's always been my best friend and he will always be my fucking best friend. Leave it alone, y'all. All right?"

All three of them stare at me as if I've lost my mind. Although they do as I ask, and one by one, they nod their agreement.

My stomach is churning sickeningly. The sharp pains in my heart are unrealistically strong, but I take a deep breath and beat down all these awful feelings.

"I—I need to be alone." I grab my glass and shove past Zeke and Gabe toward the door. I shove it to the side and step outside into the still too-hot evening air.

The party is going strong. It's barely eight in the evening, and a glance at the cupcakes on the sweets table tells me one thing: I'm better at baking than I ever assumed I was. They're almost all gone, and it makes me glad that Cain's parents have a huge yard, because there are at least one hundred and fifty people here.

Okay, huge is an understatement. I rarely pay attention to it, but now, I am. The yard is beyond massive, and I know everyone here is thinking how a builder and a hair stylist have such a big property. Well, they worked hard and bought at the right time. A little inheritance and moving from Atlanta to Barley Cross didn't hurt them, either.

Despite the people here, there are pockets of the space that are empty.

Good. That means I don't have to go climb up to the roof. *Yet.*

I slip into one of those pockets. It happens to be a table in the corner of the yard, not far from the built-in grill that's still smoking from the coals Cain's dad insists on using. Various bits of meat are still sitting on the table next to me, and I'm not gonna lie, it all smells real good, but I don't feel really hungry right now.

Does everybody know more about Cain and me than we

do? Than I do? Than he does?

Apparently so.

And I have no idea what to do about any of this shit.

seventeen

LIFE TIP #17: ALCOHOL IS BAD.

Drinking seems to be the way to go.

Honestly, when you're screwed, alcohol works. It's probably not wise, but *watching the alcohol table* seems like a real excuse for sitting here next to it and drinking my way through the cocktail jugs before Mandy wisely fills them up.

Okay, maybe wisely is a long shot, but she keeps filling them up and she knows I'm drinking it, so I'm blaming it on her.

I grab the jug of Cherry Popper and pour the bright red cocktail into my glass. If you were wondering, my sister demoted me from a full-on cocktail glass to a martini-style glass an hour ago.

Like that'll slow me down. No, no. I'm drinking quicker, if anything. Just to be a pain.

I haven't seen Cain for hours. I don't even know if he's still here anymore. Was he ever here? I don't know.

The worst part about this is that I'm not even drunk. Not in the slightest. Apparently snacking all day seriously reduces your ability to get blind drunk, which really sucks. I could definitely use the black void of that right now.

"You're hiding." Mom takes the seat to the left of me.

"Nope. I'm in plain sight." I lean forward on the table as Carly takes the one to my right. "Not hiding."

"Darlin', you're hiding," Mandy says, sitting in the seat opposite me.

My sister slides into the only empty chair at the table.

"You're not doing it very well, Brooke."

"That's because I'm not hiding." I offer her a wan smile and gently wave my glass from side to side. "I'm just sitting."

"I think you've had enough." Mom moves to pluck my glass away from my hand.

I move it out of her reach. "I've not had nearly enough. Trust me."

"I'm sorry," Billie says, leaning forward. She clasps her hands around her own glass and meets my gaze. "I shouldn't have pushed you earlier. I know this whole thing is hard on you."

"Thank you." I finish my drink and push the empty glass into the middle of the table.

"But now we don't care." Carly shuffles in her seat.

I glare at her.

"Oh, come on, Brooke!" she says in a low voice. "Enough is enough. You've been in a foul mood all day. You need to talk to him and tell him everything."

"No, no I don't." I sit back in my chair.

"Yes, you do," Mom insists. "Honey, you've been dancing around this for years. Now, he's made a move on you—"

"No, he hasn't."

Mandy snorts. "Brooke, darlin', I saw him moving on you."

I groan and slump forward onto the table, sinking my hands into my hair. "It didn't mean anything. Stop yelling at me, please. It was nothing. It was an accident. He slipped."

"Right," Billie drawls. "And that's how I got pregnant all three times. Marcus's penis just slipped into my vagina."

"Billie!" Mom gasps.

Carly hides her laughter.

"Happens to the best of us." Mandy pats my sister's hand. Then she turns to me. "Brooke, if you don't tell him, I will."

"Tell who what?" Cain appears out of nowhere, right behind me. He grabs both mine and Carly's chairs and leans forward.

"Nobody nothing," I say too quickly. "They've all had too much to drink."

"Says you," Carly mutters.

"I'm sober enough to shove your head up your ass," I warn her.

"Eh, you're probably more coordinated after a few drinks."

I'm hard-pressed to disagree with her.

"Tell who what?" Cain repeats, tugging on a thick lock of my hair. "What are you hiding, B?"

"Nothing! I'm hiding nothing!"

Mandy coughs behind her hand.

"No." I point my finger at her. "No. Stop it right now."

"Stop what?" She smiles sweetly.

"I need a drink." I push Cain's arm off the back of my chair and shove it out.

Nobody says a word as I get up, and I'm glad. I don't want anybody to say a single word. I want everybody to leave me alone.

God, why did he have to kiss me in the kitchen this morning? Why did his parents have to walk in?

Why did I ever allow myself to see him as something more than my best friend Cain?

Damn it.

I never picked up my glass. I grab a fresh one, fill it with a cocktail, and put the big jug back down. I think this is the Blow Whoa. I don't know.

I sip.

Whoa.

Yep, this is the Blow Whoa.

"B?" Cain comes up next to me and grabs a bottle of Budweiser from the big beer tin on the table.

It's full of ice and beers and actually, the cold is kinda nice. I kinda wanna hug it to cool down because I'm hot.

Okay. Maybe I'm a little drink.

Drunk. I mean drunk.

Shit.

I take a bigger mouthful of my drink and swallow it. Hard.

"Brooke, what's wrong with you?" Cain gently takes hold of my arm and turns me to look at him. His green eyes capture mine. "You've been avoiding me all night. Did I do something wrong? Shit—is it the towel thing from this morning?"

"No it's not the towel thing." My voice comes out much snappier that I'd intended.

He winces a little.

"I didn't—I'm sorry." I cover my eyes with my hand and take a deep breath. "Look," I add, dropping my hand. "I just…I didn't mean to…" I sigh.

"B, tell me what's up." Cain's voice is soft, and he runs his hand down my arm. His fingers tickle my wrist before ghosting across my fingers and dropping away. "I *know* you and I know something's wrong."

Oh god. I'm gonna have to do this. I am, aren't I?

I take another big mouthful of alcohol and swallow it. "Can we go inside? I need to…I need to talk to you about something."

Cain pauses. His eyebrows draw together into a frown. "I…Yeah, sure. Come on." He cups my elbow and guides me across the yard toward the house.

I can feel the eyes of my mom, sister, best friend, and Mandy on me, but I ignore them and go where Cain drags me. They can all kiss my ass. They all got me into this. They can all suck a donut while I have to get myself out of it.

But not before I bury myself alive, obviously.

Hi, my name is Brooke Barker, and I'm about to go dig the hole I'll surely bury myself into, because I might be about to tell my best friend that I'm hopelessly in love with him.

"Did you mean the house or my apartment?" Cain pauses at the door to the kitchen.

"Uh, where are we less likely to be eavesdropped on?"

"My apartment it is." He pushes me in the direction of his apartment.

Without a word, I follow him. I think my heart is about to throw up. Seriously.

It's my heart or me.

I'd put fifty bucks on both me and my heart vomiting.

Hundred.

I'd put a hundred.

I could do with some more alcohol.

Now. Right now.

"All right." Cain opens the door to his apartment and stands to the side to let me in.

I walk through, passing him. I'm almost disappointed that I'm barefoot because I'd find real satisfaction in kicking off a pair of shoes right now. The clunk as they hit the floor, the freedom…

And this is me putting my drink down now.

I set it on the coffee table and perch on the edge of the sofa. My stomach sinks as Cain takes the seat next to me.

He's too close.

God, this is stifling. I don't…I don't want to have this conversation. I'd rather ignore it and go on with stupid questions spinning crazily inside my head.

"Brooke. Talk to me." Cain shifts so he's looking at me. "What did I do?"

I look at him out of the corner of my eye. "Why do you think you did something?"

"Because the last time you ignored me this deliberately, you were buying your senior prom dress and I told you that yes, your ass looked big in the dress you liked because I was fed up of shopping."

Yeah…I remember that.

"Well, you were a dick that day." I smile slightly.

"I'm a dick every day. You should know that." He nudges me. "Seriously, what did I do?"

"I…you…ack!" I bury my face in my hands, slumping right forward. I'm a mess. Literally this time.

Cain shuffles across the sofa to me and rests his hand on my back. "It's the towel, isn't it?"

"No, it's not the freaking towel!" I slap my hands down against the sofa cushion and propel myself to standing. "If I cared for a damn second about the towel I'd have taken it off there and then and whipped you with it. It's not the towel." I press my hand against my forehead and rest the other hand on my hip.

"Then what is it? Jesus, B. Tell me what I did."

"You kissed me!" I clap my hand over my mouth.

Slowly, he frowns, confusion clouding his green eyes. "I…yeah, I…shit." He leans forward and rubs his hand over his mouth. "Fuck, I screwed up, didn't I?"

Oh look, there's the hole I just dug myself.

This could not be more awkward.

"Why?" I pause. "Why did you do it? And don't tell me it's because you wanted to. That's the worst excuse ever."

He takes a deep breath. "It's the only one I have."

"Well, it's terrible!"

Cain sighs heavily. He stands and comes toward me. "Come here." He pulls me over to the sofa, sitting me exactly where I just was. He sits down next to me and runs his hands through his hair. "Can you listen to me for just a minute?"

"That's exactly what I want to do," I say quietly.

"Okay." He cups his hands over his nose and mouth for a moment before dropping them. His gaze finds mine easily and just like that, I'm lost. "Brooke, I kissed you because I wanted to. Both times. I don't have another reason for it and I'm not going to try to find one. I just did it."

"That's not a reason!" I slide back from him. "Damn it. That's like me saying I ate an entire pizza by myself because I wanted to and not because I was hungry."

"That's usually the reason you eat an entire pizza by yourself."

I snap my fingers in front of his face. "Cain. Focus."

He laughs quietly, hand in his hair again. "I don't know what you want me to tell you. I'm sorry, okay? I made it awkward. I shouldn't have kissed you."

"I'm not…" Why can't I talk properly tonight? "I'm not mad at you," I say softly. "You don't have to be sorry. It's awkward, but that's because I'm making it awkward."

His soft pink lips curve into a smile. "No, it's straight up awkward."

"Yep, totally." I smooth my hair back behind my ear and look down at my bare feet on the rug. "How do we make it not awkward again?"

"We stop talking about it."

"But that doesn't stop it up here." I tap my finger to my temple. "And that's where I really need it to stop, because it's on loop in my head going over and over and over and over and it's driving me crazy!"

"Brooke—"

"No, don't Brooke me!" I stand up again and dive my hands into my hair. I run them right through as I pace toward the window and look out at the yard.

The party is still in full swing, and the sky is almost completely black now. As much as I want to put this off and never do it, I know I have to.

Mostly because nobody will set fireworks off without me. They know hell would break loose. I love fireworks.

In fact, it's the only thing I like about this stupid holiday.

"You can't Brooke me because you just don't get it." I let my hands fall away from my hair and spin to meet his gaze. "Okay? You just don't get it."

"That's because you're not explaining anything to me."

"Just—ooh! I'm done. I can't do this." I throw my arms out to my sides and storm through the room.

"Brooke! Shit."

I throw the front door open. My eyes are stinging, but I'm not going to give in to the urge to let the tears break through. I won't do it. I'm not going to fall apart like that.

Not here, anyway.

"No." Cain grabs me at the top of the stairs and yanks me back into his apartment.

I protest the entire time, but he ignores me. He slams the front door shut and shoves the bolt across. My heart skips a beat as he throws me back against the door and stares at me.

"No," he repeats, his voice low. "No, B. You're not running away from me. There's never been a thing we couldn't tell each other, and we're not going to start now."

That's what you think, buster.

"Let me go," I whisper.

He grabs me by the chin and forces me to look him in the eye. "Why did I kiss you? I kissed you because I wanted to. Because I had to. Because I knew that, even if you hated me after, I would regret it if I didn't. If I walked away without kissing you on the beach and in the kitchen when I had the chance to, I'd regret it for longer than I want to think about. So there, B. There. I kissed you because I couldn't fucking *not.*"

My heart is in my mouth. My ears are ringing and I can't think or breathe or—

"What about now?" I swallow hard. "Do you feel that way now?"

"Do I want to kiss you right now?"

I nod. Barely.

"Yes. But I can't. I won't. Because it's just going to make this worse and you're going to hate me."

I drop my eyes, turning my face so he has to let go of my chin. "You're right. It will just make this worse, but not because I'll hate you. I could never hate you, Cain. That's the part you don't understand."

"Then tell me." His voice cracks halfway through. "God, you're the most important person in my life. I want to understand what the hell is going on in your crazy little head."

A strangled sound escapes my throat. I push around him and walk into the middle of the room. Laughter and shouts come from outside, over the sound of the music which is louder than before. They're getting their grooves on while I'm...

Well, I'm up here. And I'm rubbing my heart up and down a cheese grater for all intents and purposes.

I take a deep breath. Right now, it feels like the only thing I can control. In and out. In and out. In and out.

"I heard you. With Carly." I run my fingers through my hair. "Talking about me."

"Okay," he says slowly, apparently unfazed by this. "What

about it?"

I'm going to vomit. Right now.

"You were right when you asked her if there's another reason why I hate Nina. There is." I wrap my arms around my stomach as if it'll hold in my urge to vomit. My gaze drops from his briefly before coming back up. "A big one actually."

He doesn't react for a moment. My heart is in my throat as I watch him stand and look at me until he opens his mouth to speak.

"Please don't make me say it," I whisper.

211

eighteen

LIFE TIP #18: BE HONEST. ALWAYS. SOMETIMES THE REACTIONS ARE SURPRISING. UNLESS YOU KILLED YOUR SISTER'S CAT. DON'T BE HONEST ABOUT THAT.

"Brooke." Cain doesn't move, but he keeps his gaze locked on mine. "Are you saying—"

"No, okay? I'm not saying anything. That's the point. I don't want to. I've never wanted to."

He pauses with his lips slightly parted. I swallow hard and shuffle on the spot, letting the super-soft rug tickle the soles of my feet. We're saved from awkward silence by the party outside, and I'm thankful for that. I don't know if I'd be able to cope with this situation without the backing noise.

Cain rubs his hand down his face and looks up to the ceiling. "Shit," he mutters into his hand.

I tighten my arms around myself. "I'm—I'm going to go, okay? I'll...I'll call you tomorrow. Or never. Whatever." I duck my head and walk toward him standing in front of the door, but he doesn't move out of the way for me. So I look up and into his eyes. "Can you let me pass? Please?"

He says nothing. He simply stares at me, a storm in his eyes. I can actually see the silent battle waging inside in his head thanks to his eyes, and it makes my throat go dry.

"Cain. Move." I reach out to push him out of my path.

He doesn't.

He wraps one hand around the back of my neck. He sinks his fingers into my hair and grips it at the base of my skull.

Then he pulls me against him.

And he kisses me.

The ferocity both shocks me and sends tingles down my spine. This is nothing like the other kisses—this isn't gentle or unsure or testing. This is hard and deep and, damn it, it's soul-consuming.

Cain wraps his other arm around my body, and all the instincts to flee leave my body in one exhale. I lean into him, into his kiss, and for the first time all day, I relax. He pulls me even closer, and I rest my hands at his side.

I don't know how long he kisses me. I do know that I feel it everywhere. In every hair standing on end, in every beat of my heart, in every short, sharp breath I take.

"Don't leave right now," Cain whispers, pulling away from me. Just slightly. His arm is still around my back and his hand is still in my hair. "Stay. Please?"

I take a deep breath and slowly let it back out. "I don't know." I blink, focusing on his face. "It might not be a good idea. I'll probably say something stupid."

His lips slowly curve. "As opposed to your usual, intelligent conversations."

I try to glare at him, but it doesn't work because I smile. "Shut up. You're an idiot."

"I know." His smile widens briefly before dropping. "Don't run away from this—from me. All right, B? I think we have to talk about this."

"I don't want to talk about it. I've successfully avoided it for a number of years."

His eyebrows shoot up, and he leans back. "Years?"

"And there was the something stupid." Damn it. Damn it. *Damn it.*

"Then we definitely have to talk about this." He relaxes his hold on my hair until he releases it entirely and his hand rests on my shoulders. His fingers tickle the back of my neck. "Now."

"Really? I can think of tons of other things that would be better than talking about something I don't want to talk about. Like watching Harry Potter. Ordering pizza. Going

213

back to the party. Digging a grave so I can bury myself alive."
His body vibrates with his deep laugh. "The first three I
agree with, but I like you alive. And unburied."
"Then you've officially lost your mind."
"You are the authority on crazy."
"I'm really starting to dislike you, Cain Elliott."
More laughter escapes him. "Yet here you are, talking to
me. Hugging me."
I jerk back, dropping my hands from his waist. "No I'm
not."
"Yes, you are." He pulls me right back. This time, he
releases my neck and reaches out to push my hair from my
face and tuck it behind my ear. "B, listen. If you don't want to
talk, that's fine, but I'm going to. All right?"
I clear my throat. "Um, okay."
"I'm not going to lie to you and tell you I've had feelings
for you for years," he says quietly. "But I've had them long
enough to know that doing something about them is a bad
idea. Kissing you the other day was a horrible decision
because I knew it would be awkward after. You're my best
friend, Brooke. The last thing I want to do is lose that
relationship with you because I decided to do something
stupid and act on things I shouldn't have."
I blink up at him and bite my tongue before I say, "Then
let me go home. Tomorrow it'll have never happened and
everything will go back to normal."
"But it won't, will it?" He searches my gaze. "Because even
if you pretend it didn't happen, I won't be able to. I won't be
able to forget how it feels to kiss you."
"Cain—"
"I don't want to forget what kissing you feels like." He
strokes his thumb over my cheek. "And I'm not going to stop
wanting to kiss you again. And I'm probably going to do it."
"It's a bad idea," I say softly. "A very bad idea, Cain. We
can forget it."
Liar, liar, pants on fire!
He stares at me so intently my stomach flips.

"Okay, we can't forget it." I slump. "But we can move past it. It's just kisses, right? No big deal. People kiss all the time."

"True, but they don't usually semi-admit to having feelings for their best friend for years."

Ah…Shit.

I step back, forcing him to drop his arm from my waist. "I didn't admit anything like that."

"Yes, you did."

He's right. I did. Ugh.

"It doesn't matter," I say quickly. "The point is, it's never mattered until now. Why does it have to matter now?"

"Because you're avoiding me."

"I'm not avoiding you."

"Brooke, you're avoiding me." He scratches the back of his neck. "So we have to deal with this and we're going to do it right now."

"But I don't want to."

"I don't care."

"You're mean."

"Yep."

"Ugh." I walk back into the front room and perch on the back of the sofa.

Cain follows me silently, stretching his arms out in front of him.

I need to do this. This is the best chance I've ever had and ever will have. And…hey, he's been honest. He's right too. There's obviously an issue here the size of a herd of woolly mammoths, so being honest is the best thing to do.

"Okay," I say on an exhale. I look at my feet. If I'm being honest, I'm not looking at him. "I'm going to say this really fast."

"Good. I'm bored of waiting for you now."

I glare at him quickly, ignoring his smile, and turn my attention back to my feet. "I've had feelings for you for a long time. Carly knows. Actually, I think everyone but you knows and has for a while now. I never said anything because I couldn't. That's what Car meant when she said I've been screwed by my feelings. I've watched you date woman after woman and done nothing."

"Why?"

"Because," I say sadly, finally looking up. "I didn't want to tell you and lose you. It was easier to ignore it and hurt than it would be to not have you around. But now you know and it's awkward and we're never going to be the same again."

"Hot Mess…" He sighs and steps forward. He frames my face with his hands, looking down at me. "Maybe I don't want it to be the same as it has been. Maybe I want a new normal."

"And when it goes wrong?"

"Who says it'll go wrong?"

I raise my eyebrows. "Cain, it's me. Of course it's going to go wrong. I'm a disaster of epic proportions. Hell, you actually call me Hot Mess. That's pretty damning."

"Yeah, but if we try a new normal, you won't be just *a* hot mess. You'd be *my* hot mess."

My heart flip-flops at that. "I don't want to lose you." A lump forms in my throat, and I blink hard. "Don't you get that? There's no way out of this that means I get to keep you in my life."

"I'm not going anywhere." He steps closer to me, nudging his way between my knees. "Don't *you* get that? You'll always be my best friend. Nothing will ever change that."

"But it will. If we run with this and it doesn't work, there's no going back."

"There's already no going back." He dips his face close to mine. "Our friendship is never going to be the same again, B. You have to accept that. Pretending that we never kissed or had this conversation tomorrow isn't going to make me stop suddenly wanting you."

"I don't even understand why you do." I sniff. "You've seen me do some really stupid stuff."

He raises his eyebrows and half-smiles. "Yeah, and I want you anyway. That either makes me a saint or crazy."

"Both. Definitely both." I smile back. "I just…I'm scared."

"I am too." He drops his hands down to my neck, his thumbs brushing against my jaw. "Shit, B. I'm scared of this. But I think I want you more."

"I want you to do it properly."

"Do what?"

"Date me," I say slowly. "What, you think that just because you're my best friend you don't have to do that? Um, no. If you want to do this, you have to do it right."

"Right…"

"I mean it. Proper dates. I want dinners and dancing and movies and gentlemanly…stuff."

"Gentlemanly stuff." His lips pull up the the side. "What is that exactly?"

"Um." I pause. "I'm not entirely sure right now."

He looks at me for a second before he bursts out laughing. He steps back, dropping his head, laughing all the time. "I don't even know how to respond to that."

I shrug a shoulder. "You should know I'm hard to please. Step up your game, Cain Elliott."

"You really are crazy, aren't you?"

For the first time in hours, I grin.

"So, gentlemanly stuff. Does that mean I can't kiss you again until I've bought you dinner?"

"Bought me dinner? You mean ordered it to my apartment, right? Don't try that fancy-schmancy shit where I have to shave my legs and wear real clothes."

"Noted." He steps back into me, a playful smile on his lips. "If I promise to order dinner to your apartment for our first date, can I kiss you again?"

I smile, and before he can do anything, I do. I stand up, grab his shirt, and press my lips to his.

He smiles against my mouth and wraps his arms around me.

"Um, guys?" Carly's muffled voice comes through the door, and she knocks lightly three times. "Cain, your mom wants to do the fireworks now. Marcus wants to take the kids home because they're getting tired, but they don't want to miss them."

"No worries. Tell her to go ahead. We won't miss them."

"Uh, okay. Are you…is everything okay?"

"Yes," I answer. "Quick, go, because Danny is a little shit when he's tired and is probably driving everyone crazy."

"Gotcha."

The sound of her footprints leading away from the door slowly peter out.

"Come with me." Cain stops. "Wait, put some shoes on first."

"Good thinking." I tap his chest and run into the spare bedroom where my shoes are. I slip the ballet flats on and come back out.

Cain's standing in the kitchen with a wine bottle in his hand. "Is it ungentlemanly if I don't drink this shit?" he asks, turning around to face me.

"Given that's my favorite wine, I'm going to go with letting me have it all is the ultimate gentleman move." I grin, take it from him, and pull down a wine glass.

"So your idea of gentlemanly is different to every other woman I've dated in my entire life."

"I should think that by now, you'd know I'm nothing like most other women." I put the bottle down and pick up my glass. "Now let's go see fireworks before your mom loses her mind. And my sister loses hers."

Cain picks up a beer bottle and walks toward the front door. There's a mischievous glint in his eye, and the curl of his lips reflects that. "Follow me."

"Uh…okay."

I do as he says. He doesn't lock the apartment door behind him, but he does step in front of me and turn toward the door to the house instead of the one to the outside. I frown, but I follow him through it and toward the attic.

"Oh my god. Are we watching from the roof?"

Cain, halfway up the stairs, looks at me over his shoulder with a big smile on his face. "We are."

"You said to Carly—" That we wouldn't miss them. Oh

my. "But why the roof?"

He turns the key in the door. Then he opens it and holds it for me.

"Very gentlemanly," I quip, stepping out past him onto the roof.

"Ha." He snorts and shuts the door. "And the roof because I know Dad has all the fireworks set up right at the end of the yard. We'll have the best view up here."

"But…why?"

"Shit, you're full of questions, aren't you?"

"Yes." I sit down and cross my legs. I hold my wine glass in my lap as he sits next to me. "So why?"

He shrugs a shoulder and puts the beer down. His leg brushes mine. "Because you like fireworks and I'm calling this an impromptu first date?"

"This can't be a first date. There's no pizza."

"Is that a requirement for a first date?"

I raise my eyebrows. "For me it is."

"Of course." He smirks. "Pre-first date, then."

I nod. "That wor—oh holy fuck!" I jump as a loud bang slices through the air followed by an ear-splitting crackle right above our heads. I fall sideways into Cain as the sparks from the firework fall down and disappear into thin air.

He laughs, wrapping one arm around me. "You really are a hot mess, aren't you?"

I sigh, plastered against his side. "It scared me."

"Easy to do."

"For a pre-first date, you're not being very nice to me."

"Have you ever dated anyone longer than a month who has been nice to you on a first date?"

"I'm not sure I've dated anyone longer than a month for three years regardless of the first date, actually." I pause, frowning slightly. "Nope, definitely not." I pause for the second time. "I now realize that makes me kind of a slut for putting out so quickly."

Cain opens his mouth to—hopefully—argue that point, then stops himself. His expression says he agrees with me. I'd hate him if I didn't know it to be true. Or, you know. Love him.

"Or that makes you really, really fun to date," he offers.

"You think I'm a slut, don't you?"

"That depends. Do I have to wait longer than a month for you to be naked in my bed?"

"You know," I say slowly, only jumping a teeny bit at the next firework. "I've actually thought about having sex with you a lot—"

He grins and interrupts, "Keep talking."

"—But talking about it is kinda weird. Can we not? I'd rather an impromptu fuckfest."

"An impromptu fuckfest." He looks at me, desperately attempting to keep a straight face if the way his mouth is twitching is any indication. "Can I quote you on that when said fuckfest happens?"

My cheeks burn red hot. "Um, I didn't mean to say that out loud."

"I know. That's what makes it great."

"Cain? Shut up, or I'm going to demand fancy shit for the first date."

"Hey, you can demand fancy shit if you want fancy shit. Most women do. They want to be wined and dined."

"Is that dining courtesy of Dominos by any chance?"

"Never once have I ever been on a date consisting of Dominos."

I turn into him and slap him on the chest. "Get ready, Elliott. Tomorrow night I'm going to show you the best first date ever."

"Why? Will the fuckfest happen after that?"

"You're obsessed with that comment, aren't you?"

Slowly, he nods, looking me dead in the eye. "I'm male, B. And you're hot. You mention fuckfest and I start thinking with this." He points to his dick.

Don't look. Don't look. Don't look.

I look.

I cough and look away. *Lord, he's hard.* "Um, okay."

His laugh tickles across my skin and he pulls me right into him. "Get used to it," he says into my ear in a low voice.

"But it's awkward," I hiss back.

"B, we're gonna be awkward no matter what we decide. But this awkward ends in an orgasm at some point and that's better than the alternative."

I hesitate. Well... "Still awkward."

"Good thing that's your middle name. Now sit down and shut up because Dad's finished with his test runs."

"I'm already sitting down."

"Then just shut up." He tugs me into his side, leaning us both back against the sloping roof behind us on the little balcony.

I do as I'm told, leaning into him. No sooner have I rested my glass on my thigh and my head on his shoulder than the first whee of a rocket screams through the air. It explodes in a burst of scarlet red and vivid blue, a stark contrast against the dark night sky.

For the second time tonight, I relax completely. And while we watch the fireworks, there's no awkwardness. It's all disappeared. Probably just for now, but I'll take it.

Because oh my god, he wants me.

My focus shifts away from the fireworks and toward the man sitting next to me with his arm around me. Cain. My best friend. Who wants me. Who wouldn't let me say no.

Cain wants me.

Cain. Wants. Me.

My stomach does a flip that's a strange mix of nervousness and excitement. Can we make this work? Really? Is there any possible way to fix this situation so that it does work?

Why am I dissecting this right now? He's here with me and he wants me. He said so. Unless...

"Cain?" I ask quietly, my voice almost entirely drowned out by the fireworks cracking and banging and booming in the sky.

"Yeah?"

"Is this...am I...is this just because you broke up with

Nina? Is this a rebound thing?"

"What?" He shifts, relinquishing his grip on me a little as he does so. "You think that's what this is?"

"I don't know," I whisper, looking down.

"No." He puts one finger beneath my chin and brings me back up so I'm eye-level with him. "I wanted you before I ever met her. You trust me, don't you?"

I nod, beating down the uncertainty.

"Then trust me." Now, he's the one whispering. "Trust me that I mean it when I do this."

He dips his face and presses his lips against mine before I can respond at all, kissing me for the fourth time today.

Not that I'm counting.

I rest my hand against his chest, gripping my glass tightly, my eyes shut, my heart thumping against my ribs.

And I feel that his is doing the same. Beating crazy fast, thundering against his chest, right beneath my palm.

He means it.

This is no rebound.

This is…real.

We manage to escape having to go back down to the party with a well-timed text to Carly that I'd had too much to drink and needed to go to bed immediately.

So…perhaps it wasn't a total lie, but I do hold a little resentment to the fact I was the excuse. Then again, we'd also made one other decision on the roof.

Tell no one but Carly.

Taking our friendship to the next level will be easier without the gossip train chugging along behind us. In such a small town it's going to be nearly impossible, but the fact we're so close will make it easier.

Apparently.

I don't think so, but hey. I get a first date tomorrow with pizza in my sweatpants, so I'm not going to complain.

I slip into Cain's spare room after one more gentle kiss and shut the bedroom door. Staying here at his place tonight might not be the greatest idea I've ever had, but it beats having to get a cab home.

I change quickly into my pajamas and pull a hair tie from my make-up bag. Perching on the edge of my bed, I braid my hair into one long plait before flicking it over my shoulder.

Tonight has been the craziest, most insane night of perhaps my entire life—except the one I was born. I imagine that's insane, coming out of a vagina and all that.

I sigh heavily and climb into bed. The cold sheets are a welcome reprieve from the horribly humid air we've been in all night.

I click off the light from where I'm lying in bed and pull the sheets right up over me to beneath my chin. They clump in my hands, but I unwind my fingers from it and roll to the side.

My phone vibrates from its place on the nightstand.

I reach out and grab it. I wince at the brightness before quickly turning it down and unlocking it with my fingerprint. The new message is from Cain.

Cain: *I can't sleep.*
Me: *Why is that my problem?*
Cain: *Because you're the reason.*
Me: *Just call me insomnia. I'm here all week.*
Cain: *Ugh…*
Me: *What? What did I do?*
Cain: *I don't want it to be awkward. I feel bad that you feel bad. Fucking hell, B.*
Me: *It's not my fault it's awkward. You started this.*
Cain: *If you don't shut up, I'm going to come in there and finish it.*
Me: *Please don't kill me.*
Cain: *I don't know how to reply to that.*

I stare at my phone. Shall I? Can I? Um…

Me: *I'm thirsty.*

Apparently I can.

Cain: *So…*
Me: *I'm going to get a glass of water. If you happened to meet me there…*
Cain: *Are you hitting on me, Brooke Barker?*
Me: *Hug yourself to sleep, you asshole.*

I huff and get out of bed. Screw him. I do actually want water now, so he can keep his stupid comments to himself while I go have fun in the kitchen with his fancy fridge with the ice maker.

I use my phone as a light as I pad my way from the bedroom to the kitchen. I can still hear the party going outside in the backyard and the distinct sound of my mom's laughter.

Well, shit. She's drunk then.

I pull a glass from the cupboard and use the dispenser in the fridge to get ice and water. The little light in it cuts out as I lift my glass and sip from it.

"Are you hitting on me?"

"Oh, holy motherfucker!" I slam my glass down on the counter, splashing water and ice everywhere.

"Shit, Brooke. You're jumpier than a class full of kangaroos."

I turn and blink at Cain in the crappy light. "Then stop scaring me, you dick! You've wiped ten years off my life today!" I flatten my hand against my chest. "Jesus Christ."

He shrugs one shoulder. "You hit on me."

"You're the one whining you can't sleep."

"Can you sleep?"

"I barely had a chance before you started texting me!"

"You hit on me."

"I flirted. It was awkward. I hate myself. I want water. Go away." I grab my glass of water again. "Goodnight, Cain."

"Wait." He puts his arm out for absolutely no reason whatsoever given that he's on the other side of the room. "I can't sleep. Really."

"So take a pill or…something? I don't know. Have a hot bath or a cocoa."

He walks to me and stops right in front of me. He avoids the fact I'm holding the glass in front of my face and pushes my hair behind my ear. "Or…"

"Or what?"

He reaches behind his neck and scratches. "Or sleep on the edge of my bed until I accidentally spoon you in your sleep."

I've had worse offers. Much, much, worse. "I, um, okay."

"It's weird, right?" he asks, still rubbing his neck.

"Very weird. But if you'll stop texting me and let me sleep, I'm okay with it." I walk toward his bedroom and then stop. "Oh, and please keep your cock under control."

"That's the first time a girl I'm dating has ever said that."

"We're not dating. We haven't been on a date. I'm only here to get sleep. Be quiet and control your cock."

"I don't know if I can."

I perch on the edge of the bed. "Do something, Cain. Turn it off. Power down. Run it out of battery. Just control it."

"Is my cock a robot in your mind?" He gets into bed before I do.

"Well…" I put my glass on the nightstand and slip beneath the covers. "It would be helpful. It'd have a power off button if it were."

The bed ekes and creaks as he moves and shuts off the light. "Can we hook your mouth up to be one of those robots?"

"Go fuck yourself, asshole." I huff and roll onto my side, facing away from him. "Stay on your own side of the— whoa!"

Cain wraps his arm around me and pulls me back against him so we're spooning. His body fits almost perfectly against mine. Except the thighs. Lord, he has long legs. Why have I never noticed this?

"*Whut* are you doing?" I whisper.

His chest shakes against my back. "Did you just say 'whut?'"

"Yeah. What didn't cover the emphasis I needed."

"I'm spooning you, Brooke," he answers, deciding apparently to get straight to the point. "Now shut up and go to sleep."

I snuggle down, pushing further against him. "You've told me to shut up a lot tonight."

"That's because you talk a lot." He kisses beneath my ear. "Seriously, shut up."

I freeze, feeling his heart thump against my back. He feels good here, against me, wrapped around me. He feels perfect, actually. And he smells like warm cookies for some reason. I don't know why, he just does.

"Cain? This is awkward," I say into the darkness.

"Brooke," he responds, pressing his face into my hair. "Shut the fucking hell up and go to sleep."

I close my eyes and focus on the warmth of his body instead. "Got it."

nineteen

LIFE TIP #19: DON'T SLEEP WITH A GUY ON THE FIRST DATE. LITERAL OR IMPLIED.

Three hours ago, I snuck out of Cain's apartment while he was in the shower.

Yes, I'm a shitty person. This is common knowledge, so don't sit there and act all surprised, okay?

I did it because it was awkward. There we were, newly agreeing to date, and waking up together.

Do you know what that makes me? A prize slut. Even if I've spent the night with him before. That was then and this is now and it's all completely and utterly awkward.

Like the rest of my life. Mostly because I'm fielding calls and texts from my mom and sister about what happened after we spoke.

That's right. My mom is so desperate to know that she's texting me. My mom does not text. *Ever.*

It also explains why I'm day-drinking with Carly.

Well, maybe. It's either that or I'm using it as an excuse.

So here I am with my strawberry margarita, staring into it, pretending I didn't just agree to totally fuck up my friendship with Cain. Because that's what'll happen.

"You don't know it'll mess up," Carly says, dipping her straw into her Blue Lagoon cocktail. "You might surprise yourself."

"No." I lean across the table, pointing my little umbrella at her. "You know what's going to happen, Car? I'm going to do something so monumentally fucking idiotic that he's going to look at me and say, "Well, shit. She was right. She's a better friend than girlfriend.'"

"Well, I can tell you that," she replies. "Given that you have little to no experience of being someone's actual girlfriend."

"You make it sound like I'm a relationship reject."

"You are. Kinda." She drops her eyes to her drink where she's still playing with the straw. "I mean…not in a bad way."

"How can that possibly be anything but bad?"

"You're right. It's bad."

I peer up at her, narrowing my eyes. "You're an asshole, Carly."

"I prefer honest." She pulls her cocktail closer to her. "Listen, Brooke. You've fucked all your relationships because you've always wanted to be with Cain. Now, you have that chance. If you don't start believing it could work, it won't work."

"I don't want to lose him." I voice the exact same fear I said to him last night. "I'm scared. I don't want to mess up what we have, and I know that when he realizes what a mess I am to live with, that'll happen."

Our waitress brings over a plate with six slices of cheesy garlic bread on.

We both grab one.

"I mean, hello, I ran away while he was in the shower." I bite into my bread.

"I wouldn't date you," she says honestly, dabbing at her mouth with a napkin. "But you're forgetting one really, really important thing about Cain."

"He prefers blonds over brunettes?"

She stares at me as if I've just grown two heads. "No, dickhead. He knows you. He's already used to your…quirks."

"My quirks? Like my inability to cook or unpack my things or work a vacuum without electrocuting myself?" I'm not saying I've done that, but I don't think my left pointer finger has ever recovered from a certain incident a whole four days ago.

"Right…those quirks." Carly cracks a smile. "But the other things that would bother guys."

"Like the fact I'm always late, sometimes miss the back of my hair when I use my flat iron, or occasionally mix up my almost identical black flats?"

"Or that you sing horribly, never lock your front door, and are more likely to burn down New York City from hundreds of miles away than successfully heat up a ready-meal?"

I lean forward, resting my chin on my hand. "Seriously. Who let me adult? My fairy godmother needs firing."

"That too." Carly's lips tug to the side. "But those things…Brooke, he already knows them. He knows you're clumsier than a drunk person on a gym ball with handles."

"You mean a hop ball?"

"Yes. That." She waves her piece of garlic bread at me. "He knows all your crappy qualities and he wants you anyway. There's no surprising him. Didn't he buy you tampons once?"

"It wasn't my proudest moment," I admit, taking my straw between my finger and thumb. "But I was desperate and he was close to the store." And on the toilet, but she doesn't need to know about that.

"Right. But my point is, he knows you're more than your…*special* moments."

Special moments. Right. Her birthday is next month. I'll remember that asshole comment.

"Excuse me while I lick the back window of the bus," I mutter.

She laughs. "Brooke, you're a fucking disaster. But beneath your klutzy exterior, you're so much more. You're strong and loyal and dependent—"

"You're describing a dog, you know that?"

"Shut up. You have the biggest heart and the best soul I've ever met. I'm pretty sure that's what he sees when he looks at you. Not your lack of ability to remember your trash day."

"Tuesday," I say. "It's Tuesday. I have a reminder on my phone."

229

She smiles, propping her chin up on her hand. "See? You're growing up."

I flip her the bird.

Her smile widens.

"Seriously." I drop my eyes and spin my cocktail glass. "What if we do it and he realizes I'm really, really not the girls he's used to dating? I won't shave my legs just to have sex. Nor will I put on sexy panties at the potential for sex. I won't dress up just to visit a fancy restaurant or cook a stunning fucking three course meal for a night in."

"And I'm pretty sure he knows that."

So am I. Didn't I just tell him that?

"Oh god," I whine, leaning forward and sinking my hands into my hair. "I said this last night. What's wrong with me, Carly? I told him what to expect and then this morning I ran away like the giant, pathetic creature I am."

"Creature is a strong word."

"Animal! I'm a giant, pathetic animal!"

Her gaze flits across the room. "People are looking at us."

"I'm in love with him and I just went and ran away because I'm useless and pathetic and America's biggest chickenshit."

"Say it a bit louder. I'm not sure everybody heard you."

"Oh my god, I said it out loud." I flounce down onto the table, throwing my face into my arms.

"You're so dramatic."

"I want to die."

"No you don't."

"You're right. Just call ET and tell him I'm waiting for him right now."

"You want me to phone home?"

"Yes. Clearly Earth is not my destined residence so call home and let them take me." I sigh and sit up straight. "I really need to get my shit together, don't I?"

Carly grimaces, nodding.

"Brooke?"

I turn at the sound of my voice and look at Penelope Argyle, one of my mom's friends. "Mrs. Argyle. How are you?" I stand and greet her the way she greets everyone—a light hug and a peck on the cheek.

"I'm just fine, darling." She holds me at arm's length, smiling widely. "Now, I have a question for you. I was going to call your mother and ask for your number, but this cuts out the middleman."

She also likes to state the obvious.

Carly silently excuses herself and heads for the bathroom.

"Sure. What's up?" I say and rest my hand on the table.

"I was at Mandy's yesterday for the party. She told me you made those gorgeous cupcakes."

My cheeks flush lightly. "Well, yeah. Baking is about the only thing I'm really good at."

"Good? Oh, darling! You're underselling yourself." She leans forward and touches her hand to my arm. "They were wonderful, really."

"Oh, well, thank you." I smile, blushing again. "I'm glad you think so."

"I want to hire you."

I blink at her. "You...you do?"

Penelope shoots me a dazzling smile. "Annabelle's sweet sixteen party is July twenty-fifth. You know what girls are like—they all have to have the biggest and fanciest party." She sighs, her smile dropping. "I've been looking for catering, but would you believe all the bakers I've contacted in the past month can't do it? Three hundred cupcakes and a three-tier cake and they all said no!"

I can see why, if I'm honest.

"As you can see I'm in huge trouble. If she doesn't get the cakes..." She waves her hand in front of her.

"That's what you want?" Is my panic showing? Am I sweating? Is it obvious? "Wow."

That smile returns to her face. "Could you do it? Would you? She already knows exactly what she'd like."

"I...I've never done that many before, but I could." I think. I hope.

"Wonderful!" She claps her hands together. "How much

would you charge? I can write you a deposit check right now to cover your materials." She reaches into her purse, presumably for her checkbook.

"Oh." My heart thuds. "I couldn't, um, I'm not sure off the top of my head. Why don't you send me the designs Annabelle wants and I'll let you know from there?"

"Perfect." She pulls her hand out of her purse with another beaming smile. "Why don't you give me your card and I'll email you this evening?

Oh. A card. Right. Um. "I don't actually have one," I admit, shrugging sheepishly. "I generally just do it for fun for Mandy."

"Oh! Of course. You did say." She laughs lightly and opens her purse once more. She pulls out a small notebook and pen and hands them to me. "There, Brooke, darling. Write it down and I'll get everything to you."

"Sure." I take them and put the notebook on the table. My hand shakes slightly as I write it all down, and I hope she hasn't noticed.

That's a lot of cakes. A *lot* of cakes.

"Thank you, darling! You're saving my life here." Penelope puts the notebook and pen back into what is apparently her Mary Poppins purse. "I can't thank you enough."

"It's no problem. I can probably get the time off work."

Ha! Right!

"Ah, wonderful! I'll leave you to your lunch with Carly. My sister is waiting for me." She hugs me and kisses my cheek for the second time.

"See you soon, Mrs. Argyle." I smile and wave as she heads back across the restaurant to her table.

Carly slips in seconds later and takes her seat. "What was that all about? You're pale as shit. Spill!"

She cares so much about me. Can't you tell?

"I...I think I just got a job," I say slowly. I reach back behind me and sit down.

"You have a job. Remember? With Jet? Asshole boss?"

"No. Not that kind of job." I push my hair from my face

and meet Carly's gaze. "Annabelle's sixteenth birthday is in three weeks and she doesn't have a baker for her sweet sixteen. She wants me to make three hundred cupcakes and a three-tier birthday cake for her."

Carly's eyes bug out of her head.

"And she's going to pay me. Car, she offered to write me a check right now to cover materials."

"Holy shit!" Carly whispers. "How much is she paying you?"

"She's going to send me pictures of what Annabelle has chosen so I can price and give her a quote."

"How much do you think it's going to cost?"

I stare at her blankly. "I have no idea. I've never charged anyone anything before. Mandy just buys the stuff and I do it. I'm going to have to call bakeries and pretend to be a buyer to find out what they charge."

"All right then. Let's eat lunch and get to work."

"Hi! My cousin is having a sweet sixteenth party on October thirtieth," Carly says into the phone. "You were recommended to me by a friend for sweets. Could you possibly give me a quote for three hundred cupcakes and a three-tier birthday cake? Uh-huh…wow, that's great…of course, of course…I sure will. Thank you so much, ma'am."

"Well?" I say, pen poised above the notebook.

Carly puts her phone down on the arm of the chair. "Well, a surprising number of bakeries are open on a Sunday in Georgia."

"And Florida. And South Carolina." What? We're spreading out. Market research and all that.

"Cupcakes'N'More on the Georgia-Alabama border said they would charge at least five hundred dollars, but the price could increase dependent on design and decorations needed.

Apparently, though, they live in a small town where that would be considered both expensive and way too big of an order for anyone who lives there."

"Right."

"So we have anything from five hundred dollars to twelve hundred."

"Yeah, I don't see me charging twelve hundred. Ugh!" I sink forward, burying my hands in my hair. "This doesn't help at all, does it?"

"Not really. But there is one thing we could do. You have the designs, right?"

I nod and turn my laptop around so she can see it again. "It's probably going to cost one hundred and fifty dollars just for the decorations alone. Not to mention the things I need to buy that I don't have. Cupcake casings, boxes, stands, a base for the main cake..."

"Okay, so, breathing would be helpful right now," Carly says, scooting forward on the table. She picks up her calculator. "Let's add it up. Go on eBay and price up all that stuff."

One by one, I search through eBay listings to find decent prices. She adds it all up on the calculator and writes each total down on her notebook.

"Okay. So, all that is a little over two hundred dollars. Less than we thought since we can bulk-buy a bunch of it."

I nod. "Right. That's good. But that doesn't take into account the things to actually bake the cakes."

"Let's do that now. Tell me what you're going to need and what it usually costs."

I rattle off approximately how much flour I'm going to need, followed by the other ingredients.

"Huh," Carly says, writing it all down. "Amazing. You can calculate all that in your head and remember it, yet your phone number is an impossibility."

She has a point.

"How much is that going to cost? Am I going to have to find a wholesale place to buy this?" I look at the notebook.

"Shit, I am, aren't I? Otherwise it's going to not be worth it."

"Yeah, but there'll be one nearby. Get Cain to drive you there in his work van and put it all in the back. And for cost…" She types on her laptop. Her eye twitches after a minute. "There's a wholesale place half hour from Atlanta. It's gonna be around two hundred, two fifty."

I lean back on my sofa. "Four hundred and fifty for everything. I'm going to have to charge her at least six hundred. Carly, that's too much. I can't do this."

"Whoa now." She puts her laptop on the coffee table, eyebrows raised, and looks at me. "You charge her eight hundred."

"That's way too much!"

"No, it isn't! Break it down. You're going to need two days to create the decorations. It's going to take two days to bake everything. You're going to have to take time off work, possibly unpaid. And you're going to have to get Cain to help you deliver the finished cakes. This is not too much to ask for. It's a lot of work and on short notice."

"I…" I can't argue with that. She's right. It's a lot of work. And I'm not sure if I can do it or not. "Car, I can't do this. I don't have a place to bake the things, for a start."

"Ask Billie. Doesn't she have that fancy kitchen with a double oven?"

"I can't take over her kitchen like that."

Carly picks up her phone.

"Do not call my sister!" I shove my laptop to the side and get up.

Carly's quicker than me. "Hey, Bill!" she says, getting up and darting out of my reach. "Brooke needs your kitchen to bake enough cakes to feed the five hundred."

"Carly!" I bury my face in my hands.

She peels my fingers away. She's holding out her phone. "She wants to talk to you." She finishes off her sentence with a grin.

"I hate you so much." I take the phone from her and hold it to my ear. "Hey, Bill."

"Hey," my sister says. "What's happening? Why do you need my kitchen? You know you're only allowed to look and not touch on account of your awful kitchen skills."

"It's not cooking. It's baking. I ran into Penelope Argyle this morning." I reel off the entire story, including everything about our research and the costs and my panic. "So, yeah," I say after a good few minutes of constant talking. "That's the long version of why I apparently need your kitchen."

She doesn't respond immediately. In fact, she doesn't respond at all.

"You know what? Don't worry. Forget Carly called and I asked. It's—"

"Brooke, this is amazing," Billie says quietly, but there's a hint of excitement in her voice. "She's really hiring you to do this?"

"She wants to," I reply awkwardly. "But I'm not sure."

"Of course you can use my kitchen for that. I'll even help you if you need it. This could be amazing for you."

"Really? I can use your kitchen?" A grin spreads across my— "Hold on. Why would it be amazing?"

Billie laughs. "Because Penelope knows everybody in town. If you do a great job and people ask her…Brooke, you could be onto something big here. We don't really have a sweets bakery here but we have a hell of a lot of demanding teenagers."

"You think if I do this I could do it for real?" My heart flip-flops its way up to my throat where it gets stuck. "That's crazy talk."

"Everybody loved the cakes last night. A few couldn't believe you were behind them on account of your, well, usual way of presenting yourself."

"The fact I'm awful at everything but baking."

"You said that. Not me." She laughs. "Look, do it. I have the Mom-mobile to deliver the cakes from my house. You can't do that in Cain's dusty work van. I can help you decorate them. Marcus' mom and dad will be happy to have the kids for a night or two."

"I can't. Damn it, Bills. I can't interrupt your life like that."

"Please do," she says quickly. "His parents have been asking me for three weeks to have the kids for a weekend. Marcus keeps saying no because his promotion means he's working tons and he likes to use kid-free time for us. I'm going crazy, Brooke. They're all fighting all the time and all those stupid after-school activities and I need a break. You'd be doing me a favor."

"Fine, but if you help me, I'm going to pay you."

"You're going to do nothing of the sort," she shoots back. "You're my sister, and if this can maybe open some doors for you, you're going to need every dollar you can get to make it work." Then, right on cue, screaming and yelling sounds. "I have to go. Call me when you know everything for sure, all right?"

"Uh, okay."

She clicks off before I can even say bye.

"Well?" Carly grins smugly at me.

I flip her the bird in response. "I guess I have some work to do."

Twenty

LIFE TIP #20: THE TWO MOST AWKWARD THINGS IN LIFE ARE ASKING FOR MONEY AND FIRST DATES. ESPECIALLY IF YOU GET AN UNINVITED GUEST.

I cringe as I dial the number Penelope gave me in her email. It's my fault for promising I'd call with a quote instead of simply thanking her and letting her know I'd email her back.

I bite the inside of my cheek as the rings echo down the line.

"Argyle residence. This is Penelope," she answers.

"Mrs. Argyle, hi. It's Brooke."

Butterflies erupt in my stomach.

"Brooke, darling! Hello! I wasn't expecting to hear from you so soon."

"Carly helped me after I got your email, so it didn't take as long as I thought it would," I tell her. "I do have a rough quote for you, but it's a little high."

"Fire away."

"It would be eight hundred dollars including delivery."

She's silent for all of two seconds before she replies. "That's perfect. Will you be at work tomorrow? I'll write you a check for half as the deposit."

My mouth goes dry. "I…yes, I will be. I'll take lunch around twenty-thirty if that's convenient for you."

"Absolutely. I'll be in the cafe opposite waiting for you. Does that work?"

Who am I to say no? "That's fine. I might be a little late if I'm with a customer."

"Don't worry, darling. Thank you so much. Annabelle will be thrilled. I'll see you tomorrow."

"See you tomorrow, Mrs. Argyle."

"Goodbye, darling." She hangs up.

The dull monotone of the dead line rings in my ear.

My phone falls out of my hand and onto the sofa cushion next to me. Is that for real? Did that just happen? Did she just agree to pay eight hundred dollars for freaking cakes?

Then again, I'm pretty sure my mom did that for Billie's...

I lean back on the sofa and cover my mouth with my hand.

I have a job.

One I love.

Oh my god.

And I have absolutely no idea how to make a three-tier cake.

"YouTube, if this goes wrong, it's on you," I warn my laptop, fiercely glaring at it.

Low and behold, apparently my mom is the proud owner of the things I need to make a multi-tier cake from several years ago. And, apparently, the moment she heard from Billie that one of her good friends was hiring her youngest daughter to bake for her, she rushed on over here with it all.

I literally had to push her out of my apartment with a promise of lunch on Wednesday. I can't wait. I'm sure it'll be full of my favorite things, aka, her endless questions.

So now, here I am, the base cake cooled and sitting on the board. The second cake is also just about cooled, but the third is still baking away in the oven. It smells so good in my kitchen right now, and I'm so hungry, I kinda wanna just make this cake myself.

I insert the wooden cake dowels into the base before turning to the second cake. I have everything else ready to go when there are three knocks at my door.

I pull the baking paper up out of the cake tin, freeing the middle section of my cake. "Who is it?" I yell.

"It's me." Cain's voice rumbles through the door.

Cain.

Shit!

I drop the cake on the side and look at my microwave oven for the time.

Our date.

Double shit!

"Oh, shit!" I say, a little too loudly. "I'm coming!"

Shitty, shitty, shit, shit! How the hell did I forget this? Oh, I know. I have something else to be freaking about other than this.

I wipe my hands on a cloth and head for the door. I can smell pizza even before I open it, and one look at my black t-shirt confirms exactly what I thought—I'm covered in flour. Crap.

"Hey." I swing the door open with a grin plastered on my face. "I didn't realize it was six already."

Cain's lips pull up to one side, and his green gaze examines my face and upper body. "What the hell are you doing in there? Is that flour?" He wipes his fingertips across my stomach. "Are you baking? You forgot I was coming over, didn't you?"

"Boy, that's a lot of questions." I laugh nervously and step back. "Baking, yes, yes, and I didn't forget, per say. Just forgot the time."

Cain steps into my apartment, holding tightly to our pizza boxes. "What are you baking?"

"Oh, you don't know? I assumed my mom would have put out a public service announcement. This might be the only time in my entire life she's been so proud of me she couldn't yell at me." I go back into my kitchen and turn off the oven. The cake is done, so I slide my hands into my oven mitts, open the oven door, and pull the tin out.

"Why? What did you do? Bake a cake without burning

240

yourself?" He sets the pizza boxes on the opposite kitchen side to where I'm putting the hot cake on the cooling rack.

"No. There's a Band-Aid on my pinky finger." What? Are you surprised? I'm not.

"Ah. Of course there is." He's still half-smiling at me.

"Penelope Argyle was at your mom's party yesterday and hired me to bake all the cakes for Annabelle's birthday party in three weeks including a giant three-tier cake I've never done before and I'm practicing and yes I forgot you were coming over and my finger hurts and I really am a mess because look at me." I take a deep breath from my non-stop stream of words and wave my hands up and down my body. "I have flour everywhere. My hair looks like kangaroos have made out in it, I have a pimple on the crease of my nose that is really bugging me, and I have flour everywhere."

"All right. I'm going to start this again." He comes over to me, takes my face in his hands, and bends over. His lips warmly brush over mine. "Hi," he says with a crooked smile, looking into my eyes.

I smile like a fool. No, seriously. "Hi."

"Now try that explanation again without suffocating yourself."

I laugh into my hand when he steps back and repeat everything I just said, this time with less hysteria.

His eyebrows shoot up. "No way? She hired you? That's awesome. What do you have to make?"

"A three-tier birthday cake and three hundred cupcakes."

He blinks. "That's a lot of cake."

"Uh-huh. So much so that Billie is lifting the Brooke Ban on her kitchen and letting me use it. She's going to help me deliver it all too."

"You've never made a three-tier cake, have you?"

"I'm making one now if that counts."

Cain grins. "Come on, flour girl. Come and eat something. Your cake will be there in half an hour."

"Fine. But let me go clean up first." I run my hand through my hair. "I literally look like a mess."

He picks up the pizza and smiles at me. "I really don't care, B."

"Have you seen what I look like?"

"I'm looking at you right now."

"Then you know I need to go clean up."

He shrugs, walking into the front room. "So go clean up if you really want to. You don't realize how beautiful you look."

I pause, staring at him as he sits on the sofa and sets the two pizza boxes side by side on the coffee table. "You…you really think that?"

Cain sighs and slowly turns his face toward me. "B, you're the scattiest person I know. Honestly, it's a little alarming how all over the place you are sometimes. Then you get into the kitchen and you bake, and you're a different person. You're put together and in control. You're completely at peace when you're covered in flour and have butter smudged across your shorts. You're freakin' gorgeous anyway, but there's something else about you when you look like this."

My lips part ever so slightly, and I take a deep breath in through my nose. "Is that why you kissed me yesterday morning? Really?"

He nods, still with his eyes on mine. "I told you. I just wanted to. And I want to now."

I bite the inside of my cheek. "Then why are you over there?"

A smile stretches across his face. Without another invitation, he gets up, crosses the space between us, and scoops me against his body. He's going to be just as covered in flour as I am by the end of this, but he doesn't seem to give a shit at all as he lowers his face to mine.

I push up onto my tiptoes and meet his lips. My hands creep around his neck, and I hold onto him so tightly I'm scaring myself.

This kiss is everything.

He tightens his grip on my waist, sliding one of his large, rough hands up my back to cup my head. His tongue flicks out and teases the seam of my lips, and my heart skips a beat

242

when he takes a chance and deepens the kiss.

I press my body harder against his. If I get any closer, we're going to meld into one person, but right now, not even that seems close enough.

This could work, a little voice at the back of my head whispers. *Because he thinks you're most beautiful when you're covered head-to-toe in flour.*

He wants me most when I look a mess.

The kiss slows, and I savor every last sweep of his tongue against mine and every last brush of our lips. I'm warm everywhere. My stomach is flipping with the warm fuzzies, and all the hairs on my arms are standing on end. I'm sure there are goosebumps too—and, um, an uncomfortable ache in my clit.

I'm not the only one turned on by that kiss.

Now my brain isn't so fuzzy, I can feel it. His cock is hard and pressing against my lower stomach, and all that does is send a tingle of desire bolting down my spine.

"Come on," he says quietly. "I know you hate cold pizza."

"Cold pizza is only acceptable for breakfast." I drop my arms from around his neck and don't say a word when he takes my hand and drags me toward the sofa. "And you have flour on your shirt."

He looks down at his body and shrugs. He drops down on the sofa, tugging me with him, making me squeal at the quickness I hit it with.

I recover quick enough to grab my pizza box and get comfy. The strangest thing about this is that it doesn't feel like a date—it just feels like any old thing we've done hundreds of times before.

"Harry Potter seven. Part two, right?" He gets back up and goes to the DVD player.

"Does this feel like a normal pizza night to you too?"

"Yep," he answers without turning around. "Except this time, I have a fucking painful erection."

For some reason, that makes me burst out laughing. I don't even know why. Is this the transition from the awkwardness of our new relationship? Or is it because, goddamn it, I have the female equivalent of an erection? I kinda wanna say it's that…

I lift my pizza box off my lap as Cain sits down with the finesse of an elephant. Yep, this feels exactly like normal. Like nothing's changed.

Except for the erection thing. That's definitely changed. The opening credits of Harry Potter roll out around the room. Cain shifts a few times on the sofa before he finally settles with the pizza box in front of him.

I wrinkle my nose as he kicks off his shoes and puts his sock-covered feet on my coffee table. "Do you have to take your shoes off?"

"Did you shave your legs?" He peers sideways at me.

"Like two days ago."

"That's why I've kept my socks on."

I don't have a response to that. It's actually a good argument. Damn it. I hate it when he makes a good argument. That means I don't get to be right and I like to be right.

"Wait. I thought you said you were bringing wine too."

"Shit," he mutters. "It's in the car."

"I'll get it." I slide my box shut and put it onto the table. "Get me your keys."

He adjusts the box and reaches inside his pocket for his keys. "Stop looking at my cock, Brooke."

I blink and look away. "Sorry. It's hard to avoid."

He laughs and puts his keys in my hand. "I am aware."

"Oh god," I groan. I stand up without looking at him and rush, still barefoot, to the door.

I barely remember to slide my feet into my flip-flops before opening it and rushing out to the sound of Cain's laughter.

I can't believe I was just staring at his cock. And apparently, I didn't even realize I was doing that. This is not normal behavior, even for me.

Then again, he was the one who kissed me so hard he turned me—and him—on. It's really all his fault. And, you

244

know. If I had my boobs half out he'd be looking, right?

Human nature when you're attracted to someone. That's my story and I'm going to stick to it until the pages fall apart.

I push open the apartment building door and turn toward the small lot. His car is in the back corner, and I almost trip on a loose rock as I skip over the little bit of grass. My toe stings a little, but I successfully manage to make it to his car in one piece.

I hit the button on Cain's key fob, and instead of unlocking the car, the alarm blares out at me.

I freeze.

How did that happen? Am I honestly that much of a disaster that I can't even unlock his car?

I pat my pocket for my phone, but it's empty. I don't have my phone. It's in my apartment. With Cain. And I'm here. With his car. Screaming at me.

"No, no, no." I jab at all the buttons on the key, but it does nothing. The car is still blaring obnoxiously loudly, and its lights are flashing so hard it may as well be coordinating a school dance in the parking lot.

"What did you do?" Cain yells from behind me.

"I unlocked it!" I shout back. "Make it stop!"

He takes the keys from me and presses a small silver button on it. A long, silver key flicks out from the plastic fob, and he inserts that into the driver side door. He opens the door, sits inside, and turns off the alarm.

"Is everything okay, ma'am? I was driving past and heard a car alarm."

I turn and stare into the face of a concerned police officer. I open my mouth and close it again several times.

"Ma'am?"

Cain gets out of the car, takes one look at me standing and gaping at the cop, and laughs. "Sorry, Officer. My girlfriend is technologically challenged and apparently can't unlock my car without setting off the alarm."

"My sister is the same. As long as everything is all right here."

"It's all good. Thank you for checking, sir."

The officer waves, bids us goodbye, and walks away, presumably back to his car.

Oh my god. I just gaped at him like I was doing something wrong.

But Cain called me his girlfriend.

"You just called me your girlfriend." My voice comes out squeaky.

Cain pauses by the trunk of his car. "Yeah, it kinda just came out. Are you bothered I said it?"

"No. I mean yes. I mean am I your girlfriend? No, I'm lying. I don't know what I mean. Goddamn it, Cain. You know when to make me stop—"

His lips against mine do what I was about to yell at him for not doing. Stop me talking.

"There," he says, pulling away. "That's way more fun than putting my hand over your mouth," he muses, stepping back to the car and popping the trunk.

I'm hard-pressed to disagree.

"Yes it is," I say, waiting as he pulls a plastic bag from the car. "Well, I hope I never see that particular cop again."

"I hope I never agree to let you unlock my car again."

"That's a little drastic. I didn't know that silver thing made it into a real key."

He laughs and locks the car. Then he puts his arm around my shoulders and pulls me into his side. "Of course you didn't. Can we go upstairs and eat the pizza now?"

"Is it still going to be hot?" I ask, following him up. "Maybe."

We walk through the main door and turn toward the stairs. We take the flights up to my apartment in silence. Where I freeze, because the door is shut.

"Oh, shit. We're locked out. I'll have to call the—I don't have my phone!" I turn to Cain in a panic.

With an amused smirk, he pulls his keys back from his pocket, selects one, and inserts it into my lock.

"Right. Spare key. For this reason," I mumble.

He only laughs in response as he turns the key and pushes my front door open.

It's just further proof that someone needs to fire my fairy godmother. I know he has a spare key because I remember him taking mine to get cut in case I ever happen to lock myself out of my apartment.

Although technically this time, he locked us out. I didn't do it.

I go back to the sofa and my pizza while he opens a bottle of beer and pours me a glass of wine.

"So," he says, sitting down. "You're actually going to earn money for baking."

I pick a slice of my—thankfully—still-hot pizza and nod. "Quite a lot of money too. She didn't even bat an eyelid on the phone when I told her."

"Why would she? Her husband is a millionaire. She's not likely to be fussed over, what? A couple hundred dollars for cake?"

"Eight," I say around a mouthful of pizza. "Eight hundred dollars."

He chokes and hits himself in the chest. "Eight hundred dollars on cake?" he wheezes out. "Who in their fucking right mind would pay eight hundred dollars for cake?"

"Penelope Argyle."

"All right, smartass."

I grin and tear a bite off my pizza. "You asked."

Slowly, he nods his head. "You're right, I did. I should have known better."

"I agree. You really should've."

"Brooke? Shut up and eat."

I roll my eyes. "Lord, that's romantic. Excuse me while I swoon all over the place."

"I offered you romantic and you turned it down. I assumed you'd be happy with my usual asshole responses in this case." He shifts on the sofa, pizza slice in hand. "Did I assume wrong?"

"Your first mistake was assuming. But yes, you did. I can

247

have a little romance without a romantic date, can't I?"

"Do you really want me to be romantic?"

"You could try."

"Fine." He puts his pizza down in the box and turns back to look at me. Then he takes my slice from me and puts it in mine.

I look at the pizza and then at him. "Wow. I'm swooning again."

"B." He reaches over and literally slides me across the sofa to him. "Really, now, shut up," he whispers, his eyes on mine.

The wolfish glint in his gaze makes me take a deep breath. It's a darker, sexier glint than I've seen before, and right now, I'm guessing that his idea of romance is whole lot hotter than I ever thought it would be.

I'm guessing right.

Our lips come together in a hard kiss. Maybe I shouldn't do this and maybe I should make him stop, but I know one thing.

Kissing Cain Elliott is addictive. It's like opening a bag of chips. You can't have just *one*. You have to have more and more until your hand is groping around in the bottom the bag and coming up with nothing. I think I could happily kiss Cain until my lips are puckered in thin air and attempting to find his yet again.

Cain's arms circle my body until I'm moving up and over him. My legs settle either side of his body, and I sink my hands into my hair. His hands move across my back until one is cupping my ass and pulling me closer into him. His cock presses against my aching clit, and while my initial instinct is to move away because *this is Cain,* I also can't.

Because *this is Cain.*

This everything right and crazy and wrong and perfect all at the same time.

So I kiss him. I kiss him until my ass is sore from his grip and my lips are dry from his kiss and my heart is beating so quickly I doubt it'll ever be able to slow down.

Until I don't want to stop at just a kiss.

248

"Shh." I press my thumb against his lips when he opens his mouth to speak. "Don't do it."

He smiles against my thumb and whispers, "Run. Now."

I do as he tells me. I climb off him and run to my bedroom with him on my heels. No sooner have I walked through the door than he grabs me, hauling me to him, and propels both of us toward my bed.

This isn't awkward.

It's slutty.

But it isn't awkward.

I grip onto him as we both fall backward onto my bed. "Cain."

"No talking," he whispers against my mouth. "You just said it. No, B."

I nod and curl my body around his. With every heartbeat, I fall a little bit more in fucking stupid love with him. I want him and crave him and need him more than seconds before. Because with every ticking second of the clock, he embeds himself deeper into my skin.

He makes me want him.

The more I taste and feel and touch him, the more I want him.

It's dangerous. God, this is so dangerous. It's treacherous waters. An emotional tsunami.

But *I can't stop.*

"Brooke? Are you here? I left my phone in the kitchen."

"Holy shit!" I whisper, staring at Cain. "That's my mom!"

"Oh fuck." He gets off me so quickly that at any other time, I'd be offended.

As it is…

My freakin' mom is right there.

I sit up and stare at him. When did he take his shirt off? And, no. I can ogle him in a minute. "Get in the bathroom! Quickly!" I grab his arm and shove him toward the door.

He goes, frowning at me over his shoulder.

"Brooke? Are you here?" Mom calls. "Where's my phone?"

"Hold on!" Frantically, I search my room for a towel.

Finding one on the floor by the window, I pick it up and lift it to my nose. It passes the smell-test, and I'm sure I used it when I came home earlier, so I flip my head forward and wrap my hair in it.

Then catch sight of my flour-covered cheeks in the mirror. Shit. A shower excuse won't work.

I yank the towel down and pull off my shirt. My drawer is still open a little, so I pull out a clean one and put it on. Then I grab the towel again and walk out.

"Brooke!" Mom calls. "I have plans this evening!"

"I'm here, I'm here." I rub the towel across my face. "Geez, I was changing my shirt when you barged in."

Her eyebrows shoot up. "With two pizzas?"

"Cain's in the bathroom. Not that it matters." I ball up the towel and toss it on top of my laundry basket. It hits the wall before it lands on it.

"Right." She says it so dryly I know she knows it does matter that he's here. "So, my phone? Where is it, Brooke?"

"Oh, yeah. Here." I walk to my drawers and pull it out of the second one. "I put it here to keep it safe."

"Thank you." She takes it from me and peers toward the bathroom. "He's in there a while."

"Mom?"

"Yes?"

"Didn't you say you had plans?"

She smiles, walking toward the front door. When she gets there, she pauses and turns back to me. "Have fun." She throws me a wave and opens the door.

Almost as soon as it shuts behind her, the bathroom door opens.

I let go of a long, ragged breath and slump back against the side.

Cain walks into the room, his hand over his cock, and adjusts his pants. "Moment's gone, huh?"

I grimace. "Moments gone."

Twenty-one

LIFE TIP #21: NEVER TURN DOWN THE OPPORTUNITY TO SHOP ON SOMEONE ELSE'S CREDIT CARD.

"Your dog hates me."

"Delilah does not hate you."

"Delilah is of the devil and she wants me dead."

Carly rolls her eyes. "That's the most dramatic thing I've ever heard. This week at least."

I drop down onto the park bench. I've been working all day, and now I do not want to be running around the park with a Jack Russell snapping at my ankles when I could be lounging around at home.

I also don't want the third degree on my date with Cain. Not that it's stopping Carly.

"Can we go back to your date?" she asks, right on cue.

"No."

"Why not? I'll just ask him."

"Then go ask him."

"Did it go bad?"

I sigh heavily. "No, it did not go bad. It went fine, Carly."

"Fine? Uh-oh. Fine isn't good."

"Fine is perfectly good." I grab Delilah's ball from her slobbery little mouth and throw it.

So what if I couldn't look Cain in the eye again after my mom left? And not just on account of his lack of a shirt. Maybe I was right from the start. Maybe this is too awkward.

Can friends as close as we are—were? —ever really be more successfully?

Or is it just me?

Am I using it as an excuse because I'm too scared? I don't want to admit to that, but damn it, it's getting more and more likely.

Getting. Got. Is. Whatever.

"I can't help but think you'd be a lot happier if you simply threw caution to the wind and got on with it," she says as if she's reading my mind. "Cain might accept that you're a mess, but that doesn't mean he's going to wait for you to tidy up."

"Myself or my apartment?"

"Neither are likely."

I hate it when she throws the truth at me. "I know. I thought it'd be easier to get past the awkwardness."

"Stop calling it awkward. You wouldn't call the Himalayas a hilly park, would you? You're scared of being in a relationship with him. Accept it."

I swallow hard and focus on Delilah coming back to us, the ball in her mouth. "So what if I am?"

Carly shrugs a shoulder. "Get the fuck over it."

"Easy for you to say." I cut her a dark look. "You're not the one who could ruin everything."

"Goddamn it, Brooke!" She stomps her sneaker-clad foot on the ground and turns to me. Her dark eyes are blazing in a peculiar sympathetic annoyance. "Look at me. Listen to me."

"Yes, Mom."

She hits me.

"Ouch!" I wince back, rubbing my upper arm.

"Then listen to me, Brooke Alice Barker." Carly tucks one foot beneath her butt, wrestles the ball from Delilah, and then throws it. "I've watched you have heartbreak after heartbreak because of your feelings for him for years. Now, you have that chance you've always wanted. It's right here in front of you, and you don't swallow your fear and grab it, you're gonna break your own heart."

I open my mouth.

She cuts me off with a raise of her hand. "I can't distract you. I've tried. All those dates and perfectly nice guys that never went anywhere? Simon? I tried to get you over him, but I couldn't. So by fucking god, asshole, I'm not going to let you turn this into a disaster too."

"I don't know how not to," I admit quietly.

"Talk to him." She squeezes my hand.

"And say what? 'Hey, Cain, this might be a surprise to you, but to you, we're dating, but to me, I'm already in love with you.'"

"Ahem."

I jump and jolt around. My heart thumps against my chest, but I slump forward when I realize our apparent eavesdropper is Zeke and not Cain. "Asshole," I say, hand pressed to my boobs.

He chuckles and, gripping the back of the bench, leans forward. "Don't worry, Brooke. Your secret is safe with me." He winks.

"It's hardly a secret," I grumble.

"It is if he doesn't know."

"Doesn't know what?" Now Cain appears.

"Brooke's a virgin," Carly pipes up.

I get her back for her earlier punch to my arm by shoving my fist into her thigh.

"Owwww!" she whines, leaning forward.

"Payback. Dick." I flip her the bird and look back around at Cain and Zeke. "What are you doing here?"

Cain gives me a lopsided grin. "Looking for you. I have to show you something."

"Ew," Carly mutters. "Save it for the bedroom."

Zeke snorts. He quickly coughs into his hand to hide his amusement.

"Shut it," Cain says, flicking her ear. "No, seriously. This is a big deal. Come with me?"

"Fine. Can we leave the dog?" I ask, standing up.

Carly puts two fingers in her mouth and whistles, causing us all to wince. Delilah comes rushing back as fast as she can on her little toothpick legs, so I'm guessing the answer to my question is no.

"Where are we going?" Carly asks.

Zeke looks at the dog. "I was going to take you, but I'm not putting that mutt in my car."

Carly gasps. "She is not a mutt! She's pure-bred, pencildick."

His eyebrows shoot up. "Pencildick? Huh. You wanna draw a picture?"

My best friend purses her lips and looks to Cain. "My car is in the lot. I'll follow you there." Then she flounces off without another word to any of us.

I sigh as we all turn in the direction she's jogging in. "You just can't help yourself, can you, Zeke?"

He doesn't reply.

"Zeke."

Still nothing.

I turn to him and notice his eyes are very fixed on Carly. "Stop perving at her ass!" I shove him sideways.

He snaps out of his reverie and looks at me with a smirk. "Did you say something?"

Cain shakes his head, rubbing his hand across his forehead. "Try to control yourself, Zeke. You forget that when you've left, *I* have to hear it."

"You have to hear it?" I ask him in disbelief. "How do you think *I* feel? I have to hear it times two, because I have to hear how you never stick up for her."

"What is it with women in my life needing me to stick up for them? Do I look like a fucking superhero?"

"I don't need you to stick up for me. I'm perfectly capable of doing it myself."

"Untrue," Zeke says, hands in his pockets. "You want him to stick something—"

"Ezekiel Elliott, if you finish that sentence, I'm going to accidentally tell the girls in the coffee shop that you have crabs before work tomorrow morning."

He mimes zipping his lips, but his eyes are still glittering with his own self-amusement.

I know everybody thinks I should have my adult card revoked, but I think Zeke is operating on his puberty card still.

"Come on." Cain presses the button on his car keys. His car beeps and clicks with the sound of it unlocking. "Get in."

"Meet you there." Zeke salutes us and pulls his own keys out of his pocket.

"Where are we going?" I get into the passenger side seat. Cain shuts the door and grins at me. "You'll see."

I narrow my eyes at him. His are sparkling with excitement, and I can't help but smile right back at him. The last time he was this excited was when his football team got to the Super Bowl. I think. Or was it baseball at the World Series?

Never mind. Not important.

"Okay…Why are you so excited?" I ask slowly as we pull away.

"Because it's something exciting."

"Why can't you tell me?"

He flashes me another happy smile. "It's a surprise."

"Um…I'm scared." I shuffle back against the door. "Why can't you tell me?"

"Because."

Ugh. Like that's an answer.

I stare at him instead of replying. How do I reply to 'because?' Because what? Because why? Because where why what when? Because how? Because, because?

Oy, too many becauses.

"Don't look at me like that," he warns me, green eyes darting my way. "I mean it, B. This is fun, I promise. And really important to me."

"Oh god. We're not eloping to Vegas already are we?"

He chuckles. "I said fun."

"Marrying me would be fun."

"Only if I want a direct line to the mental hospital."

"I don't think I want to date you anymore. Or be friends with you."

He laughs, and at a red light, leans over and kisses me on the corner of the mouth. A shiver tickles across my skin where his lips just were.

Damn it.

"All right," I mutter, peering through my hair at him. "Shut up."

"I didn't say anything."

"Your smug smile is yelling at me. Make it stop."

He laughs and rests his hand on my leg. "God, you're so awkward. It's funny."

"I'm not awkward!" I sit up straight. "This,"—I wave my hand between us— "is awkward. I can be awkward about it but that doesn't make me awkward."

"You have got to stop saying awkward fifty times a day, B." He swallows back another laugh, squeezing my leg. "Or I'm going to make you."

"That would be more of a threat if you punched me in the mouth to shut me up instead of kissing me."

He balls his fist and lightly lifts it, touching his knuckles to my mouth with the lightest brush. "There. Better?"

"Oh, shit, I'm terrified," I say dryly. "Look. I'm shaking." I hold my hands out in front of me.

"So bad," he drawls in response.

The Barley Cross town sign comes into view, and just when I'm opening my mouth to ask him where we're going, Cain takes a sharp right. My lips still when they're parted, and I feel his eyes on me a few times as he takes another turn, and then moves onto a dirt road.

The road is lined by tall trees, and the early evening sun is dancing through the leaves and branches in bright orange streams. We drive along it for a couple of minutes before we go left at a mini crossroads. The dirt road continues along here, and we drive for another two minutes until the road comes to an end.

"Uh…" I stop.

Cain kills the engine and gets out.

I do the same thing. "Cain?" I ask, walking toward him.

"What is this?"

He shoves his hands in the pockets of his shorts and looks out at the open field. "This is…mine."

I look from him to the field. And back again. And again. And again, and again. "This is yours?"

He nods slowly. His shoulders heave as he takes a deep breath in and lets it out again. "Yep. I bought it. This afternoon, actually."

"For…wait. You bought this for your house?" I stop again, but this time, I look around the field. It's huge—bigger than one person needs. Hell, you could build three houses on this thing if the fences are the guidelines.

"Lawrence Hooper is selling off some of his land. This is one of the fields, so I sought planning permission. He held it until I got my plans were accepted this morning."

I turn and shove him. "Why didn't you tell me you were doing all this?"

He shrugs and looks at me, one hand buried in his hair. "I don't know. I guess if they rejected my proposal for the house I would have hated having to tell anyone what I was doing. Only Zeke and Dad knew and that's because they worked on the proposal with me."

"I thought you weren't going to do it yet."

"I wasn't. But Dad heard about the land from Lawrence and reminded me that I can build the house for cheap because I won't have to pay him and Zeke labor, so I took a chance."

"I…wow." I rub my palms together in front of me. "That's amazing."

He looks at me and smiles. "It's gonna take a while, but the plans are incredible. Look, let me show you." He goes back to the car and reaches into the backseat. There, he pulls out a large folder and removes two sheets of paper. "Here." He grabs my hand and pulls me forward. "We're walking along where the driveway will be built. There'll be enough room to park three cars. And here's where the double garage will go. Above it will be like an office, man cave type thing."

"Of course," I concede with a smile. Even though my stomach is turning horribly.

He shows me the plans. "This will be the front door. From here, we walk into the hallway," he says, fully sliding his fingers between mine and pulling me along with him. "Immediately to the left will be the guest bedroom. Then into the living room, which opens out into the kitchen and diner. Oh, and back this way…" He turns us around and tugs me more. "Is another spare room I don't have a use for yet and a shower room. Just off the kitchen will be a utility and mudroom."

"Sounds awesome."

"The stairs will be here." He stops us exactly where it is and looks up into the golden sky as if he's looking upstairs. "Three bedrooms. The master will have a master bath and walk-in closet with access to the man cave via the closet. The other two bedrooms will be connected via a smaller bathroom and have built-in closets instead of walk-in ones."

"That's impressive."

"And the yard…"

"My god, you're organized."

He smiles at me as he pulls me into the 'yard.' Aka, the field. "There'll be a massive back porch here. I might add a sun room too. But from here, there'll be a patio area with a built-in grill, seating, and maybe a pool."

"Are you secretly Bill Gates or something?" I look around at the vast area. "That's a lot."

"I know." He shrugs, but his grin is too wide, too infectious. "That'll all take a long time. The important thing is building. I got a little carried away."

"Perhaps." I smile.

"But that's not the best bit." He pulls me further across the field, almost to the very back. "Right there, I have permission to build a massive brick shed. Two, actually. Well, they'll be attached together and connected by a door."

"Wow." I look around at where I imagine he's picturing the shed. "How long is that going to take to build? Too long?"

He laughs, looking down. He folds up the plans he just showed me and shoves them roughly into his pocket.

Man, I hope he has spares of those...

"Sorry," he says, rubbing the back of his neck. Slowly, he looks back up at me. "I guess I'm just excited. We've been doing this for a while now and I can't believe it's going to be built right here."

I turn and look around the field. Somehow, his car seems miles away, although I know it isn't. The area is so vast and open, it seems crazy that an actual house is going to be built here.

"That is crazy," I agree, linking my fingers together before pressing my hands flat against the top of my tummy. "When are you starting?"

"I don't—hey, what's up?" He steps in front of me, blocking my view of the field, and captures my gaze with his green eyes. "Brooke?"

"You're building a house and I can't even unpack an apartment after three weeks." The words escape me before I can stop them.

Guilt punches me hard almost as soon as the final word has died on my tongue. It twists at my gut and squeezes my heart, making me slap my hand against my mouth.

"I'm sorry," I whisper through my fingers. "I just ruined this. I didn't mean to."

Cain gently cups my cheek, his fingertips brushing my hairline. His pinky finger curves beneath my jaw, and using that, tilts my chin up. With that one simple move, he forces me to look at him.

Where I should see annoyance, I see mild amusement. Where I should see frustration, I see tenderness.

"B..." His lips twitch the tiniest amount. He wraps his fingers around my wrist and pulls my hand away from my face. Then he kisses me. Softly and slowly, his lips moves across mine until all the guilt has seeped out of me. "Remember," he says quietly, "When we were in Italia's? On the roof? And I said I always imagined I'd end up with someone like you or Carly?"

I swallow hard and nod.

"I lied." He brings his other face to my hand and steps into me. "I didn't imagine I'd end up with someone *like* you. A part of me imagined I would end up *with* you."

"But—"

"I. Don't. Care. Okay?" he says firmly. "I don't care about whatever excuse you're about to give me. You're chaos, Brooke Barker. Luckily for you, I happen to love chaos."

I stare up at him for a long moment.

"You don't scare me. Your crazy doesn't scare me. Do we have to work past being friends? Sure. But I can't see any way that can make this harder for us. If anything, it's already easier. Being your best friend before your boyfriend means I already know when not to argue back at you and when to agree that you're right."

That might be the hottest thing anyone's ever said to me.

"Wait...agree that I'm right? Don't you mean *admit* that I'm right?"

Cain blinks at me, his expression not changing. "Of course. You're right."

"Thank yo—wait. I see what you did there."

His stoic expression morphs into a cocky, sexy smile that lights up his whole face. "See? I told you. I know when not to argue with you."

"That is kinda hot," I agree. Agree. Not admit. See? Difference.

"And I know all your favorite things so I'm never going to order you a meal you don't like or buy you the wrong wine."

"True."

"And," he continues, sliding his hands down my body to my waist. He pulls me flush against him. "I know what sports you do and don't like, so you won't have to watch hours of them unless I have to watch your stupid, girly movies."

"Hey." I press my fingertip to his lips. "They're not stupid, girly movies. They're hilarious, heart-warming stories of love."

"You're right. My mistake."

"Stop doing that."

He laughs quietly, bringing his face to mine. The tips of our noses touch. "No. Then I'd be arguing with you."

"By declining to argue with me, you're arguing with me."

"Brooke? Shut up." He brushes his lips over mine again.

"Boy, I hope that won't be a requirement," I mutter, my eyes focused on his mouth. "I'm not great at the shutting up."

"I know," he groans, kissing me one more time before stepping back. "There's actually a reason I brought you here. You know, if you're done with your freakout."

"I am, but I have a question."

He raises his eyebrows expectantly.

"Where are Carly and Zeke?"

He grins. "He directed her to home. Because there's a reason I brought you here."

"Oh." I tilt my head to the side. "Okay. What's the reason?"

He bites the inside of his lower lip, his teeth just showing slightly. "I want you to help me build the house."

Now *my* eyebrows go up. I think they're halfway to the moon. "I can't build a house out of Lego, let alone real bricks. Believe me. I tried the Lego. I'm awful."

"I have no doubt," he replies wryly. "But I don't mean the things that might collapse on my head. I mean the other things. Like flooring and carpets and painting...and stuff."

"And stuff." My voice is quiet. "Why?"

"Because I can build a house but not make it look like somebody lives in it?" he answers, laughing nervously and rubbing the back of his neck.

I stare at him flatly. "Now I'm a bad liar, but that was just awful. Even if I have seen the inside of your apartment and know there's a thread of truth to it."

"Maybe, one day..." He looks almost embarrassed. "You know this is my dream house. Maybe, one day...it might be yours too."

Oh.

Oh.

Oh.

"One day," he says again quickly, stepping half-forward before taking a full one back. "When it's ready and you're ready and we're ready."

My heart is beating quickly, but I manage to control my breathing enough to close the distance between us he just created. I mean to say something, but the words get lodged in my throat. So I wrap my arms around his neck and hug him tightly.

He tenses for a second, but quickly relaxes and circles his arms around my waist. He presses his face into my hair and holds me close to him.

"Do you honestly think we'll ever reach that point?" I ask, my voice scratchy. "Because that seems like it's really far away right now. Especially when just being together scares me."

"Yes," he says simply—and confidently. "It doesn't have to happen tomorrow, B. Being together isn't going to be easy. It's going to be harder than being friends, but I know we can make it work. I want you enough to make this work."

I hug him even tighter. "Me too. Okay. I'll do your flooring and carpets and painting and…stuff."

"I just unleashed a monster, didn't I?"

Grinning widely, I dance out of his arms and walk backward to his car. "You have *no* idea."

Twenty-Two

Three Weeks Later

"She's going to lose her mind."

"I'm a little afraid."

"Should we ask if she's okay?"

"I don't know. I've seen her use that frosting squirter thingy."

"You're right."

"Should we hand her wine?"

"That's a good idea."

"Food?"

"I don't know. Maybe we should just…"

"Get out of the kitchen?" I yell, brandishing my frosting pipe as a weapon as I turn to my sister and Carly. "Are you helping? No! Are you annoying me? Yes! Why are you even here?"

"It's my kitchen?" Billie offers, albeit hesitantly.

"Are you frosting?" I shout back.

"I…no. You told me to fuck off."

"Yet you haven't done it!"

Carly leans in to my sister and says in a quiet voice, "Bills, I'm scared."

"And you should be!" I point the frosting pipe in her

263

direction. "I have thirty minutes to finish icing this goddamn monster of a cake and if I don't get it done I'm never going to be hired again and my dream will be in tatters and everyone will know how horrible I am!"

"Yeah, I'm just gonna…" Carly cocks her thumb over her shoulder and quickly runs out of the kitchen.

"Do you need anything?" Billie asks, slowly edging away.

"Wine? Vodka? A Valium?"

I point toward the door.

She disappears quickly.

Silence rings out around the spacious kitchen, and I take a deep breath when I hear the kitchen door shut. I carefully put down the frosting pipe onto the island and pull out the nearest stool. My ass hits it way too hard as I drop down, but I don't much care.

I'm exhausted. I've been doing this for hours. Over a day, actually. The past thirty-six hours have been nothing but crazy, crazy, *crazy*. I'm more than ready to drop dead on my feet and go to sleep.

I don't know what I expected when I agreed to take on three hundred cupcakes and a three-tier birthday cake, but I'm not sure it was this.

In fact, I'm sure it wasn't this.

Not to mention Carly was right—my boss refused to pay me for the two days I've had to take off. If Penelope wasn't paying me more for this than I'd have earned in the past two days, I'd be really annoyed. Then again, on the brighter side, this could be everything for me.

I'd be lying if I didn't say I've enjoyed all this. I've loved making the cakes and decorating them. It's just…despite my usual insanity, I'm so afraid I'll mess this up, and it's so scary. I don't want to get this wrong. I want every cake to be perfect for Annabelle's party.

Two hands gently land on my shoulders, and familiar, rough fingers move across my skin. "You're shouting at everyone."

I sigh as Cain's voice sends goosebumps across my skin. "I

know, but they're all in my way."

His thumbs dig into my shoulder muscles in the best kind of way.

I moan.

He chuckles as he massages my tight shoulders. "You can't make people get out of your way, B."

"Do you see them here right now?"

"No."

"Now tell me I can't make them get out of my way."

Cain smirks. "Okay, you win that one. Why aren't you shouting at me?"

"Because you're rubbing my shoulders and it feels really good." I moan again.

"Don't you have to finish the cake?" He stills, looking at the three-tier monstrosity that still needs tiny flowers added to it.

"Yes." I sigh and stand back up. "Only fifty, but still. It needs to rest for a little before we leave."

"Do you want me to help you?"

I spin on the balls of my feet and spear him with my gaze.

"That'll be a no." He takes a step back. "Do you need anything?"

"Yes. To finish this cake." I look at him pointedly.

He makes to move toward the door, but pauses. "Are you sure you don't want a Valium?"

I keep my glare fixed firmly on him until he's backed out of the kitchen and is out of my sight. Then, I let out another deep breath and turn to the cake. The flowers took forever for me to make and set, and although I've been in an almost permanent state of exhaustion for the past week, looking at them now…

Well, it's worth it.

For the next twenty or so minutes, I work methodically and carefully to put the last of the flowers in place. Penelope Argyle was adamant that the cake be delivered as fresh as possible, and although I'd prefer to refrigerate it overnight, I have one major problem with that.

I don't have a big enough fridge to do it.

That may have to be something I rectify…somehow…if this goes well.

I don't know. Can I hire space? Is that a thing? Can you do that?

I put the last flower on the top of the cake, adjust one, and then fall back onto the stool. God…I'm totally tooting my own horn, but the cake looks amazing. And so it should. I've put my entire heart and whatever remained of my sanity into it.

Okay, so not a lot of sanity, but whatever.

"Are you done?" Billie pokes her head into the kitchen. "Can I come back into *my* kitchen now?"

"I'm done. And yes." I turn my face toward her and smile. "Thank you for letting me take it over."

"You're welcome. But you're making the pies this Thanksgiving. Oh, holy shit!" She gasps, going over to the cake.

"Don't touch it!" I reach out and immediately pull my hands back. I touch my face and stare at it.

"I wasn't going to touch it, you fool." My sister stares at me for a moment. "I just wanted to get a closer look."

"Oh. Right." I slowly sit back down again. I'm not taking my eyes off her though. I know what she's like.

Billie leans in to the cake the slightest bit. I can't help but wince. If she catches it, she ignores me and circles around the cake, dipping her head this way and that. She also bobs it forward a few times.

One time a little too forward.

I squeak.

"Brooke," she says quietly, moving away from it. "This is amazing. I can't believe you actually did this."

I'd be offended if I weren't kind of thinking the same thing.

"Whoa," Carly breathes from the doorway. "How did you, the queen of klutz, make something so precise and beautiful?"

266

"That's the strangest mix of compliment and insult I've ever heard." I tilt my head to the side. "But also, a really great question."

Carly pats my shoulder. "Now you just have to get it to the party in one piece."

We all freeze at that.

"Perhaps me being the one to carry it isn't the best idea..." I hesitate. "I mean, I've come this far. It's like I'm asking to drop it if I do it."

Billie slowly nods. "Cain will have to do it."

"Whoa," he says, coming back in. "I'll have to do what?"

"Carry the cake," Carly answers. "Brooke's done so well today and not klutzed at all, so there's a two-hundred percent chance she's going to destroy the cake in transit."

Two hundred seems like a long shot.

I was going to say five hundred percent chance.

That's definitely more up there.

"Seriously," Billie agrees, moving away from the cake to the fridge. She pulls out bottles of water and hands them to us one by one. "I watched her since five a.m. She didn't even drop so much as a *spoon*. Seriously. I've seen her drop a spoon eating her breakfast. Yet now? No. Not even a chocolate sprinkle is on my floor, you guys. This is not normal behavior for Brooke."

"She's a ticking time bomb," Carly goes on. "She's probably going to trip as soon as she stands up. She's been so in control for so long."

Well...Now I'm scared of myself.

"Thanks for your confidence." I swallow hard.

Cain walks up behind me and rests his hand on my shoulder. "They do have a point."

"I know that," I answer. "And I am afraid to move the cake. I don't want to do anything that might damage it."

He sighs. "I'll do it. It's probably too heavy for you anyway, isn't it?"

I look at the huge thing. "Yeah, there's no way I can lift that."

"Will the board hold up?" He leans forward and touches the solid, silver board it's standing on.

"It's wooden, so yes. Just…be careful."

"You got it." He meets my eyes and smiles. "And you…don't move. At all."

Billie and Carly giggle into their hands.

I offer him a thumbs up. "Can somebody bring me a drink now?"

I can't believe I did it.

And I can't believe I'm holding a check for four hundred dollars that is *all* mine.

I have a strange sense of satisfaction. It's comparable only to the moment you hit an orgasm after hovering on the edge for what is almost always too long.

I can't believe I *actually* did it—and well. And right. And, well, perfect. But I did—and both Penelope and Annabelle were ecstatic with what I did.

"Can you believe I had to give her permission to give my number to people interested?" I tuck my feet beneath my butt on the sofa.

Cain sets two plates of pasta on the coffee table. "That's pretty amazing. You should do some cards or something instead."

"Four hundred dollars!" I squee, shoving the check in his face. "And it's all mine!"

"You're probably still going to need cards."

"I don't know what to do with it." I should probably save it just in case, I know, but this is special. This is my first actual paycheck from doing something I actually love and want to do as opposed to something I don't care about. "What should I do with it?"

Cain's lips pull to one side as he settles in with his plate on his lap. "Buy some business cards."

I pause. "You're probably right. Are they expensive? What do I put on it?"

"Well," he starts around a mouthful of pasta. He swallows. "You should probably put your name, number, and what you do."

"Should I put a cutesy name on it?"

"For what?"

"A business. If I'm going to do it, I need to name it. Right?" Among other things. But for now...

He raises his eyebrows. "I'm impressed you thought of such a thing."

I poke my tongue out at him and pick up my plate.

"What are you going to use? For a name?"

"Uh..." I stab some pasta with my fork and, as I eat it, think. What could I call it? Something cute, like I just said. Simple. Catchy. "What about Brooke's Bites?"

Cain slowly chews. "I like that," he says after a moment. "So now all we need to do is set you up an email address for it and put that on the cards. Maybe even a small logo."

"Whoa," I say quietly. "That's a lot of things for a business card. I don't know if I can use that amount of money to pay somebody to do that stuff for me."

"Why would you need to pay somebody?"

"Because I can barely use Word Art in Microsoft Word."

He laugh-coughs into his hand. "I can do it," he says when he's done choking himself on amusement. "I have a basic understanding of Photoshop. It's not that hard."

"Really? You'd do that?"

"You think I wouldn't?"

"No, but I, well I, I don't know," I eventually settle on after stammering my way through the other words. "I didn't know you could do that. Can you stop keeping secrets from me now?"

He laughs again, putting his now-finished dinner back on the coffee table. "Okay, fine. But it's really not a big deal. Someone had to do it for Elliott and Sons, and I lost at Rock,

Paper, Scissors, so I'm the one who had to learn Photoshop."

"Seems reasonable," I say, putting my half-eaten plate down on the table next to his. "But I have no idea what to do, and I don't own Photoshop."

"Leave it with me." He smiles and holds one arm out.

I scoot across the sofa and curl into his side.

He wraps his arm around me and rests his cheek on top of my head. "I'm proud of you, you know."

"You are?" I tilt my head back, dislodging his. "Why?"

"You did it." His smile is warm and tugs at my heart. "Honestly, for a time, I didn't know if you would, you were so stressed over it, but you did. You found something you love doing and something you want to do."

I shrug. "I never considered baking. Is that crazy? I mean, I do love it, but I always did it for fun. I can't believe I could be doing this for real."

He opens his mouth to speak, but he's cut off by the ringing of my phone. It's barely seven p.m., so it has to be either my mom or Carly.

It's neither. I don't know the number on the screen.

"Answer it," Cain urges me. "You don't know after you spoke to Penelope."

"That's dumb. The party started an hour ago. There's no way someone would be calling me already."

"Answer it before it cuts out!"

"Ack!" In my haste, I almost drop my phone, but I manage to keep hold of it and swipe the green call button to the left. "Hello?"

"Is this Brooke Barker?" An unfamiliar voice asks down the line.

I glance at Cain, but he waves at me to carry on. "Yes, ma'am. Can I help you?"

"You sure can, honey! My son is at Annabelle Argyle's sweet sixteen party tonight and I couldn't help but notice the gorgeous cake. Penelope gave me your number. My daughter is getting married in six months and is struggling to find anyone in the area who can do her the cake she's fallen in love with." She pauses. "Would you be free to meet with her this week to discuss it?"

I widen my eyes and look at Cain. Sweet sixteen to a wedding is a big jump. Big, big jump.

"Of course," I answer after a moment. "I'm free on Thursday, or any evening after six, Mrs…"

"Oh!" She laughs. "Forgive me. I completely forgot to introduce myself. Loretta Henderson. Let me call my daughter and—oh, do you mind if I share with her your number? It may be easier."

"Of course, Mrs. Henderson. That's not a problem. I'll wait for her call."

"Excellent. Thank you so much, honey!"

"You're welcome. I look forward to hearing from her."

We say goodbye and hang up.

I slowly reach out and put my phone on the coffee table. I'm avoiding meeting Cain's eyes 'cause, well. He was right, wasn't he?

"Well?" he asks.

I can hear his damn smile.

"Wrong number," I answer nonchalantly.

"B!" He laughs and pulls me over on top of him. "I heard the whole conversation. Loretta Henderson isn't known for being quiet at all."

"You know who she is?" I lean back. "Her daughter is— wait, you heard that too, huh?"

He nods, grinning. "Although I must have heard it wrong, because it's far too soon for anyone to be calling you about a cake."

"Shut up." I swat him on the chest. "Is this a good thing?"

"Someone wants to pay you to bake cakes and you're asking me that question?"

"No, I mean, like…" I trail my fingertips down his body and over the ridges of his stomach. "Is she…will she *help* me?"

"You mean does she have friends who'll pay hundreds of dollars for cake and share you around like a hooker at a frat

271

party?"

"Yes. That. Exactly that. Wait. No. Don't answer that. That's shallow."

He presses his thumb to my lips. "Yes, she does have those friends. Lots of, actually. We did her extension five months ago and we got a huge uptick in work, some we're still attempting to schedule. Loretta Henderson is influential and uses that for all the right reasons."

"So…"

"Don't get carried away. There's a long time between now and then. You know as well as I do that building a business doesn't happen overnight. I know that somewhere inside your pretty little head you might be entertaining thoughts of leaving Jet, but you may still be there next year."

I thin my lips into a flat line. "Way to keep me humble, Cain."

"You're the dreamer and I'm the realist. We balance out."

He grins, linking his fingers at the base of my back.

I flatten my hands against his stomach and lean forward. I have butterflies in my own, and a crazy little bit of adrenaline pumps through my veins, lending me the courage I need to say my next words. Especially since my mom walked in a few weeks ago and we haven't actually…had sex.

"Yeah, well," I say, my voice a little on the shaky side. "I might be dreaming about you naked."

"Really." His voice drops several decibels, and the look in his eyes changes from playful to hot. "That right?"

"Maybe. And since you're a realist…"

He needs no other invitation. He shoves me to the side onto the sofa and stands. Then, when I'm about to ask him what he's actually doing, he bends forward, grabs me, and throws me over his shoulder.

I scream as he carries me through my apartment and toward my bedroom. My butt bumps against my bedroom door as he pushes it open, and I frown as I throw my arm out to stop it closing on me when he carries me through it.

"Can you try not to kill me in the process?" I ask, wriggling on his shoulder. "I should not be able to fit on your shoulder, Cain! Put me down!"

"If you wish." He throws me—literally *throws* me—onto my bed.

I bounce.

"Motherfucker!" I shout as my head bounces off the headboard. My elbow knocks it too, but the real kicker is when my foot flies into my nightstand and knocks off an almost-full glass of water.

"Shit!" Cain somehow manages to catch it before it goes over and throws water everywhere. It splashes over his hand, but otherwise, the water stays contained to the glass. "That was close."

"That was you!" I scramble up so I'm leaning back on my hands and stare at him sharply. "You can't throw me around. I don't need your help to cause destruction."

He looks at me for a moment before he laughs and comes closer to me. He grabs my ankles and pulls me down the bed toward him with the sound of another little shriek from me.

"Stop that."

Cain's grin is playful, and he leans right over me, putting his hands flat on the bed either side of my head. "I can't stop. I haven't gotten started yet."

I raise my eyebrows, linking my hands behind his neck. "Really?"

"Really," he murmurs, lowering his face to mine.

He kisses me, and…

Well.

I really don't care when I kick the glass off the nightstand for the second time…

epilogue

LIFE TIP #23: SURPRISES WILL DO ONE OF THREE THINGS: SCARE YOU, THRILL YOU, OR MAKE YOU SOB LIKE YOU'RE WATCHING A COMMERCIAL WITH PUPPIES WHILE ON YOUR PERIOD.

Four & a Half Months Later

"Close your eyes."

"I don't want to close my eyes." I pout and meet Cain's gaze. "Why do I have to close my eyes?"

"Gee, Hot Mess," he replies dryly. "I don't know. Maybe because it's your birthday and I have a surprise for you?"

I pout harder. "I hate surprises. You know I hate surprises."

"I'll drive you there in your new car just so you can drive it back."

Okay, hmm. Tempting.

Loretta Henderson wasn't the only person to call me after Annabelle's party. Apparently, people will pay for cakes for everything from a family-only first birthday to a full-of-screaming-kids tenth party to a blow out one hundredth celebration. Not to mention funerals, bachelorette parties, and family reunions.

Long story short, if I haven't been cementing bridges with my mom, hanging out with Carly, or working on my relationship with Cain, I've been baking.

274

Actually, the baking has come first. Good thing too. I've made enough money to have to register as a real, legit business—Brooke's Bites, LLC, if you freaking well please! —and perhaps my absolute favorite…buy my first car.

That's right. I'm now officially twenty-five, and my birthday present to myself three days ago was collecting my new car from the dealership.

"There's a problem with that," I finally reply to Cain. "I don't know if I want you driving my car."

"Okay, I gave you enough lessons in my car for you to retake your test and get your license back. Don't give me that shit." He taps me on the nose and holds up a black, cotton scarf.

"I hope that scarf is to blindfold me for kinky sex and not this surprise. Oh, wait. Is the kinky sex the surprise? I can deal with that."

"Brooke."

"I'm going to take the use of my name as a no."

"Come on," he says, now pleading with me in earnest. "I promise we aren't going far. You're going to have to wear it for ten minutes at most."

"This is bullshit and I don't like it," I warn him. "And you should know that for your birthday, I'm going to blindfold you and cuff you to your bed and then leave you there while I watch the Kardashians and eat your favorite chips without you."

"Big words from a girl who still sometimes kicks the lamp on the nightstand when we have sex."

"Carry on. Go on. Next time, I'll hit you with it in those couple of minutes where I've already come but you haven't."

"Truce," he calls quickly. "Please let me blindfold you?"

"Fine. But you do it for real later." I huff and turn my back to him.

"Can I eat your favorite chips and watch TV?"

"Only if you want me to take a drill to your cock."

He wraps the scarf around my eyes. "Threat heard and noted. You got it. Whatever you want." He ties the scarf.

"Come on then, let's go."

I turn around, but when he doesn't grab me to guide me, I don't move. "Uh, Cain? I can't see where I'm supposed to be going."

"Shit. Right." The sound of shuffling footsteps across the hallway of my apartment building seems louder than it should. His grip as he takes hold of me is also stronger than usual. "Come on. Your car is right outside."

"No it's not."

"I put it there."

"You drove Sheila?!"

He coughs. "I told you when you bought it and I'm going to tell you again. Sheila is a dumb name for a car."

"So is Elvis, but you don't see me bitchin' out your choice of car name."

He guides me inside the passenger side of my car. "Elvis was a legend. It's a perfectly good name for a car."

I wait until I hear the sounds of him getting into my car and shutting the door. "You know he'd be insulted by that."

"Yeah? Well who is your car named after?" he asks over the rumbling of the car as he starts it.

I'm not going to respond to that. Maybe she just looks like a Sheila. You don't always name your kids after somebody else, do you? No. You name them what you want. That's my stance with Sheila. I like her as Sheila, so Sheila she shall stay.

"How much longer are we going to be?" I shift in my seat, turning my head left and right although I know I'll see nothing but the inside of this damn scarf.

"Couple minutes," he answers.

The car veers to the right.

"Where are we going?" I ask.

He doesn't reply this time.

"Where are we going?"

Again, silence.

"Where are we going?"

More silence.

"Are we there yet?"

"Jesus, don't start that," he says quickly. "I don't want to hear that for the next two minutes."

"Are we there yet? Are we there yet? Are we there yet? Are we there yet? Are we—"

"Shut the fucking hell up, or I'm turning around and you'll never know," he threatens me. "Sound good?"

I mime zipping my lips and drop my hands in my lap. It's taking forever and ever to get to wherever the freaking hell we're going, but I'll do as I'm told and be quiet. For once.

Maybe.

This is taking a long time. I'm not sure I like having my eyes covered. In fact, I'm almost certain I don't. No, I lie. I hate it. Straight up hate it.

"Cain?" I say in a small voice. "I want this thing off my eyes now."

"One more minute," he replies, turning again. "I promise, B. Then we'll be there and you can get out the car."

"Promise?"

"I said so, didn't I?"

I nod. "Thirty seconds."

"Thirty seconds," he confirms, his voice shaking.

My god, is he nervous? Wait, he's not going to propose, is he? We haven't even said I love you yet. That would be a huge step. Oh my god, is he proposing? I don't want to remember this birthday as the one where I had to... oh god, what would I say if he proposed? Yes? No? Maybe? Okay, but in a few years?

Oh dear god.

This is ridiculous.

The car comes to a stop. I'm hyper-aware of everything around me, and now I know it's because of the scarf blindfolding me. I can hear Cain's breathing. I can feel the stillness as the engine powers down. I can smell Cain's musky cologne. I can feel the comfort of my seat beneath me and all the fibers as they press against my thighs.

"We're here." His voice wavers again, but he clears his throat. "Ready?"

"Yes. Please. Get me out."

Shuffles.

Doors opening.

Doors closing.

Silence.

Silence.

Silence.

Door opening.

One hand on mine.

"Brooke. Let me help you." Cain guides me to turn. I sigh in relief when my feet hit the ground.

"Take my hands." His fingers wrap around mine, and he pulls me up.

"I don't like this," I remind him for what feels like the five-hundredth time. "I can't see a thing."

His laugh sends goosebumps across my skin. "I hate to tell you this, but it's kinda the point."

"I hate you so much."

His lips press against mine in a perfect kiss. "Hate me. I'm at the other end of the scale."

I gasp.

"Come on," he says, amusement in his voice. "Trust me."

"Did you just—"

"Trust me." His repeated words are stronger than I anticipated.

I tighten my grip on his hand. "I trust you."

Cain pulls me across ground that feels suspiciously soft. Are we on grass? Sand?

Where in the hell are we?

Cain wraps one arm around my shoulders before setting me to a stop. A door opens, but he doesn't move, so I know he isn't alone. He can't be, can he?

No, no. He moves me forward some more and steps behind me.

My back is flush against his body, and one of his arms is wrapped around my stomach.

Slowly, he takes a step to the side, his hand trailing across the bottom of my tummy. "Six months ago, you took a risk," he says in a low voice. "You did something none of us thought you'd ever do."

"Cain, what?" I ask on a whisper.

"Sshh, please?" he asks, moving so far that only his hand now rests on the small of my back. "You took a risk and you've done it ever since. I've been there every day, watching you achieve a dream you didn't know you had. So has everyone else. Your mom, sister, best friend, dad, brother, grandpa, my parents…we've watched you come out and believe in yourself."

"I don't understand."

"Give me two seconds, okay?" he says, moving into me. His hand goes up my back and there's a light tug on the scarf covering my eyes. "So we decided to do something epic for you. We got together and decided we have one goal: to help you achieve your dream."

"I don't—"

He tugs.

The scarf falls from my eyes.

And I stare the sight before me.

I don't know where I am or what I'm standing in, but I do know I'm standing in the world's most perfect kitchen. There are chrome appliances so shiny not even fictional creatures could clean it so well, and at the back, nestled between matte, black cupboards, is the biggest fucking fridge I've ever seen in my life.

More than that, there's a calendar on the wall. An island. Kitchen utensils next to the chrome sink.

"I don't get it," I whisper, looking around.

At a cake stand.

"What did you do?" My voice is thicker now, but no louder.

Cain audibly swallows and steps in front of me. Before he can speak, all the people he mentioned just moments ago do the same and line up behind him.

Carly. Mom. Dad. Billie. Benny. Mandy. Grandpa.

And his dad. Gabe. Zeke…

But my eyes are on Cain.

"This was one half of my shed," he says softly. "We could build it, so we did. We wanted to give you the one thing you really needed."

"No," I whisper, covering my mouth with my hand.

Cain has the hint of a smile on his lips. "It's nothing fancy, but it has enough ovens that you don't need to steal Bill's kitchen anymore. It has a fridge big enough for those crazy cakes. There's a cupboard dedicated to boxes, and if you look in the drawers, you'll find stickers and business cards. And a portfolio of real pictures of every cake you've made over the past few months. We decided you needed something amazing so we made it happen."

A thick lump of emotion forces its way up my throat. Tears prick at the back of my eyes, and I lick my lips before swallowing. "I don't understand."

Cain cups my face, his lips curved, his eyes dancing with mischief. "Welcome to Brooke's Bites."

"No!" I stagger back into somebody.

"Yes," Carly says into my ear, her soft hands resting on my arms. "Welcome to your dream kitchen, Brooke. Everything you need is right here."

"Not everything," Ben, my brother, pops up. "She has to buy all the ingredients and shit."

I cover my mouth with my hand as I look at the line of people staring at me. Cain catches me when I stagger backward into him.

"I don't know where I am," I say, choking back tears.

Nobody says anything.

Slowly, I turn toward Cain. "No." That's apparently my favorite word today. "Don't tell me you did this."

He links his fingers through mine and pulls me through our families to outside the building. Where there's nothing but endless grass.

His field.

His home field.

His shed.

"Cain!"

"Happy birthday," he says in a quiet voice into my ear. "Brooke's Bites has a home. Where it's supposed to be. The other half of the shed will become an office for you. I have permission to build another next to yours."

"You can't do this." I'm shaking. Everywhere. "This is insane."

"Dad and Zeke's birthday present is the materials and labor. Your family put up the money. My mom bought your cake stands." He pauses. "I bought your packaging."

"And the land! Motherfuck, Cain!" I step away, hands over my mouth again. "Why? Why would you all do this?"

"I can't speak for them, but…" he looks me dead in the eye and says, "Because I love you, Brooke. More than my best friend. You're literally everything to me. I love you the way the center of my world should be loved. Why wouldn't I do this?"

I throw myself at him. The emotion overcomes me and I bury my face into his neck.

"Chase your dream," he rasps into my ear. "We all believe in you. We want this for you. The best birthday present we could ever give you is this."

"Stop it." My voice is thick, and fuck it, I'm done. Tears escape my eyes and I hold him tighter than I knew I could. "You did this, you shit. I know it."

"I love you." He pulls me into him. "That's all there is to it, okay? I love you. I love seeing you happy. This makes you happy. We can all do this."

The lump of emotion in my throat bubbles up and over. It swamps me, and I fall against him.

"Go be Brooke's Bites," he says thickly. "Right here in the place that'll always be your home."

I bury my face into his neck. "Love you," I whisper against his neck. "You have no idea how much, Cain Elliott."

He hugs me.

Tight.

Hard.

"Go play with your new kitchen." He presses his lips to mine and spins me toward the shed.

I do as he said. I hug the shit out of everyone. Everyone wishes me happy birthday or a variation of and after a few minutes, I settle in and look around me.

Holy. Perfect. Kitchen.

Everything. Just everything.

I wrap my hands around Cain's neck, lean into him, and press my face against his neck. "Thank you," I whisper. "Thank you so much."

He hugs me back just as tight. "Anything for my girl."

The End

ABOUT THE AUTHOR

Emma Hart is the New York Times and USA Today bestselling author of over twenty novels and has been translated into several different languages. She first put fingers to keys at the age of eighteen after her husband told her she read too much and should write her own. Four years later, she's still figuring out what he meant when he said she 'read too much.'

She prides herself on writing smart smut that's filled with dry wit, snappy, sarcastic comebacks, but lots of heart... And sex. Sometimes, she kills people. (Disclaimer: In books. But if you bug her, she'll use your name for the victims.)

You can find her online at:
www.emmahart.org
www.facebook.com/emmahartbooks
www.instagram.com/EmmaHartAuthor
www.pinterest.com/authoremmhart

Alternatively, you can join her reader group at
http://bit.ly/EmmaHartsHartbreakers.

You can also get all things Emma to your email inbox by signing up for Emma Alerts*. http://bit.ly/EmmaAlerts

*Emails sent for sales, new releases, pre-order availability, and cover reveals. Each cover reveal contains an exclusive excerpt.

BOOKS BY EMMA HART

Stripped series:
Stripped Bare
Stripped Down

The Burke Brothers:
Dirty Secret
Dirty Past
Dirty Lies
Dirty Tricks
Dirty Little Rendezvous

The Holly Woods Files:
Twisted Bond
Tangled Bond
Tethered Bond
Tied Bond
Twirled Bond
Burning Bond
Twined Bond

By His Game series:
Blindsided
Sidelined
Intercepted

Call series:
Late Call
Final Call
His Call

Wild series:

Wild Attraction
Wild Temptation
Wild Addiction
Wild: The Complete Series

The Game series:
The Love Game
Playing for Keeps
The Right Moves
Worth the Risk

Memories series:
Never Forget
Always Remember

Standalones:
Blind Date
Being Brooke
Casanova (*Coming January 24th, 2017*)

Paranormal Romance:
Mind Witch (*Coming February 21st, 2017*)

Made in the USA
Columbia, SC
18 October 2017